Praise for Judging Noa . . .

"*Judging Noa* is an impeccably researched and richly detailed story of one woman's struggle against a patriarchal system that threatens not only her freedom but her life. Noa's courage and determination make for an empowering and thought-provoking read." — Rebecca Kanner, award-winning author of *Esther: A Novel* and *Sinners and the Sea: the Untold Story of Noah's Wife*

"Noa's quest is the focus of this imaginative retelling of the brief biblical story of Zelophechad and his five daughters. With her immense knowledge of the flora and fauna of the wilderness, Michal Strutin took me on a multi-layered, sensual, and sense-laden journey." — Peninnah Schram, teacher and renowned storyteller, whose most recent book is *Jewish Stories of Love and Marriage: Folktales, Legends and Letters* with Sandy Eisenberg Sasso

"Michal Strutin's debut novel, *Judging Noa*, brings the Exodus to life in language that is spare and lyrical. Noa seeks justice from a patriarchal society that is loath to change anything in the midst of the wrenching cultural upheaval that is turning them from slaves to a free people." — Mary F. Burns, author of *J - The Woman Who Wrote the Bible*

JUDGING NOA

A fight for women's rights in the turmoil
of the Exodus

MICHAL STRUTIN

BInk

Bink Books

Bedazzled Ink Publishing Company • Fairfield, California

978-1-945805-74-5 paperback

Cover Design
by

DESIGNS

Bink Books
a division of
Bedazzled Ink Publishing Company
Fairfield, California
http://www.bedazzledink.com

For Pilar and Ami

ĀCKNOWLEDGMENTS

There Is Nothing New under the Sun
—Ecclesiastes 1:9

Some years ago, I joined a group of women organizing a weekend retreat at the Jewish Community Center ranch camp outside of Denver, Colorado. Sari Horovitz, friend and teacher, introduced Zelophechad's daughters as the subject of one program. Through our exploration, Noa's story opened for me.

Noa and her four sisters are mentioned in only a few biblical verses: Numbers 27:1-11; Numbers 36:5-12; Joshua 17:3-6. But I was intrigued by this glimpse of women's rights dating back nearly 3,500 years. Looking at life through the lens of time is a reminder of how little human emotions and desires have changed. The people of that time pursued justice, wrestled with complex sibling relationships, endured religious fanaticism and political operatives, adopted technological innovations, and likely suffered battle fatigue and PTSD.

I plunged into voluminous research: the Bible and its various translations,* *The Torah: a Women's Commentary*, Robert Alter's *The Art of Biblical Narrative*, works by biblical scholar Carol Meyers, Louis Ginzberg's *The Legends of the Jews*, and many more. My knowledge of the location's geography, flora, and fauna comes from research for my book *Discovering Natural Israel* and the help of many at the Society for the Protection of Nature in Israel.

The following friends and writers provided my first critiques: Fran Rathbun, Jean Flanigan, Joan Coogan, and Molly MacRae, whose cozy mysteries are warm and witty. Molly's sister Cam added a demonstration of drop spindles and looms. Judy Sandman, the insightful editor of *Discovering Natural Israel*, guided me then and now, urging me to stay focused on Noa's pursuit of justice. Just as she has done for her rhetoric students, Chris Buchalter offered trenchant editorial suggestions.

Thanks to members of the Northern California chapter of the Historical Novel Society for advice and encouragement, with special thanks to Jo Haraf. Rabbi Daniel Pressman's discussions on hope provided the philosophical pot of gold. I am grateful that, during the time I served as Santa Clara University Library's science librarian, the university included me in a writers' retreat at a critical point. Pilar Strutin-Belinoff provided suggestions and Ami Strutin-Belinoff helped me keep a schedule.

I am delighted to work with Bedazzled Ink Publishing, whose vision matches mine. Finally, many thanks to my husband, Michael Sinensky, for all-hours questions, from plotting and name choices to "Which adjective do you like better?"

* The five quotes based on or directly quoted from the Bible are from the Jewish Publication Society translation.

Michal Strutin

CHAPTER 1
IN THE SHADOW OF MOUNT SINAI

NOA WALKED ALONE, amid a chaos of bleating sheep, braying asses, clouds of dust, and a long shambling line of people. She preferred it. As the Israelites plodded into the desert, away from Egypt and slavery, being alone within the crowd gave Noa time to notice without being noticed.

Her mother saw her as ripe for marriage. At sixteen, Noa saw herself as ripe for the land her father promised, for streams splashing down verdant hills, for anything at all. She looked to the dry hills on the horizon, so different from the Nile delta. A tiny sunbird flashed overhead, catching her attention with its sapphire plumage. As she watched it fly to a red-flowered vine winding through a lone acacia tree, Noa heard a voice behind her.

"Like a jewel in flight . . . yes?"

Noa turned and saw a young woman about her age, stunningly different from most. Freckles sprinkled her nose and the crests of her cheeks. Golden, wavy hair framed her face. Noa stared. She had never seen anyone so pale and shiny.

"Everyone stares . . . at first."

"I'm sorry, I did not mean . . ."

"I'm used to it," she said. "My name is Yoela. Do you mind if I walk with you?"

Embarrassed that she had stared, Noa was, for once, without words, so simply said, "Please."

"What do they call you?"

"Call me?"

Noa could not seem to catch the rhythm of conversation.

"You know . . . your name," Yoela urged.

"Noa. Noa! Oh, I'm not usually this blank."

She looked at Yoela, who was biting the insides of her cheeks to keep from laughing. Then both burst into giggles.

As they walked, they told what they had brought out of Egypt and what they expected to find at the end of their journey.

"My father trained Malah and me to breed flocks for the best traits," Noa said, leaking pride. "And he tells of the green land we are returning to. There I will lie on soft grasses under the shade of trees and watch goats I bred milk themselves."

A smile lit Yoela's face, pleasing Noa.

"You have a far different father than most. We have few sheep and goats, and no name to speak of. So, I will be happy with one tree. But anything is possible."

They walked in silence for some moments, each imagining possibilities.

Then Yoela said, "I saw you with another maiden. Your sister?"

"Yes. That's Malah. She ran up to walk with the daughters of Manasseh's headmen. She prefers to walk with the highest of our tribe. My parents should have switched her name with my sister Milcah. Malah thinks she is the Queen."

"So, there are more of you?"

"You ask a lot of questions. But, yes, three sisters besides Malah. Younger. And you?"

"A brother. Two years older."

"Like my sister. But Malah would never marry a man with no name. Me? Noa is name enough for me."

"I knew a Noa. She was married to a mouse."

"Impossible!" Noa laughed.

"Truly. But she, too, was a mouse. And what happened to them in Pharaoh's storehouse?"

"Better than what happened to us, I hope."

"Listen. I will tell you . . ."

Yoela bubbled like a spring in the desert and was full of stories that helped pass the time.

THE TWELVE TRIBES had traveled beyond the boundaries of Egypt days before. After the Angel of Death took Pharaoh's first-born and the first-born of every Egyptian, Pharaoh finally released the Israelites. Setting out in darkness, their stomachs soured by fear, they took what goods they could and glanced furtively behind them. But the Egyptians were mourning their dead.

Zelophechad and his wife Ada kept their five daughters close, fearing Pharaoh's revenge. After their two older daughters were born, Ada had prayed for a son. Yet, their third child was another daughter—Hoglah. When a boy-child came crying into the world, Ada thanked the goddess Asherah. But Pharaoh had decreed death for all Israel's newborn males, a guarantee they would not rise up to challenge him. While her husband slaved in Pharaoh's quarries, the Shadows of Pharaoh stole into their mudbrick home. Two held her down as the third smothered her baby.

Ada birthed a fourth girl-child, Milcah. Then another baby boy, another death. Tirzah, the last of their children, was born writhing and bawling like a cornered cat. Ada favored her and let the honey-haired girl run wild, barely tamed by her sisters.

Exhausted by the trials of Egypt, Zelophechad spent the remnants of his energy on his two older daughters, pointing them to a future in their ancestral lands.

"We will return to these lands," he said, "where wheat and barley swell like the sea, watered by sweet streams. They are yours. Don't forget. And if anything should happen to me . . ."

Malah spit against the Evil Eye.

"Nothing worse will happen," she said, assuring herself.

" . . . if anything should happen to me, pursue your share of our land."

"But we are daughters, not sons," Noa argued. "Who will hear us?"

"Vow that you will."

Zelophechad planted seeds of the land he had never seen, and the need to claim it.

WHEN THE ISRAELITES reached the Sea of Reeds, the vast assemblage stopped. There, on the sandy banks, they huddled like animals, covered only by stars.

Lulled by the waving plumes of reeds along the water's marshy edges, Noa slept deep into the night, until she was startled awake by shouting.

"Up, *up!*"

"The Egyptians . . . they have come for us."

"We will die in the wilderness."

Surprised by the Egyptian army's sudden appearance behind them, people panicked. They crowded forward toward the water in the pale light of the moon, afraid to go forward and drown, afraid to stay and be cut down by Pharaoh's warriors.

Finally, one man, Nachshon, stepped into the water. As he pressed forward, the water rose to his waist, then his shoulders.

"He will be smothered by the sea," Noa gasped.

Hoglah and Milcah turned their heads so they would not see him die.

Then the wind rose and stroked back the waters. Wind-charmed waters fell back from Nachshon's shoulders, from his chest, until only a puddled path lay ahead. He turned and motioned for people to follow. They began to cross, feeling their way through the night with their feet. Sea creatures spangled the rich ooze. They slipped on the knobbed backs of starfish and smooth clamshells that cobbled the sandy bottom. Crabs pinched at the toes of the miracle-dazed people.

The tribes struggled across the sea bottom, they and their camels and asses loaded with goods, their sheep and goats agitated by the rumbling waters on either side. As they dragged themselves ashore in the emerging dawn, they heard the war cries of Egyptians pressing their chariot horses on. The chariots' heavy wheels churned across the sandy bottom, then lurched to a stop, stuck halfway across.

The soldiers and the people on the shore watched as the sea came roaring back, wrapping waves around warriors, horses, and chariots, white foam spewing furiously against dawn's pink glow. When the waters calmed, all that remained was the sea's placid face shining up at the new day.

In the miracle of morning, Miriam the prophet, Miriam the sister of Moses, sang a song. She danced, shouting God's greatness. She danced, in a joyful fury. She danced, keeping the beat with the cymbals of her timbrel, the weight of her age lightened by holy ecstasy and survival. A ring of women wove themselves around her, ululating, shaking timbrels, stamping the drum of the earth.

Malah watched from afar and shook her head.

"So unseemly."

Noa grabbed Tirzah's small hand, and together they ran to join the ring of women.

THE ISRAELITES MOVED south from the Sea of Reeds into arid desert. Their tongues swelled in their mouths for lack of water. Their stomachs growled, and they forgot all of the miracles that brought them out of Egypt.

"What good are miracles when our children cry for food?"

Some of the old and weak fell prey to the tribe of Amalek, who swept down on easy targets. Behind bands of Amalekites, jackals, hyenas, and leopards waited their turn.

Parents feared predators, human and animal. Some put a hand on a son's back or kissed a daughter's forehead to communicate reassurance they did not feel. Their children were exhilarated by the drama.

Day after day, Noa and Yoela found each other, happy to share their hopes and plans, and forget their dry, cracked lips and the stones in their sandals.

"All my mother talks about is marriage," Noa said. "The best matches, the best bride prices. The way she talks, it's like when my father bought our donkey."

"So, you are the donkey!"

Yoela brayed, causing those around to look and Noa to laugh.

"Of course, no one asks me what I want."

"We're so poor, my family will be happy with whoever tumbles into our tent. Not me. I want nothing to do with it."

"The same. Let us see what the promised land brings before we submit."

They spit on their thumbs, bound them together, and vowed to remain steadfast. The day they vowed was the day the Israelites stopped on a plain before the great mountain—Sinai. There, tribe by tribe, they set their tents.

THE LAST LIGHT of day seeped through the entrance of Zelophechad's tent as the wind curled around the tent pegs, beginning its nightly dance. Outside, pebbles from the desert floor clicked by, driven by the wind toward the great mountain that filled their view of the north. Here Moses had promised an event that would change all of their lives.

Ada rested her arthritic back against piled-up sleeping rugs, wearily watching her daughters settle themselves after storing cooking pots from the evening meal. In the dim light of a clay lamp, they spun thread from baskets full of wool. Tirzah, only eight, sucked her thumb sleepily, her drop-spindle buried in her bedding.

"We've heard so many promises," Ada muttered. "Yet, with five daughters and no sons . . ."

" . . . I am the unluckiest daughter of the tribe of Manasseh." Noa completed her mother's sentence, drenching the words with drama.

"Finally, you understand," Ada said.

"Mother," said Malah, "Noa is mocking you."

"I am not. But are we not as good as sons?"

"Noa, it is the way of things. Your father and I must make suitable matches for five daughters—five. To secure your future."

"Egypt is behind us, and we are on the way to the land of our ancestors. The land we have been promised. We will be settled by the next full moon. What could happen?"

"Oh, daughter, I have seen many things happen. In Egypt, we were toys of Pharaoh. And now we are toys of this One God."

Malah pulled Noa's arm and whispered, "Must you always argue?"

"We are between childhood and the life of a wife. Between rulers. Never will our strength be greater," Noa hissed back.

"But why not use your strength quietly. As I do. More cunning, and more powerful."

"That's not what father does."

"And sometimes it gets him into trouble. As it does you."

"Malah, stop whispering and bring your father some tea," Ada said.

Malah rose to ladle lemon-scented tea from the pot simmering on coals just outside the tent. With silky skin stretched over a body that bespoke childbearing, Malah was at the height of her attractiveness. She carried cups to her father's compartment, where he lounged, conversing with his younger brother, Boaz. Zelophechad, who spoke like a prophet, looked up at Malah and bestowed a distracted smile. Unlike his brother, Boaz was a man of common sense and an eye for beauty. As Malah turned to go, Boaz nodded at her with approval.

Malah blushed and returned to the women's side to hear Noa declare, "We must tie our fortunes to the tribe of Manasseh and press for our rights to father's small fortunes. After he is gone, the jackals of the tribe will try to strip us."

"Don't tempt the Angel of Death to find your father," Ada demanded.

"But our claim to father's lands would be just, and justice shines like the sun, burning away all objections."

Malah arched her eyebrow, but said nothing.

"Noa could be a judge, like uncle Boaz," said Milcah.

Hoglah picked at a callous on her foot, then looked up to say, "She can't. She's not a man."

Malah rolled her eyes at the obvious and reached to untie a small clay pot that hung from a tent pole along with spoons, awls, and waterskins. She handed the pot to Hoglah, who dipped in a finger and rubbed thick sheep fat on the cracked callus.

"You wind your reasoning as tightly as you wind your thread," Malah said to Noa. "Which often snaps. But, you could help father negotiate a good bride price for me."

"Why don't you marry Gaddi's son? That's what mother wants," Tirzah said to Malah. "His spears arc like anything."

"You know nothing about this," scolded Malah. "You're just a baby."

"I'm not. I threw Adam down and made him eat dirt."

Tirzah ground her spindle into the earthen floor to demonstrate. Her hair, wild like her, was full of knots and bits of feather from the bird she had tracked and killed that day.

"A just ruling of inheritance would protect us," Noa continued, ignoring Tirzah. " . . . even if our husbands died. Even if we never married."

"I would be happy for a husband. One who is kind," said Hoglah.

At fourteen, already the tallest, Hoglah could control nothing about her developing body. Her feet flapped ahead of her like ducks. Now that her menses had begun, she wore a long, modest robe. She complained that her right breast was growing larger than the left. To compensate, she held her left shoulder a little higher.

Hoglah did not mind that Malah considered herself the queen, but it was hard being in Noa's shadow. Noa was blessed with a probing mind, luminous eyes, and sculpted cheekbones the equal of Nefertiti's.

"Asherah squeezed all her beauty into the first two," Hoglah sighed. "And what of Milcah and me?"

On this and most else, Milcah kept her thoughts to herself.

The reed mats covering the floor were spread with bedding at night so that each daughter had a nest where she sat. Noa married hers to Milcah's and watched as Milcah worked a bone hook to weave black and red threads into a unicorn medallion.

"The sign of Manasseh," Noa whispered as Malah held forth on which was more important in a husband, power or wealth. "Milcah, you have a gift. Stories told in thread."

"Malah, we will get you both. And, now, enough," said Ada.

After her daughters wrapped themselves in coverings and closed their eyes, she smothered the lamp, entered her husband's compartment, and lay down beside him.

In Egypt, before the worst of the Israelites' slavery, Zelophechad had taken Malah and Noa everywhere: to the fields where he taught them how to care for flocks, to meetings where they heard tribal politics and their father's well-reasoned arguments. Yet, for all his logic, when he lost his sandals in folds of the rugs, Ada was the one he appealed to. It was she who picked bits of wool from his beard before he went out to greet the day and anyone who might pass his tent door.

"Zelophechad," she whispered. "Malah must be married. Her shine will not last forever. Get a good match. The son of Gaddi ben Susi—he is the one. And Noa, who you think is so clever, she is not far behind."

His eyes heavy, Zelophechad mumbled, "Ummm."

Piercing his sleep, Ada said, "You train Noa for trouble. She will have trouble...and *be* trouble. If only you could see that you have daughters, not sons."

He did not answer. From the other side of the curtain separating the compartments, she heard Malah and Noa whispering.

" . . . and, when it comes to marriage," said Malah, "the most important thing is how to change father's mind if the man he chooses is completely unacceptable."

Tired of marriage talk, Noa anticipated tomorrow's great gathering. " 'Make yourselves pure,' Moses warned us. That will be difficult in this desert."

"Perhaps Moses meant more than our bodies," suggested Malah.

"And what do you know of purity?" Noa challenged.

Malah and Noa whispered knowingly of purity as if it were like scrubbing a garment. Ada listened as she drifted to sleep. Talk of purity made her think its opposite. She remembered the feel of Zelophechad's hand on her thigh, the warmth that spread from the quick of her. Wrapped in her robe, she rubbed her own hand along her thigh, feeling something of death there, the skin yellow and thick as a camel bag.

CHAPTER 2
WREATHED IN SMOKE & FIRE

MALAH, NOA, AND Hoglah stood at the foot of the great mountain, waiting for the revelation Moses had promised. Behind them, the black goat-hair tents looked like shards of flint, arranged in dark, elliptical necklaces across the bleak beige plain. Ahead, the central peak rose sharp and gray against an overcast sky.

"Hoglah, can you see Moses?" Malah asked. "Do you see what he is doing?"

"No, just people. What should we expect?"

"Nothing," said Noa. "Then you won't be disappointed." Nodding toward the mountain, she added, "They've picked a bad day for this. A storm is coming."

Milcah and Tirzah ran up to join them.

"Where's mother?" Hoglah asked.

"Her back hurts. You are to watch us and we will tell her all that happens."

Their uncle Boaz approached.

"Stay behind your father, me, and the men of our house," he cautioned. "We want to be able to find you should something happen," he added to Malah specifically.

Gathered on the lower slopes of the mountain, Moses, Aaron, and the elders were hidden by low-lying clouds. The people waited. The sun arced into afternoon. They became hungry. Stomachs growled. They waited, but were no longer patient. Small bursts of activity erupted. Some ran to fetch a cloak as the day cooled under the darkening sky. Some drifted toward the tents, feeling they had been played for fools.

Suddenly Malah noticed the clouds atop the mountain had changed.

"Look!"

As they watched, dense clouds roiled over the central peak. None had ever seen such clouds, flashing with lightning then rumbling and groaning as though both light and sound came from deep within the heart of the mountain.

The people drew back from the mountain, now wreathed with fiery smoke. They feared that Moses and Aaron must be consumed, leaving them alone with a monstrous, angry mountain. Then, the blast of an unearthly ram's horn called them closer. Mesmerized, they approached.

The air became still. A white breath rose from the top of the mountain, curled around the darkened peak, then gathered strength as it spiraled down the mountain until it swelled and burst.

The land undulated. Malah fell, groping for Tirzah, blinded by a holy light.

Noa heard an unearthly voice: "Justice. Pursue justice."

Hoglah was caressed by the sweet odor of broom blossoms.

A scarf of bats fluttered past Tirzah, the wind from their wings tickling her arms, causing her to laugh before they vanished back into the mountain.

Laws for living were revealed and the Spirit was made known to each person. Some saw sounds. Others heard visions. One man covered his eyes and wept. Another understood an *aleph* and, from that first letter, understood everything.

A young man heard a terrible tintinnabulation and ran screaming from the foot of the mountain, past the tents, past the Midianite traders at the far edges of the camp. He ran into the wilderness howling, his hands stanching ears bleeding with holy noise.

In time, the wind that had roared from the mountain slowed. It became a breath, a sigh. Black clouds effaced to gray. Tentatively, people gathered themselves, returning to a different day than the one they woke to. Some would forget what they heard by the evening meal. Others could not remember what had happened, but were transformed. Some remembered everything.

Exhausted and dazed, Zelophechad's daughters walked wordlessly to their tent. Their mother sat rolling balls of dough for the evening meal. At the edge of the fire pit a pot of red lentils mixed with onions bubbled quietly. She stretched the first ball of dough, before slapping it onto an ashy rock in the fire pit, then looked up and noticed her daughters' shining eyes and drained faces.

"What happened? Tell me." She waited. "Tell me!"

Unusually hesitant, Malah began, "It is hard to tell. A storm of sound . . . light . . . I can't exactly . . ."

The others could do no better. Milcah had neither seen, nor heard, nor felt anything extraordinary. Ashamed to admit she lacked vision or belief, she vowed to live her life as if she had.

Finally, Tirzah said, "It was too much for us, uncle Boaz said. So Moses went up."

Noa explained, "Moses went up on the mountain, through the clouds and the lightning, to bring back something we can better understand. No one knows how long he will be gone."

"Well . . . quite a day, it sounds," their mother said with a chirpy finality that hinted it was time to prepare the evening meal.

WHILE WAITING FOR Moses to return with God's laws, people heard wisps of the new laws, but no one was certain.

"One God," said some.

"No, one God above all other gods," said others.

"No stealing, that's certain."

"But what about borrowing?"

"The Sabbath is a day of rest. Work is unlawful."

"Ah, but for me, carving a toy for my child is restful."

"No," said another, "rest is rest."

A group of Levites took it upon themselves to decide what was right and what was not. They called themselves the Guardians of Truth.

"We cannot live without the rule of law, even until Moses returns," they said.

What they said made sense, so people allowed them to make decisions while Aaron waited for Moses at the foot of the mountain. The Guardians of Truth ruled that making an image of God was false, thus evil.

"Yes, this makes sense," people said, although they continued to keep small idols in their tents.

"And what of Asherah?" Ada asked her husband. "Who will bring fertility when Malah marries if not Asherah?"

"Ah," Zelophechad said. "That is just a little idol. A goddess for one purpose. No great God would be troubled over her."

Yet, they spoke quietly about it, in their own home.

No one in the camp raised a voice against the Guardians of Truth, so their authority grew quickly. Their ruling against images of God came to include images of people because, they said, "We are created in God's image and to create images of people is to create images of God."

Tribal councils met and agreed, "We can abide by this." But they said so reluctantly.

The Guardians of Truth extended the prohibition to images of anything that experienced birth and death. They warned that women avoid any male outside their immediate family to prevent the excitement female presence provoked. And, they added, a female must obey when a male speaks to her.

One father mocked, "Does this mean when my four-year-old stamps his feet and shouts to his mother, 'I won't go to sleep,' she must bow and mumble, 'Anything you say, my honored son'? Will I have such power, too?"

His family laughed, and an older brother threw a pillow at the little boy, but they all behaved more carefully when the Guardians were near. None stood against the Guardians of Truth, who warned that those who strayed from their rules would be banished into the desert-without-end.

Bezalel, the great artist, who worked exquisite designs in metal and wood, was warned to halt his evil craft. An apprentice, angered to see Bezalel aggrieved for the loss of his artistry, chiseled a gazelle's head for his mentor, in defiance of the Guardians. When they heard of the figure the apprentice had fashioned, the Guardians of Truth cut off his thumbs as a warning to others. Bezalel found him bleeding and took him home to heal him. He seethed at what they had done to his ardent apprentice. But Bezalel was an artist, not a warrior. There were no warriors among this crushed people.

The Levites argued over how to confront the Guardians and their assault on Levitic authority. Korach, a cousin of Moses and among the most intelligent of them, was disgusted by the Levites' indecisive arguing and began planning his own solution.

"Tirzah, no one has decided anything," Malah chided. "I'm sure Uncle Boaz only said that because you were hanging on his arm, pulling and chattering in his ear until you drove him crazy."

"God is going to turn you into a boy," Hoglah shouted from within.

"Good." Tirzah picked up a long tail of tent rope and tied it around her waist with the loose end flapping in front. She waggled her penis-rope into the tent. "Then I'll pee on you."

"Mother, make her stop!" Hoglah screamed.

Noa spluttered with laughter.

"Don't encourage her," Malah warned.

"Where *is* father? He was supposed to bring mother home, not us."

"He'll come when he comes. My arms are so tired. How much more?"

Tirzah showed them the contents of the flour pot, half-filled with flour.

"A bit more and there'll be plenty of barley cakes for dinner . . . if no one eats more than her share." Malah eyed Tirzah. "Would you give me a sip of water so I don't have to clean my hands?"

" . . . and wipe the sweat from my forehead, please," added Noa.

"Tirzah do this. Tirzah do that. I am not your slave." She stamped her foot.

"Would you like to trade places . . ."

"All right, I'm going." Tirzah danced away just as a man ran up, breathing hard.

"Your father, your father . . ." was all he managed before a coughing fit overcame him.

Sensing trouble and mindless of their flour-covered arms, Malah and Noa ran in separate directions: Malah to fetch Boaz, Noa to fetch water for the man.

When the man recovered, he pulled Boaz into Zelophechad's side of the tent and told him he had found his brother's body. When Boaz pressed, the man said he believed Zelophechad had been attacked, implying beasts of the wilderness. Boaz gathered men from their clan and headed toward the rock-walled basin, while the women waited.

When they thought they could wait no longer, the sisters saw Boaz and his men in the distance, carrying something on a rug. Malah and

Noa said nothing, but each knew what it was. Boaz saw Malah and nodded toward their father's side of the tent. She and Noa ran to inform their mother, explaining what little they knew as gently as they could. Her eyes widened and her face collapsed. The three younger girls heard, but looked blank. To have a father in the morning and none by evening . . .

Malah and Noa, who lost both a father and a teacher, wiped their tear-streaked faces with floury hands and arms. Their grieving white masks frightened Tirzah, and she ran for the cloth and tried to wipe their faces clean even as they cried, holding her, making her job difficult.

In the privacy of his quarters, clanswomen washed what was left of Zelophechad and covered him with a white shroud.

"My husband," Ada said, "set his heart on the land of his fathers. I don't want him to lie here, alone. No one will be able to honor him here."

They sympathized, but they buried him nonetheless.

Anger and grief gave Noa a voice.

"Mother, I vow to you, we will carry father's bones to the land of our ancestors, to the land we have been promised."

BY THE TIME of Zelophechad's burial, word of what the Guardians had done had spread throughout the camp. Boaz called a meeting.

"If the Guardians did not hesitate to kill my brother, a peaceful and honorable man, they would not hesitate to kill any of us. If we don't stop them now, our slavery will simply be transferred from the Egyptians to these . . . these . . ." Boaz spat his contempt.

Boaz met with other judges and leaders. The meetings spread surreptitiously throughout the camp.

Korach the Levite heard, and said to members of the priestly clan, "How would it look if we simply waited, quibbling among ourselves, while others cleanse us of this plague? We, the true leaders of Israel, must lead."

Korach approached Boaz. The Levites would, Korach said, offer their good name and lead the fight. Seeing the benefit of collective action, Boaz assented.

They did not wait until the end of the mourning period. Led by the Levites, tribal leaders and young men hungry for battle gathered knives, clubs, whatever weapons were at hand and marched on the tents of the Guardians of Truth. At the sight of hundreds of armed men approaching, the leaders of the Guardians abandoned their sacred mission and their followers as fast as it took them to squeeze under the backs of their tents and race for the empty desert.

THEY HAD COVERED their mother with a soft sheepskin and she snored softly in a corner. She slept on the women's side every night now that her husband slept with his fathers.

Following the week of mourning, they were relieved to return to work, replacing the hole in their lives with familiar busyness. Hoglah and Tirzah tended the flocks, watering them at the end of the day, then driving them into brush enclosures where Boaz's men guarded the animals from jackals and wolves. Milcah sat at the loom, weaving under the eaves, while Malah and Noa patched tents, sewed clothes, and endlessly prepared food: grinding grain, cooking, milking sheep and goats, draining curds of whey.

After dinner, they teased wool into thread, winding it onto their spindles in an almost continuous motion, their fingers seeing what their eyes could not in the dim light. Before, they chattered about anything. Now they were subdued by death.

One evening, Noa gave vent to her anger. "The Levites did not confront the Guardians until our father's murder and Boaz forced them to. I say the Princes of Israel were cowards."

Tirzah sat in the V between Hoglah's outstretched legs as Hoglah combed out the tangles in her sister's hair.

"I would chase them down and slit their throats," Tirzah swore.

"Tirzah," Noa scolded. "As for Boaz, mother said he will speak with Gaddi ben Susi tomorrow, to make Malah a match with his son Hur."

"Hur may be more suited for Tirzah than for me. He's too young, too untested."

"Spear-thrower—I'll take him," Tirzah said, pulling forward so that Hoglah's comb tore out a handful of hair, causing Tirzah to howl.

The sisters laughed at the thought of Tirzah subjugating Hur. Malah shushed them, nodding to their sleeping mother.

They lapsed into silence, until Noa cleared her throat.

"Remember when we talked about getting our rights when father was gone? Well, now he *is* gone and if we don't speak up for what was due him—and us—we will never get a share in the land to come. Not all of us will be lucky. Marriage is not assured. Husbands die. Without inheritance, who knows which of us may become bondswomen, a step above a slave."

"Remember Abigail?" said Malah. "Her parents indentured her to a family who remained in Egypt. Even when she's free to leave, how will she find her family? She will be alone, with nothing and no one."

"The further we get from father's good name, the closer we get to servitude. People forget . . . quickly. That's why mother wants to marry us off fast. Our family fortunes may crumble like dust unless we find a way to hold them through inheritance."

"How will we get our share of land?" Hoglah asked.

"We'll go straight to the top," Malah cut in. "We will talk with Moses."

"Moses is still on the mountain," Milcah reminded them.

"Wait," interrupted Noa. "We must build legitimacy. What are we to Moses? Before we convince Moses and the Judges of Thousands, we must first convince the Judges of Tens. We must climb the ladder of the courts.

"The count is based on the size of the tribe," Noa continued. "The bigger the tribe, the more land. Manasseh needs us for the count."

"Well, of course, we know the numbers." Malah sniffed.

"Do we have to speak?" asked Hoglah nervously.

"Hoglah, all you have to do is stand tall as a date palm," Noa said, smiling affectionately, remembering how awkward she, too, felt when every part of her body seemed to grow at a different rate.

"I'm like Hoglah," said Milcah. "I want to honor father, but I could not speak before judges."

"I could. You two," Tirzah pointed her spindle at Milcah and Hoglah, "are like beetles that run when they see a shadow."

"You, Tirzah, probably *shouldn't* speak."

Noa tilted her head thoughtfully and said, as if to herself, "This will take patience and determination. We have a just request. But we are women, and such a request may never have been granted a woman."

moment. "So now you are wondering why your inconsiderate uncle wants to deprive you and your sisters of something of increasing value for gold that will sit on your arms and necks but earn nothing more?"

She smiled broadly, then cast down her eyes. But she could not suppress her delight in Boaz's recognition of her accomplishments.

"You know, it's not just the wool. We've also been breeding for richer milk. Before our sheep's milk goes off for the season, you should try some, fresh. And the cheese we make . . ."

She licked her lips to emphasize its goodness.

"I have eaten this fine cheese in your father's tent." Boaz laughed, but his eyes fastened on her moist lips. He noticed her arms and hands, wrapped around the lambs. Big hands with strong fingers. He looked back at her face, her eyes luminous in the failing light.

" . . . and praised the work of your hands," he assured her, his eyes praising her.

"Your praise warms me." Malah tossed her head, causing her head covering to slip off and her hair to spill out onto her robe.

"I am won over," he said, his eyes consuming Malah. "You and your sisters will keep your flocks."

Her arms were full of lambs, her head covering fell in folds around her shoulders, mantled by her hair. Boaz lifted her hair to tuck it back under the folds of the rough wool. The weight of her hair and the scent of Malah and the lambs enveloped him.

Startled by intimacy, Boaz lifted one of the lambs as though it was what he meant to do all along. With rare embarrassment, he glanced at his niece to see if she had noticed the pulse of desire. With only the light of the emerging moon, he saw that her face was flushed.

Her eyes were large with something new. Suddenly aware that she was staring at her uncle, Malah lowered her eyes.

They stood silently. Then they both spoke at once, a little too loudly, covering awkwardness with a string of "excuse me," "no, please," "what were you saying?"

Malah quickly turned, and Boaz, just as quickly, pulled the gate open so they could set the lambs down. Speaking lightly of cheese and fleece, they walked back toward the tents. He held back the flap of Zelophechad's tent to let her enter before returning to his own home. She pinned the flap shut from the inside, glad to be safe from whatever it was she had felt, yet wanting more.

FOLLOWING THAT EVENING, Malah would often excuse herself after the evening meal, explaining that she had business to discuss with Boaz. Malah and Boaz walked the inside perimeter of the ring of tents, talking about whatever happened to cross their minds, all but what stood foremost in each of their minds.

Hoglah and Tirzah accepted Malah's excuse for being with Boaz. Milcah suspected something deeper. Noa and her mother knew it, as much as Malah herself.

"Hur ben Gaddi would have been a good choice," Ada said to her departed husband in the middle of the night. "But this . . . this is better."

Noa heard, and whispered, "Except, there is Seglit."

BOAZ DECIDED HE needed a few well-spoken verses to set the seal on Malah's desire. The music of words did not come to Boaz as they had to his brother. So he practiced, walking out in the night, speaking his words to the stars, hoping they were like a song.

Those who knew Boaz knew the fire that afflicted him. Gaddi ben Susi said to his son, Hur, "I've seen this with Boaz. It's a woman, have no doubt."

Nor did Gaddi doubt who the woman was. Life within the tribe did not allow many secrets. The situation suited Gaddi because he thought Malah a bit old for Hur. And he liked Noa's looks. Gaddi's one concern was Noa's reputation for intelligence sharp as a knife. But he was sure his wife Tamar could teach Hur how to manage even a clever woman.

MALAH WAS THANKFUL her father's name still held enough weight to give her social purchase with Manasseh's ranking young women. As they lounged in the noonday heat gossiping, they talked about betrothals and bride-price gifts, who and how much. Malah could not yet talk about a betrothal but was desperate to add something of interest.

"You know my sister Noa, how clever she is. She talked about how we might inherit our father's promised land. She said, 'What if he dies.' And then our father was killed."

"No. Really?"

"Yes. She saw before it happened."

The young women's eyes grew wide, and Malah was pleased with the effect of her contribution. When the young women returned to their families, the rumor flew:

"Malah's sister Noa prophesied their father's death."

"She is a witch."

The poison Malah released as idle gossip circled around and reached into their home.

"They are saying I'm a witch."

"Who is saying?" Malah asked.

"They are all saying it. They say I willed my own father's death. How could they say that when I miss him so much?"

Milcah, seeing the pain in Noa's face, tried to comfort her. "You know how some people talk. It's just gossip."

Malah, realizing what had happened, wished she could take back her words. But she could not admit she had caused the toxic rumor. She dismissed it. "Milcah's right. The gossip will move on to something else."

The slander had also tainted Malah, but the rumor did not dissipate. Outside of her sisters, Noa found herself isolated, except for Yoela.

"People are no better than sheep, no matter how high their names. Try not to let it hurt," Yoela urged.

"It's unpleasant when people avoid you, but what is really painful is how much I miss my father. If I were a witch, I could wish him back."

"I am not he, but I am here." Yoela put her arms around Noa and let her cry.

Consumed by guilt, Malah went to work, drawing out the poison, first from the young women who started the rumor. She cajoled and chided, hoping she would not undo all the social investments she had made. Eventually, those who labeled Noa a witch reminded themselves how useful Noa's cleverness could be, subtly blamed each other for rumor-mongering, and dropped by to ask Noa about cheese-making.

Noa guessed how the rumor started and sensed how hard Malah worked to correct what she had wrought. She also decided to use the opportunity to move forward on the path uppermost in her mind.

"Malah, I know how the word 'witch' came to poison me."

"Why, I . . ."

"I am not going to make you pay as much pain as I've suffered. But you will do this for me: make sure Boaz puts me in front of the best set of judges he can find."

"How can I promise . . . ?"

"You *will* do it. Because I am sure I can find ways to make your life miserable if you don't."

"Fine." Malah bit off her response, relieved to be squared with her sister.

THE PATH MALAH and Boaz walked in the evening was leading to a formal bond. Boaz swore to her that Seglit had clouded his eyes and now he saw clearly. Still, Malah wanted to visit the competition.

"You mean you *want* to visit the Witch?"

"Tirzah! Don't call her that," barked Malah. "She's just lonely because Boaz no longer favors her."

"Malah," their mother broke in. "You have such a generous soul and it has been too long since we have visited Seglit."

"Mother, she lives near and we see her almost every day," Noa protested, annoyed by her mother's extravagant lack of logic.

Hoglah wondered, "Maybe we should warn her. There are six of us, and Seglit might need to prepare."

"She does, after all, have a bondswoman," Malah said.

Ada agreed it might be good to warn Seglit, so Hoglah was sent, spoke her piece quickly, and returned to say Seglit expected them soon.

They trooped over, Tirzah cranky about wasting part of the day on a social visit.

"Adam's brother is going to show him how to haft a flinthead onto a spear. Where would *you* rather be," she complained, as she dragged her feet, kicked at pebbles, and generally lagged behind over the short distance to Seglit's.

Seglit's compartment appeared more spacious and orderly than theirs, but Seglit and the bondswoman she had brought from her father's home numbered two to their six. Sleeping mats were rolled neatly against the walls and cushions stuffed with blankets and clothing had been arranged around the leather serving mat. On the mat, a platter displayed barley cakes and wild carrots sweetened with date honey. Nested cups stood on the side. Seglit's bondswoman asked if they would like to refresh themselves with buttermilk.

Malah sipped. "Mmmm." Her look told Noa, "But not as refreshing as ours."

Seglit sat, erect, the tan cushions setting off her small frame and soft, olive skin. Seglit's femininity reminded Noa of a gazelle. Noa glanced at her sister and saw the sizing-up in Malah's eyes. She was sure Seglit saw it, too.

She wanted to say, "Don't let her see that you want him so much."

As Seglit extended her arm and held her palm open in welcome, her robe slipped back to reveal delicate wrists and fingers full of rings. She opened with cordial formalities, repeating her condolences on the loss of Zelophechad. Then she asked after their week. They asked after her week. They hoped their numbers did not strain her hospitality. She assured them it was her honor to offer them the best of her household.

As the pleasantries wound down, a leaden silence took hold briefly.

"Your barley cakes are full of flavor," Ada offered, breaking the silence.

Seglit smiled, cautiously. Her trimmed eyebrows framed ebony eyes that remained dark and mute.

Tirzah leaned over Milcah and whispered loudly to her mother, "Momma, don't you think I'd better go check that hurt lamb?"

Her mother gave her a look, and Tirzah sank back against her cushion.

"Speaking of lambs," said Malah. "I'm sorry for borrowing so much of Boaz's time. He's been *so* helpful to us since father died."

Seglit turned toward Malah, arching her elegant neck and shaking back her hair to show off silver earrings hanging like chimes from dainty ears. She rose, stepped toward Malah, then knelt before her. She clasped Malah's large, work-worn hands in her own, looked down, then at Malah to make sure that both saw the difference.

"I do feel badly for you. Needing to negotiate marriages without a father, when time is passing," she said in a honeyed voice, implying Malah's age.

She swept her arm to take in the seated semicircle of Ada and her daughters, her tone changing to neutral.

"For all of you. If I can help . . ." She opened her palm again, and Noa noticed that Seglit looked wistful, as though she actually meant it.

The reception ended soon after and, on the way home, Tirzah pulled at Malah's robe, examining the edge of her sleeve.

"She was giving you a strange look," Tirzah said, "like she found sheep dung on your sleeve. But I don't see any."

Malah snorted and the others laughed.

"Tirzah, Tirzah." Her mother sighed as her youngest daughter ran off to find Adam and his spear-making brother.

MALAH AND NOA sat side by side on rocks within the oval of tents, carefully easing their way back to each other. Noa opined that Seglit was wily and would throw down a thousand obstacles every day.

"If not Seglit, something else," Malah answered. "No union is free from trouble."

As they talked, a man rushed up to them. "Give me your earrings," he demanded. "We will melt them all and raise an image of the god who will save us. You will be among those who are saved, if you give me your gold." His face shone with the light of a believer.

Noa, annoyed at being interrupted, ran the man off.

He shouted back, "You won't be saved. You'll die here. Help yourselves."

He disappeared beyond the wall of tents, but they heard him crying out to others, "Give me your gold. For the god!"

Noa tracked back to Seglit. "You would have to take orders from her. She is the first wife."

"Not precisely. There was the one who died. Besides, Boaz is providing me with my own tent and bondswoman."

To Noa that sounded like wishful thinking, but Malah continued, " . . . and when Boaz presents his suit to mother, he will also present marriage possibilities for you. Of course, there are a number of eligible young men, now that those awful rumors have subsided. But Hur ben Gaddi still leads the list. For your hand, not mine. Think of it, we would both be so well married, and soon."

Malah's announcement staggered Noa.

"Married? Me?"

Noa had no thought to be married. She and Yoela had vowed they would not abandon each other for husbands.

"Hur—he is handsome, wealthy, accomplished . . ."

"I am not ready for marriage."

"I know you will fall in love with Hur, as mother did with father. As I with Boaz."

Noa feared for her love-besotted sister, and for herself. She feared that family would bind her in a union she did not want.

MOSES HAD NOT come down from the mountain and the tribes were anxious and restless. The Levites complained to Aaron, 'Where is Moses? Why has he abandoned us?"

Aaron prayed every day that Moses would return. He had no answers, so the tribes held meetings to decide what do.

With Gamaliel's backing, Gaddi ben Susi called a meeting in his tent, on a night hot and airless as the inside of a fist. The walls on the men's side of Gaddi's tent were pinned up. Still, the crowd sitting on his mats fanned themselves with fragments of palm and shards of camel hide, anything that produced a slight breeze. They sat in concentric circles, with Gaddi, Boaz, and other headmen at the center. Hanging oil lamps cast flickering shadows on the men. One held a sleepy boy in his lap.

Gaddi had barely finished thanking them for the privilege of hosting the meeting, when one growled, "What is it we are waiting for in the shadow of this mountain? Every roaming band knows where we are. They can pick us off, beginning at the edges . . . us."

"If Moses still lived, he would be down from the mountain. Let's be on our way."

"I say we go back. At least the lands of the Great River bear water."

"We cannot go back," Gaddi insisted. "We must go forward. To the land of our fathers, the hill country to the east. Where olives drop from the trees like rain. Where grapes grow as big as my thumb." He cocked his thumb to show them.

"Land of our fathers," a clansman spat out. "We have heard about this land from our fathers. But I heard from a man who heard from a Midian trader—giants live in the high country."

"Giants?" asked his neighbor, just as Gaddi's youngest children tumbled noisily into the men's tent.

"Have you no respect, you wild animals," Tamar, their mother, hissed from the edge. She set her tray down, yanked them back, and shooed them to the women's side. Then Tamar passed in a tray loaded with a pot of tea and small cups.

"Yes, giants!" the man repeated loudly, in case anyone had not heard him.

"Moses has been gone three phases of the moon. How much longer will we wait?"

The men of Manasseh were not alone. People feared the Amalekites would amass a large force and kill them. They heard rumors of babies stolen in the night, wives snatched for slaves. Tribe leaders decided to air their concerns to Aaron.

"What we need," demanded one, "is a god who will show us favor, who will assure us that we will live. We want a god of vigor—Apis, the bull. Not a god living in a cloud who we don't know and who knows nothing of us."

CHAPTER 5
THE GOLDEN CALF

"I WANT TO go. I really *do* want to go," Tirzah pleaded.

"No you don't, Tirzah," said Milcah. "You don't even know what it's about. You just want to go because anything that sounds like you shouldn't do it is exactly what you want to do. You are staying here with me. Anyway, I would be scared to stay here by myself."

"What? Mother's here. And Boaz is nearby. What are you talking about?"

"Mother's nearly asleep, and Boaz is probably with the Witch."

"Oh, all right," conceded Tirzah. "I'll stay and make sure the Shadow People don't come and eat you up." To the three stepping past the tent door she demanded, "But you have to tell us everything that happens. Promise?"

"Promise."

The day before, Noa and Malah learned that the man who called for their gold was part of a cult that had formed. Tonight the cult would be performing a ceremony for Apis, the bull god.

"I heard there will be wild dance and who knows what else," said their friend, Bat-Sheva.

"We must see," said Malah, and the others agreed.

The three sisters exited casually, as if to take a stroll, then quickly stepped over a set of guy-ropes where they met Yoela and Bat-Sheva. From there, the five made their way past the tents of the tribes of Efraim and Benjamin, past the central Tent of Meeting, past the tents of Judah on their way toward the base of the mountain.

When they reached the lower slopes, they hid themselves among boulders so they could look down on the apron of land at the base of the mountain where the ceremony was set to occur.

Fire pits lined a broad avenue that led from the foot of the mountain to a large wooden platform. A stone altar, horned on each corner, stood on the platform. Near the altar, a pedestal rose and atop the pedestal stood Apis, a young bull, its golden skin made from the people's armbands and earrings, glinting in the rays of the dying sun.

People fixed fires in the pits, lavishing precious wood on this ceremony so that Apis, Egypt's god of fertility, rampant and ready to seed the world, would save them and give them life.

When the night quickened and the fires blazed, the cultic assemblage emerged between boulders at the base of the mountain. At the head walked a woman whose hair was twisted up into horns. Behind her came a line of seven priests wearing long, loose robes, advancing between the lines of people and fire, thrumming hand drums with each slow step. On either side of each priest, priestesses shook rattles made of painted gourds and pebbles, rough copies of the sacred sistrums used by Egyptian priestesses. As they passed, the women touched the rattles to the outstretched hands of the people, ensuring them long life.

Moving to the insistent beat of rattle and drum, the priests and priestesses advanced toward the altar. She with the horned hair and the lead priest stood, facing each other, next to the low platform.

Hidden among the rocks, the young women held their breaths, awed and excited by this exotic ceremony. They watched as two of the priests laid the platform with foliage. All the while, drums and rattles sounded.

When they were done laying a bed of leaves and grasses, the high priestess and priest stepped onto the platform. Two priests removed her robe, and she stood naked before them, below the golden bull-calf. Streaks of blood-brown henna undulated down her arms and legs like waves of life-giving water. Henna circled each breast in concentric rings and arced in bows that pointed toward her vulva, her body mapped for the life force.

Because the young women saw her from afar, the priestess appeared less than life size.

"She looks like mother's Asherah." Hoglah giggled nervously.

And she did look like the palm-sized goddess figures that women kept by their hearths. In the dark, Noa and Yoela gripped each other's hands.

Then, the drums and rattles were silent and the priestess, throwing back her head and opening wide her arms, chanted:

"I am Field made by the god. Who will plough and bring forth life?"

"I am Ewe made by the god. Who will rut and bring forth life?"

"I am Woman made by the god. Who will enter and bring forth life?"

The young women could not hear her words, but watched, riveted, as two priests removed the robe of the head priest, his rod of life stiff with anticipation. He approached the priestess. And they began the strange, pulsing jig of life.

The young women hiding among the rocks had seen goats and sheep mating. They had heard their parents' low groans. But none had ever seen two people couple. Watching from above, they felt damp and desirous, confused and horrified.

As the sacred coupling peaked, priests, priestesses, and the ecstatic crowd drummed, shook rattles, and beat timbrels in a wild cacophony of sound broken when the priests' voices swelled: "Send down life."

The people howled to the god whose grace they craved, "Let it be so."

"Let life rise."
  "Let it be so."
"In earth."
  "Let it be so."
"In flesh."
  "Let it be so."
"In us."
  "Ya! El!"

Sound and penetration climaxed, and the women ululated the triumph of the life force as they lifted their robes and whirled ecstatically. The union was complete.

Then, people came forward with lambs and birds for sacrificial offerings. The smell of burnt flesh filled the air, rising to please the god of life, the golden bull-calf. The priests ate from the charred meat and handed the rest to the crowd. The smell of the roasted meat meant to please the god, pleased the people. Some were hungry for roasted flesh. Others, spurred by a primal pulse, were hungry for other pleasures of the flesh.

Drumming and shaking timbrels, the crowd danced and shouted, men and women pulled off what they wore and fell on each other in an orgy of ecstasy. Like eels swarming in the sea, bodies twisted together in fierce, frantic couplings backlit by fire, doing what every animal is designed to do: make more, make more. So urgent was his to connect, one man ploughed himself into the sandy soil, copulating with the earth, plunging needy fingers into the sure breast beneath him, crying as he planted his seed.

Noa and Yoela loosed their hands, touching tainted by what they saw below. Hoglah turned away, repulsed. Sweat pouring off her, she retched violently as Noa and Malah rushed to their sister, each silently regretting they had brought her.

In Hoglah's distress they found their reason to leave. The young women helped each other down the rocky slope, then picked their way across the plain, keeping as far from the bonfires and the writhing people as possible.

As she tried to swallow the sour taste in her mouth, Hoglah vowed, "Never, even when I marry."

The sisters crept into their tents and wrapped themselves tightly in familiar blankets. They never spoke of that night again. Waiting for sleep, Noa tried to suppress images of frantic, crazed couplings warring with the Guardians' brutal stones and knives, extremes that made her fear entering adulthood and wonder if the seesawing poles of people's needs ever settled into balance.

AS THE YOUNG women fled, they had not seen Moses descending the mountain. He looked down and saw wild pricks of light and motion. He carried with him two tablets that would seal the bond between seekers and the Sought, a holiness code for life. When he saw the abomination at the base of the mountain, the tablets of the law fell from his hands and broke. Some say the words themselves fled back to the heavens.

Moses looked for Aaron, to learn the cause of the cultic atrocity. Aaron, his eyes darting everywhere to avoid his brother's gaze, mumbled, "They demanded a god. They gave me gold. I hurled it into the fire. And out came a calf."

Moses turned from Aaron. He charged the Levites with cutting down the leaders of the idolatrous cult, as one cuts a rotting branch from a healthy tree. Before he returned to the mountain for a second set of tablets, Moses called on Korach to lead the way.

Korach did not relish his work. It was beneath him.

"But," he reasoned, "if this God is now our champion and told Moses to rout out the canker and if I am the router, I will gain merit."

So Korach called out the Levites.

"We will clean up this pack of pigs. For the sake of our souls," he exhorted, as they ran to round up the idolaters.

The cult priests shouted curses upon Korach and his men and, when that did not stop the Levites, the priests slashed at them with knives as the cleansers closed in. Howling to strange gods at the center of the carnage, the priestess whirled a rope threaded with metal balls. Korach pointed two of his men toward her. They brought her down and garroted her with her own rope, but not before she shattered the cheekbone of one, bequeathing him a new face. Afterward, the Levites washed themselves, laving away their deeds and the stink of slaughter.

The idolatrous priests were not dead a day when a plague visited the rest of the participants. Those who consumed on that corrupted night were consumed—with fevers and chills sucking life from them, leaving yellowed skin wrapped around bones. The smell of the dead oozed throughout the camp.

Hoglah dragged herself through her chores, subdued and depressed.

"The cure is as awful as the sin," Noa said.

"Your father always said that finding the right path is never easy." Her mother folded her hands in her lap as tidy as her homily.

Noa did not hear. Thinking of the extremes of orgy and Guardians, she asked, "What does God want of us?"

"'HONOR FATHER AND mother.' And how better to honor our father than to have his name continue on the land he would have inherited—by inheriting for him?" Noa asked.

Committed to pleading their case for inheritance before the Judges of Tens, she finished her practice session with a flourish. Her audience, Hoglah, sat on her heels in front of the sheepfold and clapped in appreciation, creating a slight flurry among the sheep.

"You are convinced?" Noa asked.

"Who can reason like you," Hoglah enthused, then remembered her role as a critic. "But maybe say father's name with more force, so the judges will be reminded that we have an important name."

"Yes, excellent hole-poking, Hoglah. But I think our argument alone will win it. I will simply step in front of the judges and modestly present our plea. Who could deny justice?"

Noa pulled Hoglah up and they walked toward their tent, their arms around each other's waists, their feet kicking up dust.

"Will Malah really marry Boaz?"

"Yes," Noa answered, "but I worry. She does not see the troubles she will have with Seglit. Boaz says she will have her own tent, but . . ."

"You think Boaz does not mean what he says?"

"I think he means it, but look where we are." Noa's free hand swept toward the vast wilderness. "And this is not our destination. We will be picking up, leaving at a moment's notice again."

Hoglah was quiet for a few steps, carefully composing her next question.

"Do you think there will be another marriage soon?"

Noa's laugh was layered with resignation. "You mean Hur?"

"I WOULD CHOOSE no one else," Malah said.

"But I am too old to be a good husband. You deserve better, younger," insisted Boaz, hoping she would refute him.

"No," she assured. "You are he."

They perambulated slowly around the perimeter of tents: tall Boaz, with his loping gait, and Malah, an erect, determined young woman, the top of her head reaching only to his shoulder. By now, most had guessed there was more to their evening walks than talk of sheep breeding.

Boaz, realizing his position of authority, did not want to be accused of taking advantage, so tried to keep a semblance of propriety. But tonight, his restraint broke.

He twined his fingers with hers and said, "Beholding your eyes is like . . . drinking from a well of sweet water."

Although he was secretly pleased with his expression, Boaz dipped his head in apology. "Poetry does not come to my tongue."

They laughed, to dissipate their desire.

"Malah, you make me feel like a young man," he exulted. "A man who would do anything to make you happy forever."

"So, when?" she demanded.

Days before, Boaz had stolen a look at himself in Seglit's copper mirror and saw a blurred image of the man Malah saw, with a solid jaw, but graying hair. He surreptitiously mixed charcoal and fat in a small bowl and rubbed it into his hair and beard to blunt the specter of age. Seglit saw and said nothing. She knew she would soon have a rival wife.

CHAPTER 6
BETROTHAL

THE FORMAL BETROTHAL took place a week before their marriage. Boaz displayed the bride-price items he had pledged to his sister-in-law. Although his gifts officially went to Malah's mother, Ada would dispense most of them to Malah as marital insurance. Ada sat on Zelophechad's side of the tent, surrounded by a semicircle of her daughters, who she vowed to marry off quickly before Zelophechad's tribal stature faded and she became a pitiable widow-woman.

She was determined to secure Hur, the son of Gaddi, for Noa and she had pressed Boaz to proceed with negotiations for Noa's hand.

"The match will be a triumph," she told Noa, earlier that day. "And by agreeing to speak at your sister's wedding, Gaddi has practically told us he agrees to the match."

Noa said nothing, but her mother was too busy to notice, fingering the linen cloth that Boaz handed over for her inspection. Linen was rare and precious now that they were far from fields where flax grew. As she ran her hand over the smooth cloth, her face clouded. She knew she could stay with Malah and Boaz if she could not carry on by herself. But she knew of one widow who became a bondswoman when her daughter died in childbirth and the husband married a heartless new wife.

Noa, seeing her mother's thoughts had wandered, lifted the linen from her and put it aside as Boaz offered tanned leather, the color of toasted grain, soft and pliable, not the coarse hides that most used. Next, a small copper mirror, its round edges etched with a repeating flower pattern. Earrings and bracelets of gold, a silver toe ring. A silver headband to hold the veil that Malah would wear during the week between betrothal and marriage. A pure white ass tethered to a stake at the door.

Tirzah flung herself upon it, crying, "Oh, my beautiful white one. I want you."

Boaz promised Malah she would receive her final gift not long after their seven days in the marriage booth.

"Your own tent. A home shared only by you and me."

Her sisters had worked to finish their daily chores early so they could complete Malah's bridal robe and prepare food for the wedding feast. They trimmed wool cloth with bands of red and yellow, dyed and designed by Milcah. Noa had used some of their cloth to purchase small gold earrings for Malah, the sisters' present to her. Shaped like pomegranates, the earrings promised as many children as the seeds of the fruit.

"One more thing," said Noa. "A reminder. Have Boaz secure a hearing before the best Judges of Tens—the first step on our journey of inheritance."

"This wedding is about me, not some legal problem."

"Malah . . ." Noa warned.

"Yes. All right."

In the evening, after Boaz had presented his gifts, Tirzah snatched Malah's veil, filmy as a cloud. She flung it over her head and twirled, the long cloth hanging nearly to her knees.

"I am a bride, a beautiful, *beautiful* bride," Tirzah sang in a fruity falsetto as she spun. Blinded by the veil and her own careening speed, she stepped on a corner of the veil, tripped, and fell in a laughing heap onto a floor mat, with her sisters yelling and scolding.

Malah retrieved her veil and her mother groaned. "Tirzah, Tirzah . . ." She turned back to Malah and said, "Now, here is a most important gift."

Ada handed a small clay idol to Malah—Asherah, the goddess of life, with tumid breasts and belly.

"Keep Her near at night to bring down the Goddess's grace and give you children."

ALL EYES WERE on the wedding canopy, its poles twined with vines. With guests waiting, the sisters and their mother gathered around Malah to escort the veiled bride to the happy canopy with song and timbrel. Tribesmen formed a processional around Boaz as they set forward with shouts of "Behold!"

Near the canopy, in the lee of Boaz's tent, stood a small, temporary bridal booth. Thatched with palm fronds and walled with a weave of limber branches, the structure would allow breezes and light to caress the couple within. Family and friends would bring meals and the couple would know each other as much as they wished for the next seven days.

As Malah and Boaz stood together under the canopy, the men cheered and the women ululated until Gaddi ben Susi held up his hand for silence. He spoke words of celebration, of a glorious future made possible by wise leadership in the tribe of Manasseh. After Gaddi's speech, part marriage blessings and part political advertisement, others added their blessings, and poets sang songs. Children raced around the poles of the canopy, while women bustled out food, setting down platters at either end, one for men and one for women: barley cakes, flatbread seasoned with oil and herbs, onions stewed with lentils, chickpeas flavored with cumin, dates stuffed with pistachios, and, as it was a wedding, succulent chunks of roast lamb.

Weddings were among the rare days that no one's stomach growled with hunger. Killing a lamb was a sacrifice to families whose wealth was counted in livestock, so weddings, with their guarantee of a meat dish, were doubly joyous.

Noa had feared Seglit's presence would add a sour note to the day, but at the last moment Seglit remembered a reason to return to her clan's compound. Humiliation was not a dish she savored.

When the time came, the women shooed the couple into the marriage booth. Once inside, Boaz loosened the pin that held open the cloth door. The covering fell into place. They heard the world outside celebrating their marriage and saw splashes of sunlight and blue sky through the open-weave structure. Near the bottom of the booth three sets of small eyes stared in at them.

"Out, out, out! Or I will take a broom to your bottoms," a woman with a deep voice shouted as three little boys darted off.

Malah laughed, tightly, at the boys, but more at what would happen next. Boaz carefully lifted her veil, folded it back, then pushed it so that it dropped to the mat. After waiting for weeks with this in mind, he sank his hands into her hair as they pressed together.

"What must we do now?" she whispered, knowing.

"Whatever we want."

They stood, arms around each other, until Malah reached up to touch his cheek and the bangles he had given her slid down her arm. One looked like a twin to a band Seglit wore.

"You," she said, carefully, "have had two other such weeks."

Caught off guard, Boaz stumbled, "Yes, but . . ."

"What should I know?"

Racing to recover, he said, "The first time I was too young to know. The second I was taken in by . . . by beauty."

Malah stepped back, her arms crossed, glaring at him. Boaz realized he had just compounded his mistake. Suddenly the marriage booth felt tight and airless.

"Beauty only for the eyes, not for the soul. What I mean . . . before, I was blinded. You, you have both. Had I known, I would have waited for you."

"I was right there, under your nose, the whole time," Malah returned, anger heating her face in hot waves. She turned from him, hoping he would appease her.

He saw that she required entreaty and immediately knew his role. He bent to the bowl of fruit the women had left and chose a ripe pomegranate. He ripped open the leathery red skin. Clusters of ruby-fleshed seeds arched up, bursting from their seedbed.

He offered her a section of fruit and said, "Let's not argue. I love you. It is the only reason I am here." He pressed the fruit into her hand. "You must be hungry. Here, a rare treat, even if I am not."

She allowed herself to be coaxed and bit into the fruit. Juice trickled down her fingers and spilled onto her wedding robe, staining it with drops of red. They each thought of the night ahead. Malah blushed. Boaz took her free hand.

"Come. Sit. We have time for everything."

They ate and talked, carefully avoiding the subject of former wives. With darkness, they lay down, exhausted. He held her, and they fell asleep to the sounds of men telling stories into the night. In the middle of the night, Boaz awoke and could wait no longer. Relaxed by sleep, she was open to him. He entered, and she became a woman. They slept again.

Sometime later, Malah awoke, sore and startled by the vestigial throb of her torn hymen. She rolled over and there, her swollen clay breasts and belly lit by the moon, Asherah stared at her with unblinking eyes.

THE NEXT DAY, the cloth was taken up and examined. The bride had been a virgin and the marriage had been consummated. All was as it should be. Malah's mother examined the pattern of bloodstains, looking for signs and portents.

Noa, who did not allow her fate to be ruled by omens, reminded Malah of her obligation.

CHAPTER 7
JUDGES OF TENS

DURING MALAH'S BRIDAL week, a boy ran to Zelophechad's tent and waited to be acknowledged. Milcah, who was beating the weft on her loom, did not hear him. She jumped, startled, when he coughed and announced, full of self-importance, "The Judges of Tens will hear Zelophechad's daughters."

Caught off guard, Milcah stared at the dusty boy, then panicked and cried out for Noa.

"What is it?" Noa answered, fearful the Guardians of Truth had returned.

"They're ready for you. The Judges of Tens."

"They are? Well, then, come. We'll not let them wait."

"Me? What can I do?"

"Stand near me, to give me courage. Your presence will give my tongue strength."

She bid the boy lead them to the *bet din*. He brought them to a clan circle not their own, where the three men of the Judges of Tens sat on a carpet before a large tent, sipping tea.

"Here are Zelophechad's daughters," the boy announced.

No others waited before the judges. Noa and Milcah were the only two present. The fleshy face of the middle judge was partially hidden by a full black beard. Bushy eyebrows peaked in the center, giving him a fierce look. His hand beckoned them closer. Milcah was rooted, so Noa stepped forward.

"Having no brothers, you want to inherit land promised to your father. So your uncle Boaz said. Have we understood you?"

"Yes," she said, flustered, then remembered to add, "Sir."

Noa felt awkward standing and looking down as they sat. She did not know what to do with her hands, so she clasped them in front of her. Behind her, Milcah had done the same.

"Your case is not without merit. It is just that there is no precedent for such a request. Sons inherit land. And this land is not in hand nor in sight."

He was silent for a moment. Milcah heard the whirring of locusts in bushes beyond the circle of tents. Noa looked at the other two judges. One dug in his ear, then looked at what he had excavated. He did not bother to acknowledge their presence. The other seemed half asleep.

"As you know," the middle judge continued, "the three of us must agree on a judgment. One of my colleagues," his eyes slid toward the Excavator, "believes that when the law says sons, it means sons. You will have to get land through your husbands, I'm afraid."

"But, your honor, we have not even had the chance to present our case. We have a worthy presentation. It is surely not an idle request, nor a greedy request. It is a just request."

"Without a precedent, we are not qualified to make a judgment."

"Why did the *bet din* call us to come? Why let us hope?" Noa could not temper her frustration.

"I am sorry, there is nothing more we can say or do," he said with cold finality.

He then tipped his head to one judge, then the other. They all rose and the two silent judges departed. Noa stood respectfully as they left, biting back anger.

Judge Blackbeard turned so that Noa saw only his back. When the other two judges were out of earshot, he ordered, "Come inside."

Noa did not know whether to follow him or not. She had almost forgotten Milcah, but now turned to her and gave her a questioning look.

Milcah had never seen Noa look uncertain. She found something of Noa's spirit in herself and whispered, "I'm with you."

Noa turned, and the two sisters followed the judge into the tent. Immediately they realized they were on the women's side.

"For reasons of propriety," the judge offered.

He waved them to pillows just inside the tent door. His wife and a daughter-in-law sat spinning, apart from one another in the dim tent. Neither gave more than a sidelong glance to the guests. The trapped midday heat was stifling.

The wife raised her head, directing her eyes to the water jug. The daughter-in-law scuttled over to the jug and brought small cups of water to Noa, Milcah, and the judge. Judge Blackbeard, barely noticing the silent interchange, directed his attention to Noa.

"Boaz, son of Hefer, is your uncle," he said, opening the conversation.

"Yes," Noa breathed.

"He is an upstanding man, of good judgment."

Noa waited for the judge to continue.

"I have heard of you as well."

Noa stiffened, fearing he would level the charge of "witch."

"Unusual skills . . ."

Milcah grasped her sinking sister.

"Boaz praises your husbandry."

As the sisters recovered, the judge said, "Young ladies, you have a difficult journey. I am not saying it is without merit. That you pursue your plea is a testament to your father."

Noa lowered her eyes, accepting the compliment and allowing her father's memory to fill her momentarily before she reset her attention toward the judge.

"As I said, your way is difficult. You saw the reaction of my colleagues."

The judge raised his shoulders and his peaked eyebrows as if to say, "What can I tell you about those two?"

"Judge Ploni-Almoni, with his finger in his ear, does not see the value in women asking for anything except leavings from the dinner platter. That's his prerogative. The other does not like to question the way things have always been. That's his prerogative. Most people, including judges, hate change. There's your problem."

"Please, sir, tell us what to do."

He leaned toward them and narrowed his eyes, so that his eyebrows were all they saw. "Sometimes the best path to justice is under the back of the tent."

They looked toward the back of the judge's tent and, in a corner, they saw another woman, shrunken into the oppressive dark. Noa did not know what to make of the judge's words. His next words dragged her attention away from the dark form.

"You have come before the Judges of Tens and have not found satisfaction. With my approval, you may make your appeal before a higher court. The Judges of Fifties hear complex cases the fourth day of every new month. I advise that your uncle arranges for you to appear before a rotation of the Judges of Fifties known for being open-minded. He knows who they are. There is where your path lies, although I cannot offer much hope. And now," the judge rose to usher them out, "I wish you good fortune."

The sisters took their cue, rose, and backed out of the tent.

"We cannot thank you enough for your advice and your kindness," Noa said, hoping not to trip on her robe.

"It is for your father, my old friend."

"Yes, thank you," Milcah mumbled.

After exiting, they turned and walked quickly out of the judge's clan circle, then turned to each other. Noa grasped Milcah by the wrists. "He does not see hope, but I do. I have not even presented our full plea. Milcah, we have an opening."

Milcah, delighted by the outcome and by the lucky chance to be included, smiled like a new moon.

UPON RETURNING FROM the judge's tent, Noa went straight to Malah's bridal booth to tell her the news. Malah, entertaining three young married women under the canopy that fronted the booth, looked up.

"Noa, where have you been? We expected you."

"Wait until you hear." Then Noa looked at the shiny young wives and tamped down her enthusiasm. "Oh, I had an errand. Important enough, but mostly I could not get away," she said, just remembering Malah had invited her to join them.

"Well, sit. Enjoy some of these dainty cakes my friends have brought. I don't know how Boaz and I will be able to finish all this food in the few days left to us."

Malah smiled a knowing smile, and the three other women smiled the same smile back, all quite pleased with themselves. Noa wondered when they would leave so she could pour out her news.

She endured another round of food, husband talk, and strange flounces of heads and shoulders. She was bewildered by this cake-nibbling, gossiping, tittering woman who had emerged from her sister.

"Is there a special society of married women?" Noa wondered. "Will I have to belong?"

Finally, the women left, and Malah turned to her sister. "You look bursting to tell me something," she said brightly.

"Malah, the Judges of Tens turned us down, but the main judge took us aside and said our case had merit. He said it would only take Boaz's say-so to put it before the right Judges of Fifties." She spilled out the words in a single breath. "You must ask him."

"Boaz?"

"Yes. Who else would I be talking about?"

"Well, this is not the best time. After all, Boaz and I are still in our week and I already asked him to speak of you to the Judges of Tens. I fulfilled that obligation.

"And then there will be the new tent to furnish and invitations to the women you saw here today, plus others, to secure my station in the community. I'm sure this can wait. After all, we barely know where we are going or when we will get there."

"No, it cannot wait. If you will not, then I will speak with him."

"Boaz is *my* husband. You will speak with him only if I say so."

"What?"

"You heard me."

Noa rose in fury and stubbed her toe on a rock. She refused to cry out and give Malah the satisfaction of hearing her pain. She set her jaw and headed home.

Their small spats of the past had never left her so rigid with anger, and Malah had never flung words with such high-handedness.

When Noa told her mother what had happened, Ada said, "When I first married your father, I was so foolishly in love with the idea of marriage and my new position. Oh, I thought I was so important. Now, if only I had a few hours with him . . ."

THE NEXT DAY the camp was astir with the news that Moses had finally descended the mountain, his face glowing with an unearthly light. Some muttered that he had the white disease that causes fingers to fall off. Others said he was imbued with the sign of God. This light so disturbed the people that Moses covered his face with a veil, and Tirzah declared that Moses was now a bride.

Moses brought down the laws and told the laws to the people. But the telling was long and people drifted away. Milcah, who saw no vision when the mountain had roared, listened well and vowed she would follow the new laws that numbered in the hundreds: fair weights and measures; judging rich and poor equally; leaving the corners of the harvest for the poor.

"Very sensible," said their mother.

"What harvest?"

"We'll have a harvest when we reach our land, Tirzah."

With the laws, Moses also brought a plan for a grand Tent of Meeting that would house the tablets of the law. Bezalel, the master craftsman, would build the new Tent of Meeting and the objects within it.

Noa said to Milcah, "People need something grand to see."

Remembering the Golden Calf and echoing something her father said, Noa continued, "We learn from God, and God learns from us."

Milcah's eyes widened, and she looked around, afraid someone had heard what sounded to her like blasphemy.

Bezalel chose Oholiav, he of the blessed hand, to help direct the work. Oholiav, examining the products of the best weavers, chose Milcah as one of the dozen or so who would fashion the hangings for the Tent of Meeting. Her sisters saw that Milcah glowed in the great artist's light.

"You will be at the very center. Think of the things you will hear. You must tell us everything," Noa insisted, wondering if the new laws said anything about brotherless sisters.

THE DAY MILCAH was chosen as one of the weavers was the last day of Malah's bridal week. She was in her father's tent, packing her bedding and household goods to transfer to her new tent, but as the day progressed she saw no new tent being raised. Boaz was sitting as judge in another part of Manasseh's camp, so she could not question him.

"Where is my tent?" she hissed to the wind.

As the day progressed, Noa sensed unpleasantness ahead. She nudged her mother, who had just awakened from a nap.

"Mother, remember you wanted to visit the wife of Hanniel? Come, let us find out what it was she had to tell you."

Before her sleep-dazed mother could protest, Noa hoisted her, hooked her arm around her mother's spongy waist, and prodded her out the door.

That left Malah alone in the tent. Suspecting no new tent would appear, she dragged bedding outside and, as she beat the bedding, she honed her fury to a knifepoint.

Hearing dull, fabric thuds as he approached Zelophechad's tent, Boaz hesitated. He had not forgotten Malah's tent any more than she had. He exhaled slowly, then stepped within her view.

"Malah . . ."

That was all he managed before a storm of words struck him.

"You promised . . . you lied. You shameless liar."

Malah flung a blanket at him.

Boaz dodged, then rushed her, grabbed her arms, and held them at her sides.

"Wait. Just wait," he demanded, but Malah kept spewing verbal venom.

"What was I thinking?" Boaz shouted back, his breath hot on her face. "You behave like a child. Everything is you, you, you."

Malah, having run out of words and startled by Boaz's, stopped, then gathered herself and began again, but more quietly. "You promised a tent and there is no tent. Do you want to humiliate me?"

"Malah, please understand. I will provide you with a home, one that will please you. But we will leave this place shortly, traveling to who knows where. It will be hard to protect two separate households . . ."

"So. I will have to live with . . . the Witch?"

"She is no witch. She is my wife, just as you are. Perhaps I love you more, but people cannot be thrown away."

"*Perhaps* you love me more?" Malah blistered. "So you do still love her?"

"Once, perhaps," he said, stumbling over the word again, hoping to mollify her, "but I have my obligations. Please, Malah. You two will have to make your compromises with each other eventually. Why not start now?"

Furious, Malah realized she had no recourse, but resolved to get something for herself. She remembered her father's promised land, and Noa's demand.

"*Perhaps* I will trust you again if you help us secure a place with the Judges of Fifties."

WHEN NOA AND her mother returned home, they noticed Malah's things had been removed. Ada was thankful that Zelophechad could not have focused on more than one wife. The ways between a husband and one wife were difficult enough.

"Yet," she said, "Malah will manage."

CHAPTER 8
THE SHEEP SHEARERS

TWO SHEARERS STOOD in the center of Boaz's clan circle, calling out, "Sheep sheared. Newest tools. Nothing like it." Next to each stood a nervous ewe pulling at its rope.

The taller of the two was in his early twenties, a narrow man with a mass of copper-colored hair and a redhead's complexion. The sun had melded his freckles so his arms and legs were a brown mosaic.

The other shearer was about the same age, with a moon face. Although his face was soft and round, his manner was rough.

They quickly drew a circle of people. When the crowd ringed them, the redheaded man pulled a strange tool from the belt of his tunic and held it aloft: two bronze blades joined at the top by a flexible metal band. He scissored the blades together for the crowd to see.

"These from the Kenites, known to all as master metalworkers. With these we will shear your sheep," he asserted, his hair glowing like embers in the late afternoon.

"Why choose the old way? Combs that only pluck out tufts of wool. These," he waved the shears, "can cut a whole coat as one. Takes less time. Good for me." He thumped his chest for emphasis. "And gives more wool at better value. Good for you." He stretched the shears toward the crowd.

"Watch," he insisted as the two men each grasped the head of a ewe. Each made long strokes up one side of his sheep, then sheared the other side. The ewes, their bellies bulging slightly with the hint of lambs, jumped aside when released and shook themselves, surprised at their own lightness as the two shearers held up whole pelts.

"Here. This is what we can do. From sunup to sundown, more than fifty sheep each."

"How much?" one man called out.

"One pelt for every ten."

"Too much."

"Not if you get half-again as much wool, which you can trade at greater value."

"One pelt for every fifteen," called another.

The round-faced shearer laughed and, with his staff, tickled the two sheared ewes in a dance around his legs.

"One for twelve. First-time price for you," the ember-haired shearer pointed around the circle, "and you and you and you."

Many, including Noa, decided to try the shearers with their new shears.

The next day, shepherds stood or squatted near their flocks, waiting their turn. The ripe smell of sheep and the sweat of the shearers competed with the baa-ing of edgy animals and a low undertone of conversation. A pair of girls threw a camel-hide ball back and forth. Two old men, sitting on a pile of fleece, waiting for the shearers to finish the rest, reminisced about their days in Egypt.

Tirzah sat on Malah's bride-price donkey, leaning her head against its neck as she watched, mesmerized by the zzzt-zzzt-zzzt of the shearers' blades.

Hoglah had taken the goats up the slopes to graze. Before she left, she checked how many flocks came ahead of theirs, then estimated when to return. "I will return in plenty of time."

Tirzah had eyes only for the shearers' blades.

"Tirzah . . . are you listening?"

"Yes. I'm listening. I'm listening," she answered as Hoglah turned to leave, shaking her head.

Soon after, Adam ran over and pulled himself onto the donkey, right behind Tirzah.

"Look what I've got," he said, reaching his arm around her and opening his fist to display a handful of round gray stones. "Let's play."

Tirzah twisted to face him. "I am busy," she said, turning back to the shearers.

Noa had shown Hoglah and Tirzah which fleece to give in payment, cautioning them not to let the shearers get away with the best the sisters had. Tirzah kept her eyes on the shearers.

"I'm not going to let them get away with a thing," she whispered to Adam.

"We can play right in front of your old donkey and the shearers won't be able to slip anything by you. Come on, Tirzah," he cajoled.

"I'll even find stones for you while you spear those shearers with your eyes."

Tirzah liked the offer and the fierce image.

"All right. But make sure you get round stones. Not ones with sharp edges that bounce off the mark."

"You'll have them."

Adam slipped off the donkey and dashed off to find a set of dark stones. When he returned, he cut a circle in the hardpan as wide as a well cover.

Tirzah slid off the donkey and opened her hand for the stones. Adam poured them in and she grinned. "Let's go."

They stepped off seven paces from the circle where Adam scratched a "start" line into the dirt.

"I go first," Tirzah said.

"Fine."

She took a quick look to make sure the shearers had not touched her sheep then threw. The dark stone hit near-center, then rolled to the far edge of the groove Adam had cut.

"No! Too hard," Tirzah cried. "I was thinking about the sheep. I'm taking that throw over."

"Oh, no. That was a fair throw. My turn."

Adam stepped to the line and lobbed his first stone. His bounced in the circle, then skipped over the grooved edge. He threw his hands up and groaned dramatically. Tirzah shook her head and smiled.

"Too bad."

They took turns throwing, Tirzah glancing at the shearers, until they were down to one stone each. She threw, and her dark stone stopped at the edge of the circle. Adam's last stone bumped hers into the groove, while it sat triumphant on the inner side of the circle.

"Wait. You cheated. You stepped over the line."

"I did not."

"You did. I saw you."

Tirzah, furious, kicked all the stones out of the circle. Adam ran at her, dove, and knocked her down, shouting, "I won. I won again. You are the cheater."

As they wrestled on the dusty plain, Tirzah bit Adam in the fleshy part of his forearm. He howled and punched at her, but she rolled away, and he grasped his punctured arm. The old men hurried over to break up the scuffle.

The redheaded shearer growled, "Keep those brats quiet. They're making the sheep nervous."

Tirzah sat in the dirt with her knees up, looking at Adam. Blood dripped from his arm into the dirt. He cried, then dragged his good arm over his eyes to wipe away his tears, smearing dirt on his face.

Chastened by Adam's tears and the sight of his blood, Tirzah pleaded with one of the old men, "Please help me get him on my donkey. We can fix his arm at home. Adam's my friend."

"Yes, friends, we can see." One of the men laughed.

"It's just a cut, little mother," said the other, derisively.

But they helped Adam onto the donkey, and Tirzah grabbed the animal's lead. She pulled the donkey home with guilty impatience, forgetting about the sheep. There, Noa packed a poultice of spider-flower leaves onto Adam's forearm.

Then she asked, "Are the sheep shorn?"

Tirzah froze, then turned, and took off running.

HOGLAH LED THE goats down to the shearing station halfway through the afternoon. Only a couple of shepherds remained, waiting for their sheep to be shorn. She found one of the shearers working on the second of her sheep, but did not find Tirzah. Horrified, she asked if they had seen a young girl with wild hair and sun-browned skin.

"Wild hair? Ah, her. She bit her boyfriend's arm, then took him home."

"I'll wait for that one to reach ripeness," sniggered the moonfaced shearer. "Fun comes in all forms."

Hoglah ignored him and asked the redheaded shearer, "Did she show you which fleece you may take for payment?"

"No."

Bent over the sheep, he stopped cutting and twisted his neck to look up. He saw a tall young woman, picking at a fingernail. Hoglah quickly hid the hand with the ripped nail behind her skirt. With the other she pointed.

"Those two, the one with the tan patch near its nose and the one just behind it. And that one over there with the curly rump. Those you may take."

"Not this one?" He ran his hand over the fine, soft wool.

"No."

"Who's telling me 'no'? I ask you, Miss Pole."

Hoglah gasped, thinking she heard a slight of her height.

"Ech. We are tired," he said, excusing himself. "And you must be a clever maiden to know which sheep to choose."

"No, but my sister Noa . . . she is. *And* she will win our father's promised land for us," Hoglah boasted.

"Who's 'us'?"

"The daughters of Zelophechad."

The redheaded shearer turned back to his work and threw over his shoulder, "And your brothers? What will they get?"

"We have no brothers."

"Ah." He finished and rose, holding up the fleece. "Nice," he said, stroking the wool, but looking directly at Hoglah.

She raised her left shoulder, to straighten the line of her breasts, and looked right back at him, surprised by her boldness. Then a flurry of peripheral motion caught her attention.

"Tirzah! What happened . . ."

"IknowIknowIknow," Tirzah blurted, out of breath. She darted out and grabbed the fleece from the shearer. "Not this one."

"Tirzah," Hoglah admonished. "What will he think of you? They know which fleece is theirs. *I* told them, since you were not here."

"We know what to think of her," the moonfaced shearer interjected. "She's Moloch's little sister."

"Who's Moloch?" Hoglah and Tirzah asked.

"Moloch," he paused dramatically, hastily finishing off the sheep he was holding, "is the god that eats children. There's a high place in the north with an altar raised to Moloch. A huge god with rams' horns. When Moloch is hungry, the people build a fire in Moloch's bronze belly. They throw a child in. Moloch eats the child and is satisfied. When Moloch is no longer hungry, he gives women babies and men victory in battle."

Hoglah and Tirzah sat on their haunches, listening, their eyes wide. Ignoring them, the redheaded shearer continued to work, as if he had heard all of this before.

"The people who worship him feed them their babies?"

"Oh no, they feed Moloch the children of their slaves or children they capture. Children like *you*." He lunged at Tirzah.

Hoglah shouted, "Stop, you're scaring her. Make him stop."

"That's enough," the redheaded shearer ordered.

"I was just having a little fun."

"Have fun on your own time. Let's get this done."

When the girls' sheep were shorn, they loaded the fleece onto the donkey. Tirzah jittered to tell of the terrible god Moloch and his meals. As they left, Hoglah looked back, hoping the redheaded shearer would say something to her. She was not disappointed.

"Good luck to you, Miss Landowner." He smiled at his half-formed idea.

"IN THREE DAYS' time you will be a married man," Gaddi said to Hur.

They sat in Gaddi's compartment within the family's tent. Alone with Hur, Gaddi had called for date wine, and now reclined against a stack of pillows. Hur sat bolt upright.

"Yes," said Hur. His mind full of questions about marriage and women, he could not think of more to say.

His time in the company of women, even his mother, had become limited once he put on a long robe. He knew the maiden chosen for him only by sight.

With an image of Noa prodding him, he released one of his questions.

"How will I speak with her? How does one speak with a woman?"

"Laud her, but with truth. If her stews taste like mud, praise her weaving. If her wovens look like the wandering of a goat, praise her soft voice . . ."

"But," Hur broke in, "Noa is known as strong-willed and clever. What if . . . ?" he began, loath to demean himself in his father's eyes. "What if she is more clever than I am?"

Gaddi ben Susi leaned forward, putting his hands on his son's shoulders. Hur was accomplished in so many ways that it touched Gaddi to hear his son's concern.

"Women know more than men in many ways. Husbands of any worth know this. Women understand matters of the heart. Your

Yoela caught strands of Noa's hair between her fingers and twisted one narrow braid, then another.

"Gentle, please," she cautioned. "I am not a donkey and my hair is not a harness."

"Hold still, donkey," Yoela replied.

More softly, Noa said, "I am not ready to be a wife, buried in everything a wife must do."

"Ho," Yoela said, giving the braid she was working on a gentle tug, "what about all of that 'we shall secure our land if we marry within our tribe'?"

"That is in the bright light of day. But the glow of my soul tells me . . ."

"Glowing souls . . ." Yoela turned Noa's words lightly. "I will tell you a story of glowing souls."

"I don't want to lose you," Noa insisted.

"Don't worry, my heart," Yoela said, masking the same fear. "See Malah and her friends. They are thick as a stew."

The image drew a grin from Noa as she shed her dark mood for the pleasure of Yoela's company.

" . . . or, maybe like a flock of Nile geese," Yoela continued.

Noa blew a few low honks, causing them both to giggle.

Her mother heard, shot Noa a warning look, then turned back to the dance.

Neither spoke much as Yoela twined braid after narrow braid, looping them together in an intricate pattern, at ease in each other's company, watching the dancers.

The musicians and dancers paused to catch their breath.

Seglit took her cue and rose. "I apologize for leaving early. I must attend to my husband. When they return from the groom's celebration, they are full of expectations," she said archly. One of her cousins tittered as they followed her out.

Women turned to see how Malah would react, but Malah was suddenly engaged in a deep discussion of the best remedies for a sour stomach.

The music began again. Hoglah and Milcah joined their mother and Tirzah and the four began a dance, twisting through the crowd, singing, "We are the ones who praise . . ."

A young woman caught Hoglah's hand, another linked onto the chain and another until a long line snaked around itself, women pulling each other along, breathing hard. Noa and Yoela sat silent, their own island.

"Yoela," Noa said, "I need a story. Please, take me away."

"And a story is what you shall have," she answered, as she began in a soft, lilting voice:

"A young man said to his father, 'I want to become a man.'

" 'In time, my son,' his father said.

"Like all young men, he was impatient. He asked his uncle, a man known for his knowledge of magical arts. 'In time, my son.' But he preyed on his uncle's good will until his uncle told him:

" 'Go to the cave at the edge of this plain. Enter and you will begin your journey to what you desire.'

"The young man walked for seven days to where a wall of rock edged the plain. There he found the entrance to a cave and entered. The cave was cool and dark. In the dim light, the young man saw a snake slithering toward him. He grabbed its tail, to fling the snake out of the way. The minute he grasped it, the snake became a stout staff."

"Like the staff Moses brought to Pharaoh, only the other way around," Noa interjected.

"Yes. He held onto the staff and moved farther into the cave following a glow that drew him deeper. He came to a chasm. By this time, the glow was strong, lighting a passageway on the far side of the chasm. He knew he was approaching the light's source.

"The young man threw down his staff to bridge the chasm and, carefully, he crossed. When he turned to retrieve the staff, he saw that it had once again become a snake, slithering away toward the mouth of the cave. With great dismay, the young man realized his only choice was to continue.

"Cautiously, he continued toward the source of the glow until he reached the end of the passageway and an old man who was the source of the glow. He asked him, 'What must I do to become a man?'

" 'You passed my brother on your way. He told me you would come.'

"The young man, puzzled, asked the question again. 'Please, tell me what I must do.'

" 'Be patient, and I will tell you a tale. Once there lived a wealthy man with an only daughter. One day, a tree within his walled garden bore a beautiful golden-fleshed fruit. His daughter reached up to pluck the fruit when a crow landed on the branch. The crow told her that if she plucked the fruit, it would immediately wither.

" 'The young woman sat, day after day, pining for the perfect fruit that hung from the tree, longing for its juice on her lips. On the day the young woman decided to take the golden globe, despite the crow's warning, an eagle flew down, plucked the fruit from the tree, and carried it off. As it did so, the young woman withered.

" 'The eagle flew to the other end of the world. Her aerie rested on a ledge at the top of a high mountain and, within, nestled three young eaglets. She offered the golden fruit to her young, and they eagerly tore its flesh. At the center of the fruit lay a clear jewel the color of the sky.

" 'The eagle knew the jewel was meant for man, for those who cleaved to the path of righteousness. She searched the world over, looking for those who might merit the jewel. She flew until her wings grew tired, but without success. She returned to her nest and, when her young ones grew, she gave the jewel to the strongest of them, to complete the mission.'

"The eagle flies still, each eagle passing the jewel to its young, from generation to generation. Each new eagle flies the world, looking for the people who can best care for this jewel. Perhaps, one day, the eagle will choose us. And that is an end to my story."

"But, Yoela," Noa said, confused, "what does this have to do with the young man? What became of him and his search?"

"Ah, he has not come to the end of his story. He is still discovering how to be a man—a lifelong journey."

Noa thought about her friend's story and said, "Yoela, I have learned many things from my father and my mother: how to breed sheep, how to make cheese. But you are wise in the ways of the heart."

That was the day her heart became filled. They were at an age when their hearts were open and ready to be filled.

Now Yoela was preparing Noa for marriage. She finished Noa's hair as the celebration began winding down. After nearly everyone had left, having wished Noa good fortune and many children, Bat-Sheva came to sit with them, bringing the pot of henna they had prepared earlier.

Bat-Sheva, who had set one of Noa's feet in her lap, asked Yoela, "What pattern?"

"Love knot."

Each began painting an elaborate pattern of vining flowers that twined up Noa's feet to embrace her ankles. Her feet complete, they began traceries on her hands, spreading from fingertips to wrists.

While Hoglah and Milcah tidied up enough to lay out the beds, Noa's mother and Bat-Sheva's mother sat talking about the old days until Bat-Sheva's mother said, "Come, daughter. It is late."

The women wished each other good night and, following Hoglah and Milcah, their mother withdrew to bed.

Yoela held one of Noa's hands in her own as she continued adorning it with love knots, even past the wrists, each of them loathe to part.

Tirzah, watching Yoela work, asked, "Aren't you going too far up her arm?"

"And shouldn't you be asleep?" Noa demanded.

"I'm not tired."

Tirzah watched in silence for a moment, then asked, "Why do you always hold each other's hand?"

Noa, about to scold Tirzah, changed her tone. "Perhaps our souls are bound up together. We are friends, as close as you and Adam."

"Me and Adam, we're warriors, not squeezy-hand friends."

At that moment they heard a male voice outside. "Yoela. I am here to take you home," he called softly.

"My brother," Yoela said. "Well, I suppose that is the end. I must go."

Noa walked ahead to pull the door aside for Yoela. As she did, Yoela grasped Noa's wrist, slightly smearing the henna.

"We will be as we were," she whispered. "Nothing will change that."

Lying in the dark, Tirzah whispered, "Maybe I *am* tied up in a knot with Adam, like you and Yoela."

"Our souls are bound up with each other, not tied in a knot," Noa corrected. "And what could you know about souls?"

"What could you?"

Tirzah was silent for a moment, reliving parts of the evening. "Wasn't tonight like," Tirzah searched for the right words, "like Miriam's dance at the sea?"

Tirzah's delight woke Hoglah. In the haze between sleep and wakefulness, she realized that the next night she would be the oldest sister at home.

HUR AND NOA stood in the small tent that would serve as their marriage booth, then as their home. Hur had never been this close to Noa and never alone with her. Now she was his. The most valued possession he had owned until this moment was his spear. Struck by responsibility and her beauty, he wished he had something to occupy hands that hung awkwardly at his side.

She, too, felt tense, knowing what would come next.

"Smile," Malah advised. "It will hurt a little, but it will be a good kind of hurt."

Hur nodded to either side of the tent. "Of course, we will enlarge our home as our family increases. Of course, there will be a proper screen for your privacy," he explained earnestly. He fell silent, not knowing what to say next. He remembered his father saying, "Praise her . . ." and remembered that Zelophechad's daughters were known for their fine cheeses.

"Your cheeses are worthy of great praise," Hur began.

"Cheeses?"

"They are like a taste of heaven," he continued, warming to his subject.

Noa was thoroughly confused by his talk of cheeses.

"But I do not think you have ever tasted them."

He was stumped for a moment. "Ah, but I have heard."

Noa had been so absorbed by her own apprehension she had not noticed his. Hur detected the hint of a smile on her face and, suddenly, he saw what she saw.

"Am I not doing this well?"

"You are doing well enough," Noa assured him, realizing how hard he was trying.

"You know, I can strike a target at a hundred paces."

"Your spear arm is well known."

"Well . . ." he said, expectantly.

"Yes, well . . ."

"Perhaps you would be more comfortable with your robe on?"

"Yes, perhaps."

"Here." He offered her the bed, a soft sheepskin atop a broad mat. She lay down with exquisite care, took a deep breath, and let it out slowly. He bent and lifted her skirts to her waist. This was his, he told himself.

With her arms at her sides, grasping clumps of sheepskin, Noa knew the time had come to smile.

Hur saw Noa's smiling face in a blur, his anxiety overwhelmed by animal desire. He ungirded his robe and lowered himself, fumbling at first. Then, shuttering and plunging, he lost himself in Noa.

Noa made not a sound and held her rictus of a smile so long her face hurt.

Afterward, when he saw the blood that he knew should be there, he asked anxiously, "Have I hurt you?"

"No," she lied.

"You will see," he said, as he tenderly brushed tangled braids from her face. "I will become very good at this, too."

"MALAH." LIGHTING UP at the sight of Malah's familiar face, Noa tumbled out news of camp politics.

"Hur says there is talk of a meeting. Korach, the Levite prince—he's organizing it. Something about 'our new Pharaoh,' as Korach calls Moses. He says Moses grew up in Pharaoh's court and acts it. Korach is calling for broader leadership. Perhaps he is right. But who has asked me? Not the women of Gaddi's clan. Stiff as sticks, and they speak only of weaving and . . . and . . . household. Oh, I hoped you would come sooner . . ."

"I could not. My obligations . . ." Her excuse floated in the air between them.

"No matter. Here you are. Come. Sit." She ushered her into her tent. "It's small."

"But it is yours. The favored daughter does, indeed, have her own home."

Immediately, Malah wished she could take back the bitter words. She bent her head, weighing what it would take to apologize. Then, as if nothing had happened, she said equitably, "Your husband? How is he?"

Noa let the hurtful words pass.

"Hur, oh, he is a good man . . . But good as Hur is, I do not feel as a wife should."

Malah laughed. "And how should a wife feel?"

"I fear my heart has no room for him."

"They say you will learn to love him," Malah said, thankful that Boaz was her heart's desire, despite Seglit.

Though her sister had her own tent, Malah saw misery in her eyes, and felt more magnanimous. She regaled Noa with stories told among her group of young wives.

"They all talk of the glory of marriage, but most are just polishing the truth. Not me. I tell them about the scorpion dance I do with Seglit."

"I'm sure you give as good as you get," Noa said, applauding her sister's sting.

"Of course, I polish that up, too. It makes them laugh. And then the truth pours out. Stories like yours. Noa, why not join us?"

"No, I would not fit in your circle. But, tell on. Any news interests me."

Malah described a pregnant wife and how taut her belly felt and added, "I feel the seed of life within me."

"Yes?"

As answer, Malah smiled.

"I am so happy for you."

"And, praise Asherah, you should be. Everyone knows a barren wife is worthless."

"Let's go to mother's and work together. Let the flour fly!"

Then Noa remembered what she wanted most.

"Have you talked with Boaz about the Judges of Fifties?"

Remembering the heat of her fight with Boaz, Malah replied, "I have. But he has been so busy. To mention it again, well, when you have so many wifely duties . . ."

"Ask again. Securing our father's land. *This* is my heart's desire."

"I will, I will."

CHAPTER 10
JUDGES OF FIFTIES

WORK ON THE Tent of Meeting continued: silver plates hammered, inscribed, then stored in neat stacks; curtains woven and folded, to be fitted to polished poles. When the work was finished, the people's journey would begin again. Everyone was anxious to move on. The mountain, which had once glowed with a holy presence, now glowered.

Long lines of irritable women waited at the few wells. Axes, cutting in the night, reduced the desert's thin scattering of umbrella acacias. Flocks ate away the herbage of the lower slopes. People burdened the land, as the land burdened them.

The young learned the language and the customs of their harsh surroundings. They saw Midianites and Kenites rinsing their hair in camel urine, then dressing it with scented oil. They did the same.

The young men called each other by new, strong names, not the names of Egyptian bondage. They gave themselves names of what they saw around them: wolf, eagle, snake. They girded themselves with strong words: "Before we reach the lands promised us, we will let the desert temper us, like the point of a spear."

Such talk frightened parents who had not raised their sons to be pointed spears nor their daughters to wash their hair in the stream of a camel.

Noa felt the camp's need to push onward and wanted a hearing before the Judges of Fifties before they did. One evening, a few weeks after their marriage, she asked Hur to accompany her to a meeting with Boaz and Malah for an accounting of the livestock.

As they entered Boaz's tent, Noa nodded to Seglit, who sat outside sipping tea and chatting with her bondmaid. While they took account of goats and sheep, Hur listened, and Noa took account of Hur. He soaked up information and interactions as if the whole world were full of instruction.

Israel's children, would overwhelm him. With what? With the fruit of our bodies, that's what.

"To make sure we would bear few children," their mother continued, "Pharaoh's slave masters made our men sleep in the fields near the construction. This was when they began killing the baby boys.

"But we would steal into the fields at night to sleep with our husbands. They were so tired, ruined by those accursed monuments. Before we went down to the fields, we dressed our hair as best we could, hoping in the light of the stars our husbands would not see how wretched we looked. Our mirrors helped make us desirable to our husbands.

"Get me my mirror," she said to Milcah.

Milcah obeyed, running her hand over the mirror's bronze surface before handing it to her mother. Ada held up the mirror to show off its surfaces.

"This was my mother's and her mother's before that. It helped build up your father's house. I will contribute my mirror to those building the Tent of Meeting."

Noa saw her mother in a new light and wondered at her bravery. If her mother had chanced the watchman's cane to bring them into the world, Noa felt certain her pursuit of their inheritance extended that arc.

RINA HELPED MIRIAM collect the women's mirrors, and Miriam told her brother Moses of their plan. Moses refused the mirrors as second-hand goods and trifles of vanity.

Korach's wife smoldered to her husband, "Who is he to refuse? He who was raised in the lap of Pharaoh's daughter."

"Does Moses think our wives and mothers are not good enough?" Korach said among the Levites. "Let us hear from God, not Moses."

God softened Moses's heart, and the mirrors were made into lavers.

CHAPTER 11
INTO THE WILDERNESS

IN THE SECOND month of the second year since leaving Egypt, Moses and Aaron took a census of all men over the age of twenty from each tribe: from Reuben, Simeon, and Judah, from Issachar, Zebulun, Benjamin, Dan, Asher, Gad, and Naftali, and from the tribes of Joseph's sons, Efraim and Manasseh. They did not count those from the tribe of Levi.

"Why do they not count the Levis," Hoglah asked her mother.

"Because they are the priests," answered Milcah.

"I asked mother. You do not look like her."

"Milcah is correct," Ada said, patting Milcah's knee. "She who spends time close to the seat of authority."

"Why aren't they counting us," Tirzah asked.

"The census is to count the number of fighting-age men. Soon we will enter lands rich in trees and grasses, lands that were once ours. But they say we may have to fight for these lands we have been promised."

"What kind of promise is that?"

"Tirzah," Milcah admonished. "Stop this flood of questions."

"Well, even if we have to fight, I can fight as good as Adam," Tirzah prattled on. "If they count Adam, why can't they count me?"

"They are not yet counting Adam . . ."

Tirzah did not wait to hear the rest. "I forgot . . . Adam and I are after the small prickly one," she yelled as she ran into the twilight to set a trap for a hedgehog.

"Tirzah," Her mother called after her.

"I'll bring her back," Hoglah offered before running out.

"Oh," their mother sighed. "I wish Noa were here to manage my wild child."

Milcah sighed. She would not be going back to the center of camp. The work was done. Oholiav had said he hoped to see her again, and his eyes softened for her. She hoped he would ask after her, perhaps ask for her. Now that she had tasted something for herself, Milcah wanted more.

THE TRIBES PREPARED to travel again. The night before, Noa had found Boaz's watchman and offered him silver if he would unbury their father's bones. Before the moon quartered the sky, he returned, their father's bones wrapped in the cloth she had given him. Noa secured the precious package in a large hide bag, relieved to have fulfilled her vow.

At dawn, Noa and Hur took down and folded their home. While her husband went to help his parents, Noa sought Yoela.

They wandered together along the base of the mountain, choosing a path through a narrow-necked canyon that opened onto a basin whose sides were strewn with boulders. Unknowingly, they had made their way into the canyon where the Guardians had bludgeoned her father.

Sitting on a sandy bed below the boulders, Noa said, "I fear the Judges of Hundreds will not hear us until we arrive at the next stopping place."

"Is this so important to you?"

"I want the surety of my own birthright. For me and for my sisters. What could be more important?"

"More important than Hur?"

"Oh, he is kind and accomplished. I cannot find fault."

As they talked, swallows celebrated the new morning, soaring against the canyon walls in winged dance. They did not notice the swallows nor did they notice Hur, who had followed them, jealous of Yoela.

Yoela sighed. "I am to be wed to Barzel, the eldest son of Zerach. Of Efraim, not even our tribe."

"But not far. Oh, Yoela, I am happy for you."

"Happy?"

"You will be cared for. Settled. We will have husbands *and* time together."

"But what they tell of Barzel . . ."

They talked until the rising sun found a crack in the canyon and dazzled their eyes.

"Before we go . . ." Noa clasped Yoela's wrist and guided her hand over the top of her slightly swelling stomach.

Yoela gasped, "Is it true?"

"Yes. Malah and I will bear children at nearly the same time. Strange, isn't it, to think there is another soul growing within me?"

Peering down from behind a boulder, Hur saw Noa guide Yoela's hand. And this is how he learned he would become a father.

LED BY THE Levites, the people set their faces east and left the mountain of God, tribe by tribe, they and their children and their maidservants and their manservants, with their camels and their asses, their goats and their sheep, and all their goods.

The Ark of the Covenant led them, carried by the Levites and marked by a column of cloud that rose pure and white. Snaking slowly across the dry plain, the mosaic of people could always see the strangely shimmering cloud-column ahead, rising to the heavens.

Bursts of song rose up from the men of Asher, answered in song by their women. A shoving match between two groups of boys broke out among the tribe of Reuben. Knots of men discussed direction, wondering if Moses knew the way.

As they walked, Noa sought Malah. Finding her, she linked arms with her sister and said, "I am now like you."

Malah turned to her. "What do you mean?"

Noa ran her free hand over the small bulge in her belly. "You know."

They turned to each other, smiles creasing their faces.

"Have you told Hur?"

"Not yet. Like you, I want to be sure this child will hold."

Farther ahead, Hur walked with his father, Gaddi ben Susi. Gaddi wished that his own sons, rather than Gamaliel's, held Manasseh's banner. Like most, he walked dully in the waning day, hearing the flinty rhythm of animal hooves striking rock. Bone-dry plains edged by low hills. The same views all day. They might have been walking in place.

"They say there is no food to gather along the way," Gaddi said. "Already many are grumbling as loudly as their stomachs."

ewes bent their heads to sip, all but one. She stood guard, on the lookout for leopards.

The men watched, their breath shallow and tight. Haddad rose from his crouch, soundlessly cleared the concealing boulder, and cocked his spear.

The scout ewe, spotting Haddad, bleated and charged toward a steep rockslide, followed by the rest of the band. Haddad had already loosed his spear, striking the side of an old ewe. She arched in pain, then ran heavily with the rest toward the rocks. The clatter of hooves and yelling men shattered the quiet of the pool.

"To her," Haddad cried.

He sprinted toward the stricken ewe, mindless of sharp rocks spiking his sandaled feet, pulling his knife from its sheath as he ran. The ewe slowed for a moment, trying to shake off the spear. Haddad, his lungs bursting, flung himself forward. Avoiding her short, sharp horns, he plunged his hand into the loose skin at the nape of her neck and jerked the ewe's head back hard. He sliced across her jugular vein, her blood arcing dark red, staining the desert floor.

The others caught up and one of the Midianites cupped his hands under the rush of blood and drank, viscous red dripping from mouth to chin. He uttered praise to a Midianite god. As she bled out, the Midianites each drank from the fount of life.

"Drink," Haddad urged Hur. "The gods will give you her strength."

Hur dipped his finger in the now-trickling blood. His tribesmen followed his lead. None wanted to appear hesitant.

Seeing how little the Israelites took, Haddad offered, "Let me squeeze more for you."

"It is not our custom," Hur said, wiping his bloody finger on his thigh.

His hospitality rejected, Haddad said, "Custom? What do slaves know of hunting customs?"

Realizing his unintended slur, Haddad hoped Hur did not understand the Midian word for "slave."

"We are free men. No less than you," Hur challenged.

Haddad grabbed the ewe's forelegs and, looking at Hur, strove to drain the tension.

"Together, we can drag her to that slope. We'll gut her . . . as free men do." He grinned at Hur.

Haddad cut the ewe from belly to breast, then turned her on her side so her stomach and intestines slopped out. He reached inside and cut around her anus, where the large intestine was anchored, loosening a mass of soft organs. He sliced the large intestine from the coils of the small.

"Here," he said, handing the large intestine to the youngest of his fellows, "slice and clean this."

"Some day I will rise above the rank of shit-scraper," the young man asserted, smiling to show he did not take offense.

"When your brother leaves the women's side and comes out with us. Then *he* will scrape shit." Haddad laughed.

"My brother is still too young to leave the women's side," said Efram. "So says my mother. And what he sees . . ."

"Ho! We have spies like that . . ." said a Midianite.

They cleaned their kill, boasting and joking. One of Haddad's men—the silent one with the scar that wrinkled the right side of his face—chopped at a haunch with a hand axe, severing it from the ewe's body.

Two made a fire as the rest worked on the body, severing, washing, coiling, and tying. The stomach would serve as a bag. Sliced into long lengths, the intestines would be used to sew tent sutures.

A rising moon looked down upon young men too busy to notice the dark. They suspended the haunch above the fire on a pair of forked sticks. They laid the heart, kidneys, and liver on a bed of coals. Haddad parceled out the cooked organs, saving the heart for himself. He bit in, satisfaction suffusing his face.

"Yes," agreed Hur, through a mouth full of liver, "food from God."

"Delivered by my hand," Haddad reminded all.

When the haunch was ready, they gorged some more, goat grease ringing their mouths and running down their fingers. When they were finished, they retrieved their robes and wrapped themselves for sleep, their bellies distended in painful pleasure. Someone burped.

Hur turned to Haddad. "You were wise to take the old ewe."

"Past her best breeding years," Haddad agreed, warmed by Hur's praise. "The health of the herd, like the health of the tribe."

Finally, the only voice was that of the fire, crackling as it was left to die.

CHAPTER 12
HIS OWN KILL

HUR AWOKE BEFORE the sun. He remembered the ibex and the grace of Haddad's kill, years in the making. He wanted his own kill.

Rising silently, he shed his cloak and climbed upward. He hoped to find a pool above, where ibex might come, sensing that their usual watering hole was occupied. Squeezing between boulders, he tried to stay low and out of sight. The bite of morning on his skin and the thrill of ascent nearly caused him to forget his purpose until he reached a place where hill met sheer scarp. There erosion had carved a small basin filled with water.

Secreted between a saltbush and a boulder, Hur waited, watching the basin as the rising sun painted the sky pink and gold. Hearing nothing, he dozed.

The clink of hooves woke him. Three ibex picked their way down what looked like sheer rock. Squinting in the pink light, Hur watched the lead animal leap down from one hidden ledge to another, scattering gravel. The other two followed.

Three young males, two with half-arched horns. The lead animal was larger, with horns fully arched, like the eyebrows of Asherah. Hur wanted him.

He moved to the edge of the saltbush and crouched, with his spear ready. The large male raised his head, sniffing the air. His arched horns nearly met his withers and his nose was shiny with moisture.

As the three bent their heads to drink, Hur rose and pulled back his spear, aligning it with the side of the big male. One of the younger ibex moved, obstructing his shot. As he refocused on the younger ibex, he heard a rumble of rocks behind him. The ibex heard, too, and looked up, spotting Hur and his intent. Quickly, Hur cast his spear. It pierced the young male, but did not hold, falling off as the ibex fled in a haste of escape.

A second spear parted the air next to Hur's head, so close he felt the long shaft's breath.

"You son of a slave . . ." someone screamed behind him. "I knew you would fault the shot."

Hur was already bounding after the goats as he realized it was Haddad's surly, scar-faced companion. He did not care. His aim was the ibex. The Midianite's spear had glanced off the now-panicked animal. The three ibex clattered down the dry, narrow streambed issuing from the basin. Behind them, Hur lobbed rocks at the injured male, barely noticing he had scraped his shin raw while pushing past a boulder.

The streambed gullied down the hill, stopped suddenly at a ledge, then continued a few feet below. The large male took the drop easily. The other two followed, the injured goat catching a hoof on a rock and stumbling, just enough to give Hur hope. As Hur leaped down from the ledge, a protruding branch ripped the skin under his left arm. He felt blood wetting his side, but his need was fierce. He hurled rocks as he slid down the slope, one of the rocks hitting the ibex on the back of head, squarely between the horns. The ibex stopped, shook its head as if trying to remember something, then staggered on. Hur whooped at his success. Farther behind, the Midianite growled.

Gaining on the slowed animal, Hur reached for his knife. He wanted to avoid the ibex's small, sharp horns, but could wait no longer. From a few feet behind, Hur launched himself onto the animal's back. With his left hand, he grabbed the nape of the ibex's neck, as Haddad had done. He slashed with his right, feeling the knife bite flesh. Then he lost his grip, slid off, and rolled away to avoid the ibex's hooves. All he was left with was the rancid smell of the goat and its fear.

He cursed, throwing rocks after the animal as he watched it limp hurriedly down the hill. "May a leopard eat your liver," he shouted.

"The same to you, you stupid tool of an Egyptian taskmaster," said the Midianite. "I knew you would lose him. That was my animal to take."

"So. The voiceless one can talk." Hur turned to the Scarface. "And what comes out? A stream of shit."

The Midianite, seeing a bloodied foreigner before him, snarled. "Spawn of a dog, cast your eyes down when you talk to a man." He did not see how crazed Hur was at his loss. "You come into our lands. You try for our game. Next you will try for our women . . ."

Inflamed with rage, because of the goat and now because of the Scarface, Hur sprang at him, knocking him to the ground. They bashed at each other until Hur's fire abated. He pulled himself away, showing the end of the fight was his choosing. He stalked off to find his spear, keeping an eye on the Midianite. The Scarface did the same, cursing under his breath.

Hur trudged into camp first, his gouged left arm throbbing with pain.

"What happened to you?" Haddad asked.

Hur jerked his head toward the hill. "Your companion happened to me."

Efram led Hur to the edge of the pool, calling to the third Israelite, "Wet my cloak and bring it."

With the wetted cloak, Efram dabbed away the gore, Hur grimacing at every stroke.

Haddad fetched something from a bag hidden among the folds of his cloak, then tore a strip of cloth from the hem. He drew a handful of felted leaves from the bag, dipped them in the pool, and matted the leaves together.

"Press this against the wound."

Efram held the poultice against the wound while Haddad wrapped it tight to Hur's upper arm. When he was finished, he pulled something else from the bag.

"Chew this." He handed Hur a piece of willow bark. "It will ease the pain."

As he chewed, Hur offered his thanks, saying, "Your cloak . . ."

Haddad waved away the rest of Hur's words and said, "My sister now has an excuse to bind a length of her excellent embroidery around the bottom."

After binding the wound, Efram and Haddad walked Hur into the pool until the water reached his chest. Hur leaned heavily on the arms of his companions, the cold water stinging every cut and scrap as it cleansed.

"Aiyyeeee," Hur howled, releasing his pain, his fight with the Scarface, and the loss of the ibex.

At that moment, the youngest Midianite interrupted, asking Haddad, "What should we do with the animal? Cut him or leave him whole?"

"Leave him whole," Haddad answered. "Eh, I forgot," he said to Hur. "Just before you appeared, a young ibex stumbled into camp. Just escaped a leopard, I'd say. Its throat ripped and its life leaking away. The gods took the ibex from the leopard and delivered it to us. A gift."

Hur thought a minute, then realized what must have happened. A smile spread across his face.

"I am your leopard."

Shaking off their helping hands, he slogged back to the water's edge, anxious to see if he was correct. Gingerly, he clambered to the bank and asked Haddad's young man to lead him to the ibex, then turned to beckon Haddad and Efram.

They followed the Midianite to the freshly gutted ibex. Hur searched the area behind the withers.

"Here . . ." He fingered a shallow wound. "My hit that did not hold."

He began the story of his pursuit. Just as he reached the part where the branch scourged his arm, the Scarface sidled into camp, his eyes shifting to catch the mood of the scene. He saw that he had arrived too late. Hur had told his tale. But he struck a pose, arms akimbo.

"The stealer of other men's meat. It was I who stalked that animal," he challenged.

"It was you who frightened them off," Hur returned.

"Stop," said Haddad. "Hur has brought us wild goat. What is there to argue about?"

"You support his claim above mine?" He looked to the other two Midianites. "Our leader's son is leaning to the side of the stranger, the side of the weak."

As Hur watched, Haddad wrapped himself in a cloak of authority and, in an unbending voice, confronted his accuser.

"You are making a problem where none lies. You are the problem, and I know how to deal with problems. The animal is Hur's. Swallow the anger you are chewing on," Haddad swept a dismissive arm toward the wilderness, "or go!"

Scarface spat and turned aside, his neck bent just enough to indicate he understood the threat but not enough to declare the war over. The younger men returned to the task of lashing the ibex to a pole, ready for transport.

Her throat raw from vomiting, Noa whispered, "I am ashamed. I humiliated you. And I am feeling better. I can ride, and we can go right now."

Hur raised his eyebrows at her lie and smiled.

"I don't want you to sacrifice praise because of me," she added.

"Oh, the feast. My mother will make much of me in my absence. She will be free to let her praises soar. Please, drink." He handed her a waterskin. "My father, too, will feel no restraint. For me, the prize was getting the goat more than all the words that follow."

He secured the second rug atop the piles of shale, shading Noa while he told his tale: Haddad, the ibex, Scarface. The story took her away, as it was meant to.

She touched the edge of his bound wound. "You are brave. And kind."

"This is the praise I desire."

The shelter and their words separated them from the thudding feet and rumble of passing voices.

"I have something to tell you," Noa began.

Hur heart swelled, anticipating what she would reveal.

" . . . your child is growing within me."

He reached to hold her. She bowed her head. It pained her to be caught in Hur's love with none to return. She was relieved to offer a child.

"You must tell my mother," he insisted.

When she had rested, Hur lifted Noa onto the donkey and they caught up with his clan. She whispered the news to his mother, who clapped her hands and laughed.

"A feast, indeed," she crowed, and told her sister, who told her sisters-in-law and her cousins. In minutes, all knew, and Noa's shame was overspread with triumph.

CHAPTER 13
HUNGER

THE ISRAELITES JOURNEYED in spring, when storks that wintered on African savannas soared north to the lands of the light-skinned peoples. Storks and millions of other winged migrants traced the shore of the Red Sea, named for the red mountains reflected in the water. Trudging on the western side of the mountains, the Israelites knew nothing of the sea, only the mountains and lines of storks.

"Look, ten of them."

Tirzah sat on Malah's white donkey, wedged between the donkey's neck and her mother, her head craned toward the black-and-white birds.

"Ten? There's tens of tens," said Hoglah, walking alongside.

"Ten or tens of tens, who cares," crabbed Tirzah.

Tirzah rode because she was too weak to walk. Ada was thankful Tirzah had not succumbed like other children, who were hastily buried along the way. The long days struggling across the desert, the scarcity of water and food, and the heat all took their toll.

Just before lambing, when milk was scarce, hunger hollowed their cheeks. Many were tempted to slaughter a sheep, but they held off. Their flocks were their livelihood and, soon, they expected to reach the verdant land God had promised. Only *manna* kept them from starving. They scraped the light, sweet stuff from leaves and came to loathe it.

Adam ran up to tickle Tirzah's toes with a piece of reed. He glanced to see if she smiled. He patted his belly, slightly swollen from malnutrition, like hers.

"You have a little pot and so do I—just in case we have food to put in it."

She smiled at his joke, knowing he was trying to entertain her.

"I'm so hungry. I'm so tired of being hungry," Hoglah whined. "Mother, remind us about the foods of Egypt."

All through the camps, people with empty bellies remembered the foods of Egypt and, remembering, complained at their lack.

"Moses has brought us into the desert to die," Hoglah said, echoing what she heard others say.

Moses himself worried. Miriam heard him talking aloud at night to God, asking why he was chosen to lead when he only led them from trouble to trouble. After hearing these one-sided conversations, Miriam confided to Rina that she wondered about her brother's sanity. She believed her brother sometimes wondered, too.

"Moses carries our troubles heavily," Milcah said, in answer to Hoglah.

"How do you know?"

"Rina tells me."

Rina also told her that Oholiav had asked after her. Milcah did not reveal this because the last time she hinted at Oholiav's intentions, Noa cut her off with, "He is of the tribe of Dan. Not one of us."

"Your aim is for *us* to inherit, married or not," Milcah countered.

"Yes, but see clearly, Milcah. We want to put the camel's nose under the tent. The rest will follow. If we do not disturb the judges by marrying outside the tribe, they will look with more favor on our appeal."

"But the Judges of Hundreds may be from other tribes . . ."

"It does not matter which tribe. People like to stay in their fixed spheres. Just like the first judge said. They do not like change. We are asking them to change the order of things."

"So, I must be the sacrifice for your desire."

"My desire?" Noa's voice rose. "What if one of us does not marry, and must be indentured or worse. You can see how close to starvation we live."

BOAZ AND GADDI walked with their heads bent together, their voices low but intense. Hur followed, gathering as much of the conversation as he could.

"The mutterings against Moses have become louder," Boaz said.

"I, too, have heard them. As have other headmen."

"And who can blame them? Children, old ones, even young men are dying like fish on hot rocks."

"Fish. Don't talk of fish. That is all I hear. 'The succulent fish of Egypt—we long for home.' They forget the other delicacies offered in Egypt—broken bones, murdered sons . . ."

"People forget quickly the old sufferings when new ones are laid on."

Gaddi nodded. "Korach holds another meeting tonight. Come with me."

"We meet. We talk. Where does it lead?" Boaz objected.

But he and Gaddi went to where Korach designated, at the edge of the Levite camp out of sight of his cousin Moses. With other tribal leaders, they sat on the cold desert floor, lit only by the moon.

"Moses has been a good leader," Korach began, careful to set a tone of respect, but hinting at the past tense. "He and Aaron showed us God's strong arm in Egypt. We did not believe, but slowly, through miracles, we—and Pharaoh—were convinced. Such is the power of God's path . . ." Korach paused for effect.

Men nodded in agreement.

"But are we still on God's path? Does Moses know the way?"

Korach paused again, for the words to set.

Gaddi leaned toward Boaz. "Korach makes a good point," he said in a voice loud enough for all to hear.

Hur, who had wedged himself behind his father, squared his shoulders. His father had spoken first.

"Kenites say the way to the land of our forefathers is not long," said one.

"They tell us that so we will leave the edge of their lands."

"Do we know if this promised land is any good? After all, we have not been there for hundreds of years."

"Do we know if this promised land has been promised by other gods to other people, who now live on it?" asked a man from the tribe of Efraim.

The man's kinsman, Joshua, sat in the shadows behind his father, Nun. Not much older than Hur, Joshua was of proven valor, and he served Moses. He let his gaze drift to the stars. Seeing him with his mouth slightly parted and his vision focused on the heavens, one might have taken Joshua for a dreamy young man. But he heard every word.

Korach steered the discussion back.

"Again, I ask, are we on the right path? God's path? If we were, would our wives be wishing for the melons and, yes, the miseries of Egypt? Would our children be shriveling before our eyes for lack of food and drink?"

He heard murmurs of agreement and went on.

"Did not God say we are to become a nation of priests?"

Korach stopped, before exclaiming with rhetorical flourish, "Each of us a priest, each a leader."

"Amen!" called some.

"Tell us, Korach!"

"What must we do?"

"I will put this question to Moses. That we may all have a share in knowing the road to God's will."

WHILE THE MEN met, wives and daughters had fallen asleep. Wrapped in robes, Malah and Seglit remained awake, sitting on the rug that served as their traveling home, gossiping, each finessing what she had heard about this one or that.

Seglit drew a pomegranate from the sleeve of her robe, carelessly, as if anyone in an arid wilderness might find a pomegranate hidden in her sleeve. She reached for a small knife and plunged it into the leathery red skin. Ruby juice spurted from the incision and she dug her thumb into the cut to crack off a section of fruit. Where Seglit had made the cut, juice trickled down her hand. She bent to suck the juice, then looked at Malah.

The spilled ruby juice reminded Malah of her wedding night. She wanted to know where Seglit got edible treasure, but was too proud to ask. Seglit knew this. That was how it was between them.

Seglit cracked a second segment from the pomegranate and tossed it casually in Malah's direction. "Here. It's quite good."

Malah was so surprised that she missed the toss and the fruit rolled into the grit alongside the rug. She grabbed it up and covered her confusion by picking away the grit, her head bent to the task.

"Thank you," she mumbled. Fearing she sounded submissive, she said it again, head raised, nodding politely. "Thank you. It looks as good as any I've had," she allowed, as if she ate pomegranates regularly.

"So, your sister Noa is with child," Seglit said.

"Yes. We are all so happy for her. I look forward to new motherhood as well. To be a young mother, what could be more fulfilling?" Malah said sweetly, knowing her dagger of words would find their mark.

"I once bloomed with child," Seglit revealed, her voice bitter.

Malah stared, unsure she had heard correctly. She understood that Seglit was one of the barren ones.

Seglit dropped her voice. "I was in love, when I was younger than you. We loved . . . he and I. And he filled me with a child. But his family was too low for my father. My mother learned of my condition and immediately set out to marry me off to someone respectable. It was not hard," she mocked her usual coquetry, "your uncle, Boaz had no children with his first wife, the one who died. He believed the child in my belly was his."

She stopped, silent for a moment.

"Well, who knows what he truly believed. There was talk. Oh, you can be sure tongues flapped. Women 'quack-quacked' about how quickly the bride price was arranged with Boaz, as if my family were giving me away."

"Why are you telling me this?" Malah asked, extremely uncomfortable with Seglit's revelations.

"Can you not guess?"

Malah knew it would not be an answer she wanted to hear, yet she asked, "What happened to your baby?"

"Ah, my child did not hold. I lost the fruit of my beloved. Punishment for bringing dishonor on our family, said my mother. And I shall never have another."

"Why?"

"Boaz. He is the opposite of a pomegranate."

Seglit bit into the fruit, sucked the flesh off the seeds, then spat the remains into the embers.

"All juice and no seeds."

Malah let this sink in, finally realizing the implications.

"But that can't be. I am proof."

"Are you? Do you have the sickness that comes with a child in the belly? Is your belly as rounded as your sister's? Perhaps you have been pleasuring outside Boaz's bed?"

"You witch to say so," Malah hissed.

"My deepest apologies," she said lightly. "But if you are pregnant, I will host a meal in your honor for accomplishing a miracle."

Malah was quiet, then asked, "If what you say is so, why did you say nothing?"

"Who would I have told? 'Boaz has no seed. I know because I carried another's bastard'?"

"Well, you are wrong about Boaz. I am sure."

"You can be sure as sure . . . and go to the grave without a child."

Seglit leaned out toward Malah and placed the remainder of the pomegranate next to her.

"I'm tired. The rest is yours."

She turned from Malah and pulled a sheepskin over her, burying her ringed toes in the curly wool.

Malah lay down, too. The thought of the pomegranate made her sick. She hungered, but her hunger was for a child. Her mind raced with accusations, fear, and fury. She threw off her blanket and stood, took a few steps into the desert, and flung the pomegranate.

MALAH DISMISSED SEGLIT'S accusations as the fiction of a barren woman. She persuaded herself that she had been pregnant, but the trials of their journey had been too much for the unborn within her. She feared the child had stolen back to where he had come from, playing at the feet of Asherah. After a show of monthly blood, Malah commended herself on accepting the sad fate of her first, her unborn child.

One night, when she knew she was ripe, she crept under Boaz's blanket and whispered, "Now, plant your seed and I will grow us a child."

Boaz, who sensed something had passed between his wives, had been avoiding intimacy with either. When Malah came to him, his heart leaped like that of a young man.

CHAPTER 14
WELL MET

THE ISRAELITES LEFT the red mountains, continuing north. Before reaching the Wilderness of Paran, they stopped near a string of wells, none of them sweet water, but tolerable enough to slake their thirst and that of their livestock.

In the heat of the day everyone rested. Hoglah and Milcah erected a lean-to for their mother and Tirzah, who whined for soup. Ada had brought her youngest back from the brink of starvation with broth made from dried meat of the ibex Hur had given them.

Hoglah grabbed a waterskin and trotted toward the nearest well to draw water for soup. Even with a headcloth shading her face, Hoglah had to squint deeply to make out which way to go in the blinding midday sun.

No hills or mountains edged the horizon. No tumbled boulders gave form to the land. God had tilled the desert flat, breaking large rocks into small until the arid earth was shapelessly even, from horizon to horizon. Only a few sparse lines of low gray shrubs hinted at dents along the desert floor where winter water collected.

Shielding her eyes, Hoglah looked for the tall tamarisk that marked the well. Once she located it, she marched straight ahead, looking neither right nor left. At this sun-scorched hour, nothing moved and the vast formless plain scared her.

At the feet of the tamarisk, flat rocks framed the well. A thinner rock lay atop the mouth of the well to keep animals from falling in and polluting the water. Hoglah set down her waterskin and, grunting with effort, shoved aside the well cover. On one of the rocks edging the well, a great camel-hide bucket lay under a frayed palm mat. The bucket was threaded on either side by thick rope, which wound around the base of the tamarisk.

Before lowering the stiff, leather bucket, Hoglah peered into the hole. The rocky sides of the well were illuminated for a foot or two by the noonday sun. Below, all was black. Hoglah dropped the bucket onto the rock and stepped back, with a shiver, feeling unseen eyes. She shook herself to cast off the feeling and looked around. All was still. She was alone. She picked up a small pebble and dropped it into the well to hear how far down the water lay. The bell-like echo told her the water lay far below.

Kneeling, she lowered the bucket into the hole, the fibrous rope rasping her hands as she untangled it. Finally, she heard the bucket hit water and lowered it farther, to fill it. Then she stood, to gain purchase as she lifted. Hand over hand, she pulled the heavy bucket steadily upward, her feet braced, her upper arms straining. About halfway up, she stopped to gather her strength again, letting her arms slacken slightly. Again, she looked around, sure someone was watching.

When she resumed, she had lost momentum. She grunted as she pulled, sliding her left foot forward to gain more purchase. Just as she did, she caught sight of a man emerging from behind the tamarisk.

"Here . . ." he said.

But it was too late. Startled, Hoglah felt her left foot slide out from under her. She lost her balance and her feet flew forward as the bucket's heavy weight dragged her toward the hole. Sharp pebbles scraped the backs of her legs. Her headcloth flew off. It happened so fast she did not think to let go of the rope as she sped toward the mouth of the well. Hoglah gasped as she plummeted downward, the air in the well rushing up her robe. She screamed as the rope played out faster and faster, plunging her into the dark. Water bit her feet, then rose up her legs, slowing her descent and tangling her robe around her body in a wet, heavy mass as swirling water reached her waist.

The rope jerked, stopping so violently Hoglah almost lost her grip.

"Hold on," a voice above echoed. "Don't let go. I've got you."

"Please," she begged, "don't let me die."

Clutching the rope, Hoglah was suddenly aware of how badly her hands burned where the rope had torn into them.

"I can't hold."

"You must," he shouted as he pulled the rope. Slowly, she felt herself rising, the water now at her thighs, then her calves.

"See if you can touch . . . each side of the well . . . with your feet." He expelled the words heavily between labored breaths, as he pulled hand over hand. "Brace your feet." He breathed and pulled. "Let your feet . . . help you walk . . . up the wall."

"Please . . ."

"Listen to my voice."

He pulled.

Her feet were now clear of the water, but she felt her arms were being ripped from their sockets. She had a vision of falling, armless, into the black water that lay waiting to swallow her. Her moan filled the well.

"Listen to me . . . I've got you."

He pulled.

"Press your feet . . . against the sides . . . of the well."

She forced panic from her chest and took a deep breath. Then tentatively spread her legs until her feet touched the sides of the well. She pushed the balls of her feet against the sides, the sandal bottoms slipping slightly. The strain on her arms slackened, and the man above felt it.

"Good. Now walk your feet up as I pull. Press your feet when I stop for breath. Then I'll pull again."

He pulled, then held.

"Feet." He pulled, then held. "Feet."

Her face clenched with effort, Hoglah so focused on pressing her feet between pulls that she forgot her fear. Soon black faded to gray and the sunny circle at the top of the hole became larger and brighter. As the end of her effort came into view, Hoglah loosened her grip and slipped downward, gasping in horror that she might fall back into the dark maw.

"Hold on," he called. "Almost there."

Sunlight crowned the top of her head and crept down her face. Her arms bent with the rope as she was pulled across the lip of the well onto the flat rocks that framed it. The man rushed toward her, wrapped his hands around her wrists, and dragged her away from the well. Then he sat, his knees bent and his head cradled on his arms, panting.

Hoglah, cold, wet, and exhausted, lay on the pebbled ground, absorbing its warmth. She began to cry, low whimpers growing to full-throated sobbing. She did not know if this man pulled her out to save her or to sell her into slavery. She did not care. She just cried.

They remained that way for some time, Hoglah sobbing until her cries subsided into jerky coughs. The man sat a few feet away. Each sapped of strength.

When the man raised his head, he saw a wet mass. Water had twisted Hoglah's robe into dark, sodden lumps that covered all but her lower legs.

He sighed, stood, and raised her up. Fearful, she faced him. She was as tall as he, perhaps a touch taller. Then she noticed his copper-colored hair and the mosaic of freckles across his face. Her eyes widened and, immediately, she slumped, lowering herself, and he understood that she recognized him as the sheep shearer.

"You could have drowned," he began.

"You made me . . ." she began, then corrected herself. "You saved me." It was what he wanted to hear and what she wanted to say.

She looked down at her soaked robe, clinging to her, revealing her shape. She lifted her left shoulder to align her breasts. He noticed. Suddenly she realized that she stood, alone, with a man who was looking directly at her upper body.

"I must leave."

She lifted the hem of her robe just enough to allow her to run, then darted off, as he called after her, "Your waterskin . . ." He raised it above his head.

She turned, ran back, snatched the skin from him and exhaled, "Thank you." Then she lifted her skirts with one hand and the waterskin with the other, and ran like a gazelle with a wolf at its heels.

"Your servant, Asaf," he called after her, congratulating himself on saving the young woman he had in his sights, and the good fortune he might make of it.

When Hoglah returned to the lean-to, her mother, Tirzah, and Milcah forgot their torpor when they saw her damp robe and wild expression.

Tirzah sat bolt upright. "What happened to you?" she asked, delighted by the diversion.

Hoglah shuddered and wondered how she would explain. "He startled . . ." She realized she would have to explain who he was. She began again. "Yes, it was the Shadow People mother talks of. They threw me in the well, then drew me out."

"Shadow People? Really?" Tirzah looked ready for an absorbing story.

By that time, Hoglah had calmed down enough to re-explain. "No, really, it was just me. I filled the skin, then slipped, and spilled it all over myself."

"That sounds like you," Tirzah said. "But how did it soak your whole robe?"

"Did you mention a 'he,' or did I misunderstand?" asked Milcah.

"No matter," said their mother, "here you are, safe."

CHAPTER 15
A PACT IN THE GREAT CRATER

RUMORS PASSED THROUGH the tribes as quickly as head lice, people scratching and picking, wondering why the journey was taking so long, wondering if Moses had led them astray. They heard rumors about a great god's footprint in the desert. Some called the vast, elliptical crater "the Footprint of Ba'al." Others said it was "the Footprint of Moloch." When she heard the name, Milcah shuddered, remembering what Tirzah told of Moloch, the brazen god who ate living children to appease the fire in his belly.

"I hear it is colored like a rainbow," Hur said as he sat with his father near the edge of camp, looking up at a thousand small fires flickering in the night sky. He picked out familiar patterns: the goddess, the lion, the boatman. He had become comfortable with the desert night, less so with the slow pace of their journey.

"Why not go directly to our ancestors' lands? We hear they are not far and they are rich with grasses and water. Our flocks would recover."

"Suppose others now live on the land? You do not think such lands lie empty."

"We will take them." Hur slapped his thigh, his robe flapping in the wake of his hand.

"You yearn for battle," Gaddi said, remembering his own youth, when his blood boiled to take down a taskmaster. And he remembered the futility of those feelings.

"There are many ways of winning," Gaddi continued. "As great as a strong arm is a wise heart. We honor our elders for their years of wisdom."

"Just because they have lived long does not mean they are wise," Hur argued. "Their years might be only luck."

"It is God's will, not luck, that gives us life."

"Why would God choose that miserable Bar-On over Noa's father?"

They sat, silent, then Hur parted from his father and folded himself down next to Noa, whose face seemed serene in sleep. Cautiously, so as not to wake her, he slipped his hand beneath the sheepskin and slid it across her belly, swollen with life that he had made in her. At his touch, Noa stiffened slightly. Then Hur turned toward the embers that marked the dark edge of nowhere.

THE NEXT DAY, as they trod around rocky plateaus and through shallow wadis, Haddad appeared, alone. He shot Hur a conspiratorial smile.

"Want to see the Footprint of Ba'al?" Haddad asked, as they walked side by side.

"The great crater?"

"The very one."

"When?

"Now."

"Let's go."

"Take water and bread. The rest Ba'al will provide."

Hur found Noa among the women and told her he would be gone only a day and a night.

"Again?" she said. Startled by jealousy, she wondered, "Why this Midianite over me?"

As recompense, she insisted on spending the night with her mother and sisters. Hur said he would secure her request.

Haddad stood at a respectable distance and tried not to stare at the foreign women. He noticed a slight bulge in Noa's robe, then glanced at her face. He turned his back on the slowly moving troop and smiled into the blank desert. Even from a distance, he saw that she had eyes like a doe and Hur's baby in her belly.

Hur ran back to whisper Noa's request in his mother's ear. Then, he grabbed a waterskin and some round loaves and told his father of their plans. Haddad followed and assured Gaddi they would return the next day, easily catching up with the slow-moving multitude.

"I will guard the safety of my friend, as I guard myself." Haddad pulled the ring from his forefinger and handed it to Gaddi. "Here, my pledge."

Hur gave his father no chance to disagree. He waved farewell and strode off, Haddad hurrying to keep up.

Gaddi feared that Haddad had secreted others, who lay in wait for his son. He respected Hur's courage, but feared his son's impetuousness. He considered going after him, but did not want to stain Hur's honor.

AS THEY TROTTED eastward, the Israelites and their flocks became ever smaller.

Hur asked, "Just the two of us?"

"Why not?"

Hur nodded, masking his unease. He felt the weight of his knife at his waist under his robe and kept checking the margins of his view for Haddad's scar-faced cousin and others who might be lying in wait.

"Your people will stop at the wells just north of the crater. The wells are known to all. So are the springs where we will stop, deep in the center of the crater. But perhaps luck will be with us and no caravan will spoil our trip."

"You guaranteed my safety . . ." Hur broke in.

" . . . as much as I can my own." Haddad laughed.

Walking quickly, they reached the western edge of the crater before the sun had reached its zenith.

"Not here, farther on," Haddad coaxed, as the trail paralleled the long northern edge of the ovoid crater. It was past noon when they stopped. Haddad led Hur to the edge and heard him draw in his breath. Haddad was pleased to give his friend this gift.

On the horizon, across a great gulf, Hur saw a ledge matching the one on which they stood. Far below the rim lay another world: black basalt cones rose in scattered groups from the crater floor and the thin line of a riverbed twisted among them.

"To the east, the crater opens to the Valley of the Willows, where the Kenites live," Haddad explained. "When a flood rushes through, the waters are fierce. They carry away all on their way to 'the gate' of the crater."

Haddad fell silent, allowing Hur to see.

Color striped the sides of the crater: a band of cream-colored rock atop a band of rose, a band of white glinting with crystals, a layer of sea green. Here and there spikes of red rock pierced the layers, pushed upward from the core of the Earth. A griffon vulture glided past, the tips of its wings bent upward, like the fingers of a dancer. It turned its head to examine them with a predatory eye. Its gaze held them for a moment.

"Come," said Haddad, breaking the moment, as the bird drifted toward its nest on a ledge below.

They picked their way down a rocky path, reaching the wadi bed in late afternoon. They followed it eastward until Hur spotted feather-topped reeds like the ones that had framed the desert pool where he had taken his first ibex. His mind locked on the Scarface, and he looked around with a hard eye.

Noticing his look, Haddad agreed, "Let us approach cautiously, in case we are not alone."

They sidled up to the screen of reeds, the trickling water of a small spring wetting their feet.

"No one," Haddad whispered.

Water bubbled up in a sandy basin, bathing the feet of the reeds and the feet of the men before disappearing into the sand at the mouth of a smooth-walled canyon. Hur bent to drink, gulping the sweet spring water like a camel while reminding himself to draw water for Noa before they left.

Near the pool lay signs that marked the place as a stopover: fire-blackened rocks and the beginnings of a mudbrick caravansary. They gathered tinder in the waning day, then flinted a fire. Sitting cross-legged, they watched the setting sun tint the canyon walls shades of red and gold. Stars revealed themselves, Haddad peeled bits of wood from a dry stick and pitched them into the fire, and Hur allowed himself to relax.

They talked about their families. Haddad told Hur that he was being groomed as tribal leader and admitted that a part of him did not want the burden of leadership. He wanted simply to hunt and sit with companions on nights like this.

"But why reveal this to me? Is it not a sign of weakness?" asked Hur.

"Who else could I tell? My cousin, who would gladly snatch my place and give me a scar to match his? I can see you are like me. And weak? Do you think me weak?"

Haddad stood, walked to the low, mudbrick wall, and returned with a clay vessel and two small cups.

"Those who stop here know where to find these," Haddad answered, filling the vessel with water and settling it among rocks at the edge of the fire. When it was hot, he stirred in a pinch of ground berries from the bag at his waist, then poured two cups.

"Mmmm," Hur murmured, the bitter-lemon taste of sumac tea warming his throat.

He pulled out one of the round loaves he had brought, tore it, and offered half to Haddad, along with strips of dried quail meat. Haddad shaved salty cheese from a small, dry block and handed some to Hur.

"A rough meal," Haddad offered.

"But shared."

Hur noticed that Haddad's hawk-like face and wiry body looked even leaner in the fire's sculpting light.

Feeling strong within and without, Hur stood and walked in starlight to the mouth of the narrow canyon. He bent to pick up a rock gleaming like marble.

"Don't touch!"

Hur jumped back, and Haddad rushed to his side.

"Oh, prince of the desert, you still have much to learn. If you pick up rocks, you may meet the Deathstinger."

"Deathstinger?"

"The yellow scorpion. Watch," Haddad advised, as he walked into the canyon, expertly flipping a rock with his toes. The white walls of the canyon undulated like the sea as Haddad went deeper within, flipping rocks.

"Ah, a Deathstinger," he called, just as a large, silent blur leaped down from a ledge, knocking Haddad onto the ground. Hur thought Scarface, but saw a whirl of yellow-and-black rosettes. A leopard.

Hur drew his knife and charged. Fearing he would cut Haddad, he pulled at the big cat's head, slicing an ear. The leopard turned toward him. Fired by the leopard's glowing golden eyes, Hur plunged his knife, piercing until the knife wedged into an eye socket.

The leopard screamed and sprang away. Hur's knife rocking in its eye, it bolted down the canyon so fast that, in moments, it was the size of a glancing pebble, and then no more. Weeks later, a small caravan of traders found the blood-caked knife on the wadi floor and looked around nervously before scavenging it.

Hur lifted Haddad and helped him back to where their fire ebbed. The left shoulder of Haddad's robe was shredded. Beneath, so was his flesh. A scrape of teeth had bloodied Haddad's neck just as Hur had attacked.

His body and voice trembling, Haddad breathed out, "My bag . . ."

Hur eased Haddad near the fire and found the leather bag set in the sand.

"Same stuff," was all Haddad could manage.

Hur removed the felted leaves, familiar from his ibex-hunting injury. He cleaned his friend's wounds and applied the poultice. Then Haddad said, "Get a hairy leaf, toothed, from my bag. Just one . . . for pain. And one for yourself."

Hur found a small bundle, handed a leaf to Haddad, watched him chew slowly, then did the same.

"Help me into the canyon. We can sleep, protected, on the rock shelves."

"I don't think *namir* will return," Hur said, with more certainty than he felt, as they halted into the canyon.

He found a long, shallow shelf that floodwaters had sculpted over the centuries. Hur helped Haddad down and wrapped his own robe around him. He felt the cold bite of the desert night through his tunic, and wedged himself in. They lay pressed together for warmth until they both fell into deep, strange sleep.

In Hur's dream, Noa stood before him and smiled in a way she never had before, a seductive smile. She turned and floated deeper into the canyon. He arose and followed, the rock walls curving like the hips of a woman. Noa beckoned and disappeared where the canyon bent toward the left. Hur stumbled forward, trying to keep his eyes on Noa and his feet beneath him. He saw her lying on a low ledge, her belly high and rounded. He went to her and bent to kiss her.

Spots blurred his vision, rising toward him in rosettes. Noa's face melted and reformed as the fanged grin of a leopard, who wrapped his front legs around Hur and dug the tips of his claws into his back. He smelled the leopard's breath, an odor of rotted meat. Far away, Hur heard himself scream. Again, he reached for the knife at his waist. The leopard's spots danced before his eyes, and he could not see where best to stab, so he stabbed and stabbed and stabbed, as the leopard became

Noa. He threw down his knife and tried to staunch the holes he had made in her body, but he could not stop them all. From each hole, blood poured out to form a baby. Hur tried to catch each one. Some fell to the ground and ran away. His breath came hard and fast and he awoke, shivering with cold and horror.

His head ached, stars above skipped from one spot to another, and the whole of heaven trembled. He flinched at the sound of rustling. Leaning out to look, he saw a porcupine with its spray of black-and-white spines, waddle deeper into the canyon. Hur rubbed his arms to regain warmth, then curled back into sleep.

Haddad's sleep, too, was disturbed. He saw his scar-faced cousin, muttering, searching for something, finding the edge of Haddad's robe and cutting, cutting. Then he was gone.

WHEN HUR AWOKE again, a mist hovered over the ground in the pale light of dawn. His breath billowed white in the morning chill. Slowly, he unfolded his stiff, aching body, and stood. The mist reached his knees and purled along the canyon bottom like a river.

He heard Haddad stir, then answered his greeting. "Morning light . . ."

"We survived the night," Haddad croaked. He rolled from his rocky bed and stood cautiously.

"Does it still hurt?" Hur asked.

"Am I made of flesh? Yes. But now my stomach growls like a leopard." He clawed at Hur, grinning to hide his pain. Hur lightly slapped away the claw, grinning himself.

"Yes, let us eat."

They ate their loaves and drank from the spring, filling their waterskins before starting their trek out of the crater.

"My life was in your hands."

"My knife was guided by God," Hur demurred.

"You will take my knife as a small gratitude for my life."

Haddad handed Hur a sleek blade with a finely tooled handle. And that is how Hur obtained the knife of a Midianite prince.

" . . . and I will tell how you saved me. But first I will tell my wife that these 'scratches' on my back are from a fiery night with the wife of Ba'al." He laughed at his own joke.

Hur was surprised. Until now, Haddad had not mentioned a wife.

Haddad spoke of how ardent his wife was. He told Hur that his father warned that when a wife's zeal turns from her husband to her children, it is time to take a second, younger wife.

"A leader must pour his seed into a woman, who will pour her strength into the shoots that arise," Haddad declared.

"Thus, a leader builds his house," Hur agreed.

"And when the children grow, the first wife still has the lesser wives to rule over, they and their children and bondswomen, each ruler of a tiny kingdom." Haddad laughed.

Hur laughed with him, but thought of Noa. She was dutiful, but not ardent. He assumed all wives were like Noa. Haddad had told him something different.

As the trail rose, sunlight fingered its way down the canyon walls. He considered his disturbing dream and decided to see it as a good omen: he would be father to many.

"You know, I feared Scarface might be lurking when we first arrived," Hur said.

"He is always lurking. But he is cowardly. Look." Haddad spread his robe and pointed to his hem. "This cut. I dreamed he was here. I believe he *was* here. Slit my robe as a sign that he could as easily have slit my throat. I cannot be weak."

"There is always a Scarface."

"But our friendship is a counterweight," said Haddad.

"In truth."

The two headed toward the journeying tribes, and Haddad reclaimed his ring. Before they parted, they clasped each other and vowed to unite their families through their children.

NOA WALKED WITH Gaddi's women, but remained apart. She held her head high, but her spirits were low. Tamar had refused to allow her to return to her family, even for a night. Hur's female cousins seemed to set their shoulders against her as they chattered like the young wives of Malah's group. So it seemed to Noa. Or perhaps it was she who had nothing to say to them.

"I am not made that way," she told herself, at once disdaining and desiring their easiness.

Hur's two sisters treated her like a visiting Egyptian princess. Shyly, they asked her permission to speak, isolating her with their awe.

She formed no warm bond with Tamar. As matriarch, Tamar had a proprietary interest in Noa's pregnancy and did not hesitate to reach over and pat Noa's belly, talking to family members as if the belly and its contents belonged to her. Noa hated the touch of her mother-in-law's hand on her body.

"I once felt as you feel," said a voice drawing alongside. It was Tamar. "My older daughter, now a mother in her husband's house, feels the same. Separate."

"I can't help it . . ."

"You will grow into us, somehow."

"But what would one night with my family have harmed?"

"We *are* your family now. And, no, I won't allow your running back to them at every difficult moment. You must learn to live with us. As I had to. One day, you will become who I am, head of the women. And you will have to set an example. I finally fit in and—there!—my mother-in-law died. Then I had to work to separate myself, to give myself distance in order to gain respect and keep all of the women in their proper places. I deny you in order to strengthen and straighten you. That is my job. One day, it will be your job."

"But if I am not made that way?"

"You can make yourself whatever way is necessary. You must train your feelings to serve you, rather than you serving them."

Tamar nodded farewell, and strode ahead toward a knot of women her age. Noa nodded in return, but Tamar was gone.

Noa did not want to marshal her feelings. She wanted the comfort of Yoela. They were each other's refuge, caught between childhood and womanhood at a strange time, in a strange place.

Yoela's father, who could boast of little besides his daughter, could barely contain his pride that Zerach ben Efraim had chosen Yoela for Barzel, his second son. He was amazed by the ease of the match and the fine bride price Barzel brought, and he congratulated himself that his daughter's future was set. Yoela and Noa had heard the ugly rumors about Barzel. Yoela knew she was sold to his family to help hers survive.

After she had told Noa that the contract was confirmed, Noa said, "I can save you with my claim for land . . . for any daughter."

"Noa, I am not brotherless. You think winning this plea will cure all ills. And winning seems so . . . unlikely."

Remembering their conversation, Noa was interrupted by her unborn shifting within her womb.

"Once you arrive," she whispered to the child within, "you will give me strength to win over the Judges of Hundreds."

Engrossed in thoughts of child and judges, Noa did not hear Hur fall in step with her.

" . . . a most amazing journey," he finished.

"I am sorry. I was lost in thought."

"I can see, but I must tell you about this great footprint of the gods. Bigger than eyes can imagine. And the colors . . . the artists of Egypt cannot compare. We stopped at the springs where travelers rest. Here," he said, handing her his waterskin, "I've brought you sweet water."

"And what did you do there?"

"I saved Haddad from a leopard."

"Ah, you love Haddad more than you love your wife," she half-joked.

"No, truly. If you wish some meat, I will find some before the sun crowns the sky. I swear."

His pledge was so heartfelt, Noa could not help but smile. Her smile lit his face, giving him hope that, like Haddad's wife, her desire would match his.

CHAPTER 16
THE SUITOR

HOGLAH SAW ASAF'S coppery top regularly. One day, he dashed past with a group of young men and turned to stare boldly for a moment. Another time, she felt the wind at her skirt. She looked down to see his hand brush past as he walked ahead, turned, and . . . winked. She bit her cheeks to keep from grinning back at him. She liked his silent games.

One evening, at a tamarisk grove framing a well on their way, Asaf edged close to Hoglah, tied the end of a flexible branch upon itself, and, fixing her with a significant look, held the limb for her inspection. Slyly, he indicated the ring made by the looped limb and raised his eyebrows.

"Your answer?" he asked, before slipping into the shadows, knowing that "yes" would be her every answer to him.

"What could he mean?" Hoglah wondered. "Who can I ask?"

She was tied in a knot tighter than the tamarisk. She decided to question Malah as obliquely as she was able.

The next morning, she sought out Malah and said, "A friend has asked a question. Perhaps you can answer."

"Go on," urged Malah.

"If a person . . . not a maiden . . . a person, who is a man. Well, if that person showed a friend of mine a tamarisk branch knotted upon itself to make a circle. My friend wants to know what that means. He seems interested. In her."

"Why would someone knot a living tamarisk limb?"

"That's exactly my question."

"I will ask among my circle, but it sounds like something a desert-dweller would do. Hardly something one of us would do."

"Oh." Hoglah sounded disappointed.

Malah looked at her suspiciously. "What friend are you talking about? Perhaps you are asking for yourself?"

"Me? Who would be interested in me?" Hoglah widened her eyes, disingenuously.

This answer satisfied Malah, and she agreed to put the question to her young wives.

Later that day, Hoglah asked again, "Well . . . what is the meaning? My friend is beside herself. She must know."

"I was right. It is one of those quaint desert customs that our people seem to be picking up. The man ties a knot in the limb to show he is interested in a maid. The maid, if she is willing, ties another knot alongside it. Oh, the sight of that . . ." Malah loosed a long, pealing laugh. Since hearing Seglit's tale of Boaz's impotence she had little reason to laugh.

"Yes," said Hoglah cautiously, "I can see how silly that would look."

"If there are matching knots, well . . . your friend should run to her father and tell him to expect a proposal."

When the sun left only a golden glow at the edge of the desert, Hoglah walked out to the tamarisks. She tried for a careless pose, though her heart pounded and her face flushed. When casual glances did not reveal the knot she sought, Hoglah began searching in earnest. She feared he had reconsidered and undone the knot. She pushed into the tangle of tamarisk, desperately looking. Her arms became covered with the fine, dew-like *manna* that coated the leaves. Tufts from the tamarisks' flowery plumes stuck to the *manna* on her arms, turning her arms into white wings. Still she did not see the knot.

And, then, there it was. Hoglah smiled, quietly, then boldly. She looked around to make sure no one was there to see and quickly tied a companion knot at the end of the same willowy limb, then fled back to her mother, anxiously brushing her feathered arms.

The next evening, Asaf came to Boaz bearing introductory gifts and a proposal for Hoglah to be his wife. Boaz knew nothing of this unexpected young man nor who his people were.

Taking a few moments to compose himself, Boaz called for Seglit, "Bring tea, a few loaves . . ."

Tirzah, who had been running with the boys, passed the copper-headed man sitting with Boaz. She rushed on to her mother and demanded, "Why is the sheep shearer talking with Uncle Boaz?"

"What sheep shearer?"

"He was one of the shearers Hoglah and I brought the sheep to. He's fast. Zip, up one side. Zap, down the other."

"A sheep shearer?" Malah was sitting with her mother, and her face soured as she put together Hoglah's query about the tamarisk. She lifted her mother.

"Quick. For Hoglah's sake, for *our* sakes."

Malah pulled her mother along to Boaz with Tirzah dancing around them, delighted by the drama. As they approached, she heard the sheep shearer say, "I was orphaned in Egypt. I have no siblings. Yet, I made my way. I am resourceful and I will be a good provider."

Malah dragged her mother onto the rug, Tirzah slipping in behind them. Startled, Boaz introduced them, despite their breach of etiquette.

"My sister-in-law and my wife. Please, Malah, sit over there."

Boaz turned back to Asaf and asked, "And your family? Who are they?"

"You are Manasseh, yes? As I am. We are one. I will tell you:

"My uncle, Bar-On, the very one. Bent now, but his line is long and distinguished and once stood tall. And so my father was, and his father before him. My father's fathers were giants among the bowed of Egypt. They lifted up those beside them. You have heard, undoubtedly, of Eri, father of Ozni, who never left a one out in the cold. And Avram the Wise. Of Hever who did so much that his name is now gilded in our memory. And my mother, she from the family of the former gilders to the pharaohs, known for their exquisite work and she herself was. But her family, alas, perished in Egypt. They stood in the way of powerful forces. Not merely bending the backs of our people, but forces flailing them like reeds in a storm, Egyptians who wanted to win the gilders' trade from the Pharaoh. If only they, my mother's people—Shelah ben Saul ben Nahum ben Zoma, Mica with his good eye and even better hand, Zahavi the master of all gilders— were here to bring their skill, the beauty of their work to the canopy of a bride. Such as your niece, whose beauty would be mirrored in their work. But I am, for now and ever, an orphan, with Bar-On as the only other remnant of a rich history. From the mighty river that was my family, we have come down, a small stream, goodly and well-meaning with seeds of greatness and I, who would, with your beneficence, build up a house again, to blend our two families, yours whose might you have built even here, even in this desert—praise to you—would live again . . ."

Boaz, unsettled by Asaf's abrupt appearance, was drowning under the suitor's flood of words.

"I know how to buy and sell, and I am the shearer of shearers . . ."

Tirzah could not contain herself and jumped up. "You should see him." She smacked her hands, up then down. "Zip. Zap. It's done!"

"Tirzah!" Malah and her mother gasped.

Ada leaned out, as if to grab Tirzah back.

"Can no one stop this girl?" she wailed.

Malah shot a sharp look toward her mother, grabbed Tirzah, and dragged her back while apologizing to Boaz for the intrusion.

Asaf concluded with farewells, departing just as Hoglah returned from the well, struggling with a huge skin of water. Asaf rushed to relieve her of her burden and, bowing to Hoglah's mother, laid the skin before her, turned, and skipped away, leaving Hoglah with marveling eyes.

Boaz asked Ada for a moment in private. In one hand he held a limp bunch of grapes, shriveled by the heat of the sun. In the other hand, he held an ostrich plume.

"What am I to make of this?"

"It is the feather of an ostrich," Ada answered. "They say they live in the valley of the Kenites."

"I do not need a lesson on ostrich feathers," Boaz roared. The wife of his brother sometimes set his teeth on edge with inanities.

"I am sorry, sister, I did not mean to shout. I care nothing for a feather. I mean the young man . . . who arrived unannounced. He says he is an orphan, of our tribe. I could not quite follow the connections. Coming without proper introduction, I doubt we need to take this proposal too seriously."

He held up the grapes. "Grapes. Where does a simple shearer get grapes in the desert? And, indeed, what *is* the use of this?" Boaz demanded, waving the long, silky ostrich plume.

Tirzah ran to his side. She slipped the plume out of Boaz's hand and fanned it over her mother's head. "A fan for the queen of the desert."

"Are you acquainted with this young man?" Boaz asked Hoglah.

She ducked her head. "Yes," she whispered.

"Aha," seized Malah, "the young man of the knotted shrub. I knew it."

"Explain," Boaz said.

Malah and Tirzah's words tumbled over each other, telling what they knew of Asaf. At the heart of the telling was Hoglah's tale of Asaf's gallantry at the well.

Boaz plucked a grape and bit into it. "Sweet, nonetheless." He looked distracted, thinking he might have to take Asaf's bid seriously after all.

"I WILL BE called 'barren.' And I will die childless. Noa, what can I do?"

"Are you sure Seglit has not lied?"

"My body tells me she does not lie."

"Well . . ."

"Find me an answer."

"This is a difficult problem."

"You are such a well-known problem-solver. So, solve it."

Malah voiced her demand with equal parts anguish and ridicule.

"Attacking me will not make me inclined to solve it."

"I didn't mean . . ."

"Wait. I've thought of something."

"Yes?"

"Remember the story of Abraham and his wife Sarah, who was so old she offered Abraham her handmaid, Hagar, as the source of their future?"

MALAH DID NOT wait a day. After Seglit had fallen asleep, she lay down next to Boaz, covered them both, and whispered the problem and the solution. Boaz did not deny the problem, but the solution was more than he could bear.

"Mom," Tirzah whispered insistently, "Malah and Boaz are making too much noise. Why are they arguing? I know they are. I can hear."

"People who live together have differences," she whispered back. "It is just that way. They will resolve it. And please stop calling me that rude term."

Tirzah lay, listening. She could not hear their words, but their tone carried on the night air. She rolled closer to her mother. "Mom-mom-mom," she whispered, to see if her mother had fallen asleep.

"Tirzah," her mother scolded in a low voice, "go to sleep."

"How can I sleep when they are hissing like snakes?"

CHAPTER 17
A TEMPORARY HOME

THE TRIBES OF Israel trudged on in a daze. One harsh horizon looked much like all the others.

"We have passed this plain before. I remember that tree with the red flowers."

"This well cap, it is one we have opened earlier, I am certain," said another. "Moses is leading us in circles."

They tried to avert their eyes from the unyielding horizon, so all were surprised when the land softened. In the northern reaches of the great Wilderness of Zin, dry plains gave way to clusters of low hills whose water-carved crevices were veined with shrubs. Lines of date palms sinuated below the hills, creating avenues of shade under their feathery green heads. Fields of yellow and purple wildflowers greeted the travelers.

The land looked so welcoming that the first tribes to arrive hesitated, fearing a trap by its inhabitants, hidden among the hills. But the cloud above the Ark of the Covenant stopped at the broad oasis, so the people knew God had designated the place, which they named Kadesh Barnea, Holy Wilderness of Wandering.

As the Levites erected the Tent of Meeting near the center of the broad oasis, other tribes rushed to claim a shady place beneath the trees. Later tribes squeezed in where they could. Like oil in water, lobes of one tribe oozed into the edges of another. Fights broke out, boundaries were set, then broken, then set again.

By day's end, order had taken hold. Tents, raised for the first time since they left Mount Sinai, absorbed the voices of the night. Transforming themselves from a Nile of humanity flowing across the desert, the people pooled in clans and tribes, just as they had at the holy, roaring mountain.

Manasseh trod farther back in the line of tribes, so could claim only an outer arm of the many-branched oasis. Those too tired to raise their tents lay down their rugs and fell asleep watching the hills glow blue and purple as the sun set.

Gaddi ben Susi and Tamar selected a spot for their tent befitting a leader of Manasseh. Hur and Noa erected theirs adjacent. After unpacking, Noa walked toward her family's tent as fast as her swollen shape allowed. Hoglah was holding forth on her anticipated engagement.

" . . . *and* he has promised me finery for my wedding day . . . *in addition* to the bride price."

"And where do you think a sheep shearer will get such finery," Malah asked, her head bent to her spindle. "A sheep shearer with no family name? How would that look in a family with a name such as ours?"

Hoglah, the sister hidden in the middle, was made bold by love.

"You will see. All the young girls will talk about how he saved me at the well. I will be married to a hero."

Noa had more practical concerns.

"What do you really know of this . . . sheep shearer?"

"You and Malah act as if you know everything," Hoglah complained. "He is what he says he is. He lost his parents and, from nothing, he made something of himself. Not like those who have everything already," she tossed off, defiant.

Noa and Malah looked at each other, astonished. The notion of Hoglah as social critic struck Noa as funny. She bit the insides of her cheeks as her face puckered with silent hilarity, infecting Malah, who sputtered laughter.

Hoglah slumped.

"Oh, Hoglah, we don't mean to mock you," said Noa, "This Asaf, is he really of the tribe of Manasseh? There are questions about him that are meant to protect *you*."

"No," Milcah countered, defending Hoglah and thinking of Oholiav. "It is to protect *your* idea of our land. You care more about this land than Hoglah's happiness."

"Not true. What if Hur died?" Noa spit against the Evil Eye. "I could be sent back, with a child and a pot or two. A burden to my family. Or what if one of us does not find a husband? What will she be left with? In either case: she or me could be reduced to servitude."

"We will get you your land, Noa. Me and Adam—we are going to fight our enemies!" Tirzah trumpeted, diving toward Noa.

Before she landed, Malah pulled Tirzah onto her lap and wrestled her into a knot of robing. "Wild one, you are trying to deprive us of a nephew."

"But why does it matter whether Asaf is from Manasseh?" Milcah argued.

Hoglah flashed a thank-you smile toward her younger sister.

"Again, because the judges will counter, 'If we allow these women to inherit and they marry outside Manasseh, the land will go to some other tribe. We cannot allow that.' If we say we will marry within the tribe, it will blunt the teeth of their opposition."

"If we win the Judges of Hundreds," Noa continued, "we've set a standard. Then we can bend the law toward true justice. Our rights to inherit whether we're married within Manasseh or not. Whether we're married at all."

THE PEOPLE SETTLED at Kadesh, anticipating that soon they would reclaim the land of their ancestors. The men spoke of planting fields watered by rippling rivers. Women dreamed of washing their bodies and dusty robes in languid pools. Before they reclaimed their land, Moses had asked each tribe to provide one man for the small group that would spy out the land and report on its plants and animals, and what peoples lived there.

In the cool of the evening, the leaders of Manasseh sat at the base of a palm, with the others arrayed around them. Each of the young men was anxious to be chosen as Manasseh's representative.

"I know these desert people," said Hur. "I spend time with one of their princes."

"To think of any of *those people* as a prince is to show how much you have been swayed by them," said his cousin Uval. "They are as ants to be scraped up and tossed in a heap. Conquered. Cleaned away from the lands of our fathers."

For emphasis, he cupped his hand, scraped it across the sand, and collected a small pile of conquered grains.

"Yes," countered Hur, "but we must spy out their ways so we may turn their strengths against them."

Focused on a role he felt should be his with vows to Haddad buried below, Hur thought his analysis sounded both tough and smart. He reached over and scooped up the mound of sand Uval had gathered and flung it into the air. "We will scatter them!"

"Hi-yah, Hur!" one called out. Others, sitting cross-legged, beat the ground to signal their agreement.

Gaddi smiled to hear his son, but the young men's boastings were in vain. Manasseh's leaders had already decided. They chose Gaddi ben Susi, proposed by Boaz and elected by Manasseh's elders.

Hur and the other young men had been certain one of them would be chosen for their youth, vigor, and fearlessness.

When Hur understood that his father was chosen, he argued, "Mother won't sleep a night without fear for you."

Hur, too, feared. He had heard tales of torture, impalement, beheading. He, not his father, could surely outmaneuver any enemy.

But the older generation had decided that wiser eyes should spy out the hill country that lay north and east, lands none had seen in more than four hundred years.

THE SPIES SET out in darkness, silently, with their shields on their shoulders and their knives at their waists. They carried little else. And the people wished them well.

These are the names of the men that Moses sent to spy out the land: from the tribe of Reuben, Shammua ben Zaccur; from the tribe of Simeon, Shafat ben Hori; from the tribe of Judah, Caleb ben Jephunneh; from the tribe of Issachar, Igal ben Joseph; from the tribe of Efraim, Joshua ben Nun; from the tribe of Benjamin, Palti ben Rafu; from the tribe of Zebulun, Gaddiel ben Sodi; from the tribe of Manasseh, Gaddi ben Susi; from the tribe of Dan, Ammiel ben Gemalli; from the tribe of Asher, Sethur ben Michael; from the tribe of Naftali, Nahbi ben Vophsi; from the tribe of Gad, Geuel ben Machi.

The people knew that when the spies returned, all of Israel would go forth onto their lands. So they set about ordering their lives, making contracts for marriage and contracts for flocks. Yoela's family arranged her marriage date to the second son of Zerach. Yoela pleaded with Noa to stay near her, and Noa pledged that she would.

Boaz, adding Gaddi's duties to his own, was busy with tribal matters when Asaf came to formally claim Hoglah's hand in marriage.

Hoglah, anxious to know her fate, made her way to the back of her uncle's tent. She flattened herself against the ground and carefully lifted the edge of the tent and peered under. She could see their knees, angled up as they sat cross-legged. She could see the bronze platter and small cups tooled with Manasseh's banner. She saw a hand reach down for one of the cups. Asaf's hand. She sucked in her breath, excited by the sight.

A stone was pressing against her rib and, quietly as possible, she slid her hand under her chest to extract it. This was how Milcah found Hoglah, with one hand wriggling a stone from beneath her while keeping the tent flap slightly lifted with the other hand.

"Get up," Milcah whispered, "lest you make a spectacle of yourself."

When Hoglah did not respond, Milcah lay on the ground to see what Hoglah was seeing. They heard only snatches of the negotiation. What they saw was Asaf's hands fumbling with a wrapped cloth at his side. He lifted some bangles that caught what light the tent afforded. Hoglah sighed with the thought of his presents adorning her body.

"Did you think he would *not* bring rings for your arms and your ears?" Milcah whispered. "It is required."

"Be quiet or go away."

Asaf's hand next lifted the corner of a sheepskin as he said, "many more."

"*Of course* he would bring those."

"Be quiet, Milcah," Hoglah hissed. "Your comments are ruining my pleasure."

"Now on your stomach. After marriage, on your back." Milcah giggled.

"Milcah . . . what is that?"

From the depths of a sheepskin, Asaf lifted out two round, flat stones coupled one atop the other, the diameter of a round bread.

"Stones . . ." Hoglah groaned. "What gift is this?"

They heard Asaf talking quickly, and Boaz responding slowly. Then Asaf stood and said, "Well, then, she will be mine?"

On the other side of the tent, two men entered. A discussion ensued. Asaf's tone slid from triumph to defensiveness.

"Do you think I am not who I say?"

Asaf then intoned a long line of names, each "son of . . ." adding a bead to strengthen the string of names.

"Bar-On, your father's brother? In truth?" one of the men asked.

"Bar-On will share his tent with us. That is what uncles do. We need only raise a curtain."

"And how do we know you have not made all of this up," said Boaz. "How do we know you are not of another tribe, or even another people?"

Asaf stood, dropped his robe, then his loincloth. The two young women gasped, quietly. Hoglah lifted the tent edge higher.

"There. Like a sheared sheep, I am exposed. Circumcised as covenant. And I am ready to make another covenant, with your permission."

Asaf turned slowly, a ray from outside lighting the bronze hair on his legs. Hoglah and Milcah saw his narrow buttocks tighten as he took each step until he had circled toward the back of the tent where they spied. Neither noticed his face. They were riveted by the sight of his genitals, hanging loosely between his thighs.

"Eh. Cover yourself," said Boaz. "We have seen enough."

AFTER THE SPIES had set out, Hoglah implored Boaz to accept Asaf's bid. Noa pressed him about approaching the Judges of Hundreds. And Malah insisted on the one thing he could not stand to think about. Worn down by the young women's barrage, he said, "yes," "yes," and "yes."

"Ach. Hoglah may have her young man," Boaz said, sitting with his sister-in-law. "Set the marriage five days from now, the next new moon."

Ada smiled. Another daughter accounted for. She ran her hand over the hand mill Asaf had presented.

"Perhaps it will save her bones from the fate of mine."

The gift was something most had never seen: two matched stones, stacked one atop the other. A peg, fixed in the bottom stone, rose through a hole in the top stone.

"What is this good for?" Boaz had asked.

"Let me show you," Asaf said, as though he were about to make magic.

He poured wheat kernels into the hole with one hand and, turning the top stone with an affixed wooden handle, he ground the kernels between the two stones into fine flour.

"Hoglah will be the envy of all the young women," Ada marveled. "Even her own sisters."

Hoglah knew now would be her time to shine. She had won a husband. And, in the bride price, she had received a gift the envy of women young and old. She also knew her time to shine would be short, so she burnished it with the promise of allowing others to try her hand mill after her wedding.

Noa knew that preparations for Hoglah's wedding would take precedence over her appearance before the Judges of Hundreds. She had time. The Israelites would go nowhere until the spies returned.

"Please, uncle, secure me a place just before the spies return."

"And if they do not return."

"Then sometime after Hoglah is wed."

"It will not be easy," Boaz cautioned. "By now, your plea is well known and few judges want to handle a case that stands on such uncertain ground."

"But . . ."

"I will have to call in a favor, but I will do it."

FEARING HE MIGHT never father a child, Boaz finally agreed to Malah's suggestion. He wanted the loathsome deed done quickly and, until it was done, he sent Seglit to her family.

He told Malah, "I will send a man to you on three nights, when your womb is most open to seed."

Malah bowed her head to show she was humbled by his hard decision.

"But," he continued, "you must veil yourself. I will wait outside the tent to ensure your safety."

The first night, when the camp was dark, Malah lay on her bed, tense. She heard a rustling not far from her head on the other side of the tent. A night creature, searching for food or a mate. The thought of strange mating made her shudder. Suddenly, she heard Boaz's voice.

"Cover yourself, Malah . . . my wife."

Malah pulled a veil over her face and lay absolutely still.

She heard someone enter the tent, then felt the man's presence at her feet as he lifted her skirts, unveiling her sex. His hands pushed lightly against the inside of her thighs, and she widened her legs. She smelled goat and strangely sweet sweat as he felt past the swollen lips guarding her vulva and entered her with his fingers. He withdrew, then grasped her shins and angled her legs into position. She sensed his heavy presence as he lowered himself into her, grunting, thrusting against her, finally withdrawing. He raised himself from her, and then was gone.

He did not cover her. Her skirts lay tangled around her waist. She felt a breeze tickle the wetness between her legs. She pulled down her skirts, but was afraid to lift her veil.

Boaz did not enter, and she could not tell whether he remained outside or not. She lay, too disturbed to move, until she fell asleep.

The next day Boaz said, "Twice more he will cover you. Then we will wait to see if the planted seed will grow."

She could not look at him, nor he at her.

"And what if it does not?"

"At the same time of your next cycle, we will try again."

"What assurance do you have of his ability?"

"He has had other 'results,'" was all Boaz would say.

CHAPTER 18
SCOUTING THE PROMISED LAND

THE SPIES TRAVELED on the shoulders of the day to avoid summer's blistering heat. They followed camel tracks across the desert, knowing they could easily dodge the few caravans they might meet. Moses had cautioned them to avoid traveled roads once they reached the hill country.

As they journeyed north and east, graveled deserts gave way to plateaus where gnarled terebinths stood sentinel near old wells. The terebinths spread heavy, green-leafed arms over the heads of men, sheltering them. The spies saw sacred stones piled near.

"These must be the trees they call *ela*—the Goddess," one said.

They rested the night under the arms of the goddess trees and, before the sun rose, they rose and trekked along cliffs scoured by wind and water. In a small hollow, a single red tulip clung to the earth, its roots fertilized by animal droppings. Farther on, Igal ben Joseph picked up a dry turd the size of a grape.

"Not camel. Not wild goat . . ."

Ammiel ben Gemalli laughed. "You think you are a desert-dweller who knows the wild. You are still like us, the son of a poor slave of Egypt."

"And you still sound like one, with that Egyptian tongue of yours."

"At least I am not a handler of strange shit," Ammiel returned.

Gaddi ben Susi laughed. "So, Ammiel, you handle only well-known shit?"

Ammiel stooped to pick up a dry turd, which he lobbed at Gaddi. Gaddi raised his shield to block it and the dry excrement crumbled and fell in grassy pieces.

"May all our enemies be so," Igal exclaimed.

"Yai!" answered others, their voices relaxed, happy to be together, on the move, unburdened of people, beasts, and belongings.

THE THIRD NIGHT, Malah again lay still, waiting for Boaz's voice. When she heard him say "Make yourself ready," she lay down on her bed and pulled her veil over her face as she had done the two nights before.

Again the unseen man lifted her skirts and opened her legs as she lay still. Again, he felt for the place in which he would plant his seed. This night he was not quick. He played there with his hands and with his mouth until her legs quivered. He whispered, "the taste of your honey." Words that made her breath catch until he finally lowered himself into her. Malah, filled with him and his scent, momentarily stiffened with guilt before a low groan escaped from her throat as he began a slow, rocking camel's gait and carried her away.

MILCAH LONGED FOR the days when the center of camp was her life, weaving curtains with Rina, exchanging looks with Oholiav, which caused her face to flush even now. She asked Hur's cousin, Uval, to escort her to the courtyard that surrounded the Tent of Meeting and asked Hoglah to accompany her. In case Oholiav happened to be there, she did not want her sharp-eyed older sisters with her, nor her sharp-tongued younger sister.

In the spirit of the Sabbath, they dressed their hair, cleaned their nails, then made their way to the broad, linen-screened courtyard. For offerings, they brought fine flour in a small sack and a lidded basket holding a rock dove.

"I will give the offerings to the priests. Then I will return," Uval said.

Hoglah looked around for maidens she might know, to announce her betrothal. She wondered if she was allowed to speak of something not holy. She feared she would be struck by an unseen hand if she did, so remained silent.

Milcah took in the courtyard: people standing in small groups or alone in prayer, the stand for the lavers full of cleansing water, the tables of showbread, and the stone ramp leading to the horned, copper-clad altar. Near the far end stood the Tent of Meeting. Her eyes followed the column of cloud that rose to the heavens from the Holy Ark enclosed within. She recognized one of the Tent's richly figured curtains as hers and felt filled and drained all at the same time.

She heard the bawl of a young bullock and turned to the altar as the knife took its life as sacrifice. The bullock's hindquarters draped one side of the altar and sticky ribbons of its blood oozed down to fill runnels in the stonework below. Levite priests clothed in white linen covered by purple tunics added balsam and frankincense to embossed incense censers. Tendrils of smoke rose from censers, masking the fleshy smell of sacrifice. As the Levites swayed over the altar, the gold bells that lined their robes chimed in time with their chants, holy and hypnotic.

Milcah trembled, light-headed from the sensual deluge. Her eyes were drawn across the courtyard, to the eyes of another. Oholiav. The intensity of his gaze, rhythm of the bells, chants of the priests, pungent odors heated by the sun . . . Milcah slumped against her sister as she sank to the ground.

Hoglah feared calling out for help in the holy place, so sank with her sister, holding her in her lap while she tried to think what to do. Oholiav came, asked Hoglah to lead, lifted Milcah in his arms, and carried her home.

THE SPIES TRAVELED north into the hill country, crossing steppes brushy with purple thistle, blanketed with yellow mustards. Rising into the mountains where their ancestor Abraham had dwelt, they passed through oak forests and small valleys open to the sun, each centered on a winding stream. Like the deer they killed to fill their empty bellies, they moved stealthily along the forest edges. In some of the valleys they saw the crumbling remains of settlements, but no people.

"What happened to the people who lived here?" asked one of the spies.

"Perhaps God cleared them away to make room for us," Joshua said, half-seriously.

On a hilltop farther north, they passed a lightly fortified Jebusite town watered by a spring in the Kidron Valley.

"This place would make a fine fortress," Joshua said.

They descended to the Great Rift and immersed themselves in a lake called the Salt Sea, marveling that they floated effortlessly in the salty, lifeless waters. From there, they followed the crease of the Jordan River northward.

Emerging into broad valleys, they saw barley ripening on slender stalks, undulating like the sea. They pressed ahead onto a high plain that overlooked another great body of water, this one dotted with small boats whose nets sagged with fish. A few of the spies sneaked down to the harp-shaped lake and speared enough fish to give each of them a taste of their future.

They trekked high into the foothills of Mount Hermon, whose head scraped the sky and whose shoulders were mantled with snow.

The next morning, when they awoke shivering, Joshua announced, "We have come to the northern reaches of our lands. Now we must return and take stock of the people who dwell here."

They picked their way down the slopes, heading south. While crossing an oak savanna, they saw a figure lumbering among the trees, larger than any of them and covered with thick brown hair. It stopped at a tree, stretched upright, scratched its back against the trunk, then dropped down. Once it reached open meadow, it galloped away through the grasses.

They stopped, their eyes wide.

Gaddi said, under his breath, "What being is this? Is this the sort of man that lives here?"

He felt a tremor of fear, as did the others. None had ever seen a bear.

They toiled south through the narrow, steamy Jordan River valley, and turned west below Jericho, an ancient town even then. Plodding up a stark ascent, they reached the hilltops overlooking the Salt Sea and, again, passed the Jebusite town that would become Jerusalem.

Their destination was the walled city of Hebron, the largest of the hilltop towns. Here, Abraham had dwelt among the terebinths of Mamre, as did his son Isaac and Isaac's son Jacob. Here, Abraham had bought a field and a cave in which to bury his dead. The memory of this place succored the Israelites during their slavery in Egypt. And now here were the spies in the land of their fathers.

Hebron was known at that time as Kiryat Arba. The forests around the walled town had been leveled to make room for wheat and barley fields and orchards of olive trees. Past the fields stood a few shepherds' huts.

On west-facing slopes, terraces held vineyards heavy with grapes. From tales their fathers told, the spies knew that if they had the eyes of God, they would be able to see the place of the sun-setting and the Great Sea.

The morning of their arrival at Hebron, the spies divided into small groups to pose as traders from afar. It would explain their strange tongue. As they approached the town's thick stone walls, everything looked unusually large.

"Is this the height of a Hebron man?" Guel asked as they neared the tower gatehouses that flanked the main gate. Near the gate, a broad oak sheltered the town's elders, who sat to see and discuss. As each group of spies passed through, the gatehouse guard demanded to know where they were from. Gaddi's group answered, " . . . land of the Kenites." Some of Hebron's elders noted that today brought many groups from the caravan trade.

Just inside the gate, a low wall fronted a caravansary where camels and donkeys were tethered in a broad courtyard. Narrow stalls, shelter for traveling merchants, lined three sides. Gaddi, Geuel, and Palti stood before the caravansary gate and agreed on an approach. Striding inside, their robes swinging as though they belonged, they noted the goods that merchants brought to sell: bitumen, linen from Egypt, balsam oil in glass bottles, medicinal herbs, tools, and weapons for every purpose. Gaddi thumbed the edge of a bronze axe head, and sauntered away quickly when a merchant approached with his eyes on a sale.

Adjacent to the caravansary, huts of prostitutes and the poor lined the inside of Hebron's walls. Stretching into the center of town, the main street was lined with merchants setting out their goods on mats. Behind them stood stalls that served as their shops.

The small groups of spies strolled through the market, noting how large the people appeared compared to them, whose frames were pinched by the desert. One pair of spies approached a woman sitting on a mat piled with dates as large as a giant's thumb. They pointed. Ammiel spread his palm to indicate "five." She looked up, the eyes of a vulture examining prey. She indicated the price and, as they exchanged copper pieces for fruit, they noticed her forearms were more muscled than theirs and scaly as a lizard.

"The people who live here are a race of giants," Ammiel said, as they turned away. "The offspring of gods and humans."

They saw a temple ahead, but were more concerned with the measure of men than of their gods.

Gaddi and his companions turned down a side street lined by meager, mudbrick dwellings with shared walls and courtyards. They saw sag-backed ewes, women wearied by chores, and disheveled children. The disorder and the stench of animals, unwashed bodies, and smoke from rancid oil made Gaddi think that desert life held some advantages.

Farther into Hebron's residential section, homes stood separated by narrow lanes, two-story homes where people dwelled above their beasts. The courtyards were larger and, in the pillared arcades that edged the courtyards, they saw grinding stones and looms, scythes and hoes. Wooden ladders served as stairs to the rooms above, and Gaddi noticed mats draped over flat, low-walled roofs where people slept on hot summer nights. A young boy pointed at him and said something to his mother. Gaddi and his companions moved on quickly.

Deep in the center of the city, Gaddi's group came upon the house of Anak, the ruler of Kiryat Arba—the Town of Four—named for Anak and his three sons. Broad trees fronted the walled compound. The spies scrambled up to hide among their branches. They saw a fine stone stairway leading to the second story and walls plastered in the manner of the wealthy. Under the arcade, Anak's daughter worked at her loom, a giant rack set on poles. The skeins of yarn at her feet were thick as ropes.

They heard men's voices, rumbling and roaring.

"I'll take on those Jebusite dogs. The Jebusite high place will be mine," boomed one son, emerging from the doorway, filling its frame.

"That's the prize of the first-born. Me. Not the likes of you," said another, cuffing his brother. The three were enormous, but none more so than the father.

Wild haired, with legs as thick as oaks, Anak ignored his sons' quarreling. He walked out the gate ahead of them, passing below where the spies hid in the trees, making themselves small lest they be seen. The sons followed their father toward the market.

The first-born threw up his arm, as if to clout his brother, and knocked it on the tree limb above his head, the very limb to which Gaddi clung. Gaddi wrapped his legs around the limb to keep from falling and gripped so tightly his arms shook. Terrified of falling into the midst of the ferocious giants, he lost control of his bladder. The youngest son felt a few drops from above, but as he looked ahead, the sky was clear.

After Anak and his sons had gone, the spies climbed down furtively and, like mice, scampered for the town gate.

On their way to the cave of Machpelah where their ancestor Abraham was buried, Joshua and Caleb passed Anak and his sons, but took no note as they discussed how best to honor Abraham. At the cave, they prayed for strength of heart and strength of arm to bring their people back to their land. They rejoined the other ten on the way from Kiryat Arba that was Hebron.

The others could not flee fast enough, but Joshua made them stop in the vale of Eshcol, where they hid at the edge of the vineyards. Under cover of dusk, Joshua cut a huge woody twist of grapevine.

"Besides what we have seen with our own eyes, let us show our people how rich the land is."

The vine was so heavy with fruit, it took eight to lift it. They hoisted it on their shoulders, then turned their faces toward the desert and Kadesh Barnea.

NOA LAY ON her bed, too tired to move. The baby within her did all the moving. Today Hoglah would wed the sheep shearer. Today was also the day Yoela would wed Zerach's second son, Barzel, a marriage Yoela dreaded. Noa had promised she would stand near Yoela to give her courage. That was before Hoglah's marriage had been arranged. Obliging her family meant disappointing Yoela. Noa did not know what to do, so she did nothing.

Hur found his wife tangled in her bedcovers and her thoughts. He ran his hand over her hair, saying, "Your family comes first."

She pulled the cover over her head to deny his hand. The heat of her belly and the cover stifled her, and she wished Hur would leave her to her misery.

"Go," she whispered to him after he left. "Go be your father, the headman. Make pronouncements. But not to me."

At Hur's request, Malah came to fetch Noa. She offered Noa her hand, her smile sweet as date wine. Noa grasped Malah's hand and pulled herself up. She had not seen Malah this content in months.

But when she told Malah to make an excuse so she could be with Yoela, Malah's sweetness faded fast.

"It's bad enough Hoglah's marrying that . . . redheaded sheep shearer. Not to have a full show of family would make us look as if we did not think much of the match."

"But, we don't. Even if he is truly of Manasseh, he does not inspire trust."

"What is the matter with you? We cannot look as if we do not support this marriage. You must be there long enough so people can see and note."

Noa went with Malah to stand with her sister Hoglah for a moment. But once she arrived at the celebration, sisters and cousins held her captive in talk and dance. Malah, she noticed, danced slowly, holding herself carefully as if something might drop.

By the time Noa slipped away, Barzel was leading Yoela toward the marriage booth. Noa ran toward the booth, hoping to catch Yoela's eye. Yoela saw her, but her eyes were blank. She did not smile at Noa. She turned her head and followed her husband into the booth.

WHILE BRIDES WERE giving themselves to bridegrooms, Malah had been calculating the phases of the moon and of her body. "Now is the time," she informed Boaz. "Perhaps this month the seed will take root and grow."

Boaz was reluctant. But he worried more that two childless wives would confirm his impotence.

Seglit, waiting for Boaz to escort her to her family's tents, said, "I know what you are up to."

While waiting for the surrogate, Malah arranged herself on her bed, her veil over her head. When, finally, the man entered her chamber, he touched her in places that made her shiver and gasp. She breathed in his odor, she heard him growl low, "Does he play with you like this?" And, "Does he pleasure you like this?"

Malah counted on two more nights and then her veiled indulgence would end. Her monthly emission had not come and her mornings were already wracked by nausea. The seed had been planted. She told herself, "Two more nights to make sure the seed flourishes."

CHAPTER 19
THE SPIES' REPORT

AS BOAZ COUNTED the end of his ordeal with the seeding of a son, the spies returned. In the chill of dawn, the eight who were bowed by the grapevine straightened as they approached camp. The four who carried other samples of the land's wealth stepped up the pace, their feet kicking up dew-laden dust.

Some saw them from afar and ran out to escort them. As they approached, the host of escorts grew. The people knew the return of the spies signaled an end to their journey and entry to the land God promised them. They hailed the spies as returning warriors.

Noa and Hur quickly learned of the spies' approach. Noa panicked. Now that the spies had returned, the tribes would be traveling eastward to claim their promised land. Boaz had agreed to pave her way to the Judges of Hundreds, when she was ready. But Noa had done nothing to forward their claim, and now she feared their case would be lost in the rush for land.

Hur anticipated being warmed by the reflected light of Gaddi ben Susi's report. He longed to push through the crowd and throw his arms around his father, full of relief and pride. But he restrained himself and walked with Noa, the vessel who would soon deliver his son.

As Hur pressed into the crowd, creating an opening behind him for Noa, he heard a spy cry out, "Yes, the land flows with milk and honey. Here is its fruit."

Ammiel broke off a small cluster of grapes and tossed it over the heads of the crowd. Arms reached up to catch the fruit. Ammiel threw another and another.

"Here, here," cried Hur, calling for a taste of grape. "My father is the one with the shield of Manasseh."

That brought a cheer from those nearby, and they passed him some grapes, which he offered to Noa. The crowd, pressing around her, threatened her heavy, unbalanced body.

She whispered to Hur, "I must leave. The crowd is too much."

"Yes," he said, facing his father, not her. "Return to our place."

Noa struggled to turn and open a path behind her.

"I cannot." She grasped his sleeve for emphasis.

Hur turned and shouted, waving his arms outward to open a wedge of space.

"Can't you see? She's weighted with a precious burden. Make a path."

The crowd parted, then closed behind her, the sea of people washing in to fill the space between Noa and Hur.

Without realizing it, Noa had come to depend on Hur and now felt unbalanced and fearful in the crowd. As she pressed toward the edge, admonishing herself for neediness, she saw Barzel. Yoela was not with him. Their time in the marriage booth must be over, she thought.

Noa broke through the back of the crowd and waddled quickly toward the camp of Zerach, hoping to find Yoela. Hur had pushed forward, toward his father and the knot of spies telling their tale at the center of a vast wheel of people.

" . . . yes, the fruits are plentiful. Wheat and barley we saw, too." It was his father talking. "With heads as big as my fist." Gaddi thrust his fist into the air for emphasis.

Igal continued, "We saw all this growing in fields and vineyards. Vineyards built by people who have our lands. Our lands."

"Our lands!" the crowd shouted back.

"Wait. Hear more of these lands," shouted another spy. "There live people to match the size of these fruits." He held up a handful of large, juicy dates. "They are mighty and their cities are built with walls all around."

"And they are many peoples. The Canaanites, the Jebusites, the Amorites . . ."

"We will take them," shouted a young man, in a muscle of young men standing near Hur, who boasted, "My father is one of them."

Another of the spies spoke. "Yes, the land flows with milk and honey, but in one great city live giants. I swear, giants."

With the memory of Kiryat Arba, Geuel said, "We cannot face such mighty people."

As the light subsided, Moses emerged and told them what God had said. "In this very wilderness your carcasses will drop. All of you who muttered against Me, not one of you shall enter the land—save Caleb and Joshua. Your children I will allow to enter. They shall know the land you have rejected."

The generation who would not believe would end their days in the desert. The spies who offered the bad report were struck by a plague of body and spirit. Only Joshua and Caleb were spared.

A host of young men, angered by their fainthearted elders and dying to prove their mettle, rushed off to the hill country, their knives and eyes flashing.

Moses called after them, "You are ahead of God and yourselves."

But they would not hear. They rushed forward, looking more for enemies than for their land. They found Amalekites and Canaanites who struck back, destroying the young men utterly.

With the decline of the spies and the deaths of the host of young men, the people mourned and wept, and were chastened. Korach, angered by the summary sentence, grew bolder.

GADDI GREW WEAK, a victim of his own doubts.

"Gaddi, he is a shadow of himself," Tamar worried. To Hur, she said, "You must sit by your father and learn leadership."

Hur sat dutifully by his father's side and learned what he could. At night, he asked Noa her opinions and saw the value in having a clever wife.

"Too clever," Tamar argued when Hur praised his wife's advice. "She must learn how to cultivate the women who will help support your leadership. Something her sister Malah can do. While Noa pursues foolishness about inheritance."

AS HE LAY on their bed, Hur's mind roared with thoughts. He reached for Noa's hand.

"Noa, do you think my father has become too old to lead? Should I wait until leadership comes to me, or should I take it?"

Noa worried that she had not stood before the Judges of Hundreds, she did not know how to help Yoela, and their child seemed ready to explode from her belly.

"It is too much."

"Leadership?"

"No, I am sorry. I was listening to my own concerns."

"What concerns? Tell me and I will fix them."

The two lay in separate worlds, linked by their hands.

NOA COULD NO longer squat to mold cheese, so Hur had built a rough table. Hur's younger sister, Liri, worked at her side. Noa had pressed one cheese, wrapped it in saltbush leaves, and set it aside to dry in the sun. Liri dipped into a cloth bag with her small wooden paddle and scooped another load of curds onto the table. As Noa pressed the curds, a gush of water wetted the insides of her thighs. At first she thought it was whey, but the curds seemed solid. She feared her bladder had betrayed her.

Then she remembered Nechama, the tribe's most accomplished midwife, who had instructed, "Call for me when the waters break."

Noa hesitated, not wanting to panic. Then more liquid trickled down her leg.

"Liri," Noa urged, "run for Nechama. Run now."

Before running to Nechama, Liri told her mother, who bustled to Noa's side.

"Where are the things Nechama told you to prepare?"

Noa moved tentatively, afraid she might shake the baby loose.

"Do you think you are as fragile as a poppy petal? Move, daughter. This child will not come out if you stop moving."

Tamar found her older daughter and Malah and pushed Noa into their arms.

"Keep her moving, but nearby," she demanded.

Nechama arrived soon after, her bulky birthing bag slung from her shoulder. She pulled Tamar into Hur's tent, the only person who would dare do so. Together they set up the tent as a birthing chamber.

Hur arrived and found himself in a flurry of women, cloths, jugs, and waterskins.

"For all her cleverness . . ." Tamar muttered, rushing past, forgetting how unprepared she was for her first child.

"What is going on here?"

Suddenly Tamar stopped and turned to him. "Oh. My son."

Tears filled her eyes and spilled down her cheeks. She raised her arms to embrace Hur, dropping the fleece that draped her arm. She looked down at the dust it raised.

"She's having your son."

Hur's eyes widened. "You mean right now?"

"Yes. No. Soon. Oh, look what I have done to this fleece. Tell Liri to beat it clean again. It will be what your son sleeps on."

Hur ran the few strides to his tent and entered.

"Are you mad?" his mother called after him. "You should not be in . . ."

By this time, Noa's cramping had begun in earnest, and Hur's sister and Malah had escorted her into the tent. Noa flashed him a distracted smile. Malah and his sister gave him looks that said, "Leave." Unnerved, he did.

He brushed past Nechama, who dragged her bag to the center of the tent. The line of Nechama's thick eyebrows met in the center, giving her a serious, foreboding look when her face was at rest. But Nechama's face was rarely at rest. She took in the three young women before her and her face crinkled into a smile.

She had learned that a sense of humor matched with the authority of experience relaxed nervous mothers. Bearing a child was often a deadly matter, and Nechama gave laboring mothers—and herself—the best possible odds.

"Noa, my dear, you look stricken. You are going to have a baby, not a battle. Oh, ho, some would say it *is* a battle to give birth, but those poor women have not had Nechama to help them. If we were still in Egypt we would have the birthing house. But here . . . well, we do what we can."

Nechama chattered on as she opened the mouth of her bag and drew out a low, wooden stool, then a slightly taller stool with a crescent-shaped seat, both brought with her from Egypt. Her energy and volubility distracted the young women. Noa was cramping heavily but was afraid to allow herself more than strangled grunts.

"Let it out, my dear. Your child is speaking through you. Let his voice be heard," Nechama urged as she continued arranging things: folded cloths, a jug of olive oil, a large waterskin, and a broad bowl, a firepan with coals, small sacks of herbs and incense.

Liri brought in the white lamb's fleece, which Nechama folded fleece-side in and put it off to one side. The edges of the tent had been lowered for privacy and let in just a glow of light.

Having pushed aside most of the clutter, Nechama secured the birthing stool atop a rug in the center of the tent. She told the women to pile up pillows behind it, and set the lower stool before it.

The crescent-shaped seat of the birthing stool had been worn smooth by straining muscles wet with sweat and the fluids of birth. Images celebrating fecundity burnished the sides of the seat. Full moon and new moon anchored the ends. Crescent moons marked the quarter-points, enclosing the sitter within a protective lunar cycle. Crowded between the phases of the moon and inscribed on the legs of the stool were images of heavy-breasted Asherah, tumid pomegranates, fish, and eggs—the icons of life.

Nechama tied a large apron around her middle, sat on the lower stool, and patted the taller one. "Come, my queen of the birthing stool."

Noa, seeing that her tent had been transformed into a birthing theatre with her as the centerpiece, cried, "My mother. Someone call her to come."

Liri, who lingered at the tent door, serving as Hur's spy, was happy for something important to do.

"I can find her," she said.

"Yes, but quickly."

Nechama then pointed to the crescent-shaped stool again.

"Please, young ladies, escort the queen to her seat."

Noa attempted to sit, but was not sure how.

"Here, squat like this. Your hands on your thighs." Nechama demonstrated. "Let your baby know you are ready to push him into life."

Noa gingerly imitated Nechama's squat.

Seeing Noa's tentativeness, Nechama said, "Do not fear. Your baby will not drop onto the ground like a stone. Asherah be praised if birth would be so easy. When the cramping stops, we simply wait for the next set."

As they suffered Noa past one set of contractions and soothed her toward the next, Liri broke into the tent.

"She's coming. But slowly. Is she really, really old? I never saw anyone move *that* slow."

"Liri, hold your tongue and run back to help Noa's mother here."

"Awwww . . ." But Liri did as she was told.

"And, you," Nechama said to Hur's older sister, "please fill another waterskin."

At that moment, Liri parted the flaps of the tent, and Noa's mother entered. Noa saw her mother's face, lined by life, magically transformed by joy. Forgetting her impatience with her mother's fatuous pronouncements, Noa burst into tears.

Her mother shuffled over and cradled her daughter's face between her hands, thankful she had been granted length of life to attend the birth of her first grandchild. "God willing," she added. She was also thankful for Nechama, whose skills were known beyond the camp of Manasseh.

The birth of a child was not guaranteed. Some died in the womb, taking their mothers with them. Some died in the struggle through the birth canal. Every child born alive was a miracle.

Nechama arranged Malah and Hur's sister on either side of Noa.

"You strong young women will hold her up from either side when she tires. And help her push. Liri, place pillows over there, for Noa's mother to rest her bones."

Nechama pulled Noa's skirts up as Noa adjusted her heavy body on the stool. The wood felt cool and smooth against her flesh.

"Liri, pour some water so that I may wash my hands."

Liri brought a basin and set it on the ground in front of Nechama's stool, then poured water over the midwife's hands.

"Set the water and basin here." She pointed just beyond where she sat. "Now you may leave."

Nechama reached for the small jar at her side, poured olive oil on her hands, and rubbed it in until her hands were well oiled.

"You are in our loving hands and those of Asherah."

Noa groaned as contractions clutched her womb again. Nechama slid her hand up to feel the position of the baby. As she did so, Noa gasped.

"Don't worry, little mother, I feel the curve of your child's head just behind the sheath. You will labor, the sheath will part and let him into the world."

As Nechama spoke quietly and steadily, she bore down on Noa's belly, her inserted hand feeling which way the child faced. Noa, caught up in the journey of her child through her body, breathed heavily, sweated, and gripped the arms of her sister and sister-in-law, transmitting the pain of her flesh to theirs.

Frightened by the ferocious focus of Noa's body, Malah drew back. Nechama noticed and regretted allowing the presence of a woman who had not experienced birth. As she massaged the mouth of the birth canal, easing it open, her voice took charge.

"Sing your songs, women," Nechama commanded. "Sing your songs."

CHAPTER 20
KORACH'S REVOLT

THE TRIBES SEETHED over God's decree that they must sit like stones in the desert. Korach saw that the moment cried out for decision and direction. He gathered men among the Levites and other tribes, two hundred and fifty in all, strode to the tent of Moses, and called out:

"Why should you alone raise yourself up if we are a nation of priests? You say God tells us we must die here in the desert. If we are truly a nation of priests, I say God tells me that we are to live, not die. Live in our own land."

As news of the confrontation spread, people ran to see what would happen. Those who heard Korach wondered why he did not lead the people.

Korach fixed their attention with a searing question to Moses. "Does God hear and speak only through you?"

Moses, anguished that he had delivered unwelcome news, fell on the ground before them, humbling himself, a reluctant mouthpiece.

"You who promised us a land of milk and honey have led us into the wilderness to die. Do you think you have the right to lord it over us?"

Moses slowly rose from the ground. Quiet roared in all their ears.

Moses said to Korach and his followers, "Tomorrow morning, bring your firepans. Place fire upon them and incense upon the coals. In the morning, let God choose who will lead the way."

HUR'S FATHER GATHERED with others to discuss what Korach had said. Korach's challenge to Moses voiced what many felt.

"We will wait only for death in this forsaken desert," said an elder from the tribe of Efraim.

"Maybe our sons, too."

"None will be able to claim this land promised to us."

Before the group broke, a few vowed to stand with Korach in the morning.

"Will you support Korach against Moses tomorrow?" Gaddi's cousin asked, as they walked toward their tents.

The silver light of a half-moon tinted the hills and spread a faint glow across the ground. The sheen of something slithering caught their eye, followed by a barely audible squeak. A night hunter and its prey.

Because of his fear of Anak, he had failed his son, trapping him between Egypt and the lands of their ancestors. Gaddi hoped he would not fail again.

Hur lay curled in his robe outside his tent, his head cushioned in the crook of his arm. He listened as the women's urgent, pulsing songs of praise to Asherah waxed and waned in rhythm with Noa's contractions, lulling him to sleep as Noa labored into the night.

GADDI STEPPED OUT into the thin light of dawn. He rubbed his arms to warm himself in the sharp morning, then walked toward the place where Moses and Korach would meet to decide the leadership of all Israel.

"To stand with Korach, or not?" His resolve tilted back and forth. "At least Korach is decisive," he told himself.

One of the elders of Efraim passed and asked, "Are you with Korach?" Without waiting for Gaddi's answer, the man said, "I will not wait to die in the desert."

Gaddi, one of those responsible for the wait, heard reproach in the man's voice.

"Yes," he said, suddenly decisive. "Yes, I am with Korach. Come, I will walk with you."

KORACH AND THE assembly who stood with him held their firepans, in defiance, against Moses and Aaron.

"Stand aside," Korach cried out. "We will make our own sacrifices to the one God. Who is Moses to make us wait until our bones bleach in the wilderness? Who is Aaron, so jealous to be the only priest? Did he not sanction the Golden Calf? Is he not of the same family as I . . . I who had no business with that wanton shame?"

Moses, fearful of Korach's arrogance, fell before God, crying, "Oh God, when one man sins, will You be wrathful with the whole community?"

Moses beseeched the community to move away from Korach. Of those that remained, each had his reason. Gaddi stood with them to make amends to himself and his son for showing cowardice in the land of their fathers. He hoped to remedy one action with another.

As Moses and the community fell back, Gaddi could not hear Moses say, "If the ground opens its mouth and swallows them up with all that belongs to them, and they go down alive into Sheol, you shall know that these men have spurned the Lord."

As he said these words, the ground cracked and roared under Korach and those who stood with him.

Those who had come to watch the confrontation fled, racing from long-fingered fissures that reached to grab them. Those who had stayed away felt the ground roll and shake. Bellowing camels rocked up to their feet and stamped at their stakes. Some broke loose and charged wildly, one crushing the leg of a young girl.

Hur, who had fallen asleep outside his tent, was shaken awake. He leaped to his feet, grabbed a tent rope to steady his sleep-shaky legs, then parted the tent door. The intensity of birthing rivaled the intensity of the quaking earth.

"Not now," his mother hissed. "We are almost there. Go. Find your father. When you return, *you* will be a father."

Hur went to seek his father.

LOOKING FOR FRESH forage, Milcah and Tirzah had led the flocks into the hills overlooking the Kadesh Barnea oasis. They had left early, even before Gaddi stepped fatefully into his day.

Perched on a rock, Milcah spun out thread from her spindle and looked toward the tents of Dan and Oholiav, her heart tight. From this distance, the tents looked no larger than the pebbles Tirzah lobbed down the slope. When she tired of pitching pebbles, Tirzah picked at a scab on her ankle.

"Do you think Noa has pushed out that baby yet?" she asked, her head down, worrying the scab.

Milcah was lost in silently mourning her dream of life with Oholiav, a dream now crushed. Rina had broken the news gently: Oholiav had been betrothed to a woman from his own tribe.

Rina had held Milcah and whispered, "My Milcah, you would have been his choice had he chosen. It was his father's decision."

Dutifully, Milcah hid her heartache.

"I *said*, do you think Noa had her baby?" Tirzah repeated.

"No." Milcah bent over her work. "Babies have big heads. Not like lambs."

"I know that."

"Then why did you ask?"

Tirzah sing-songed, "Milcah, Milcah, always right. Weaves her weaving out of spite."

Milcah leaned over to jab her spindle at Tirzah, who pulled back in mock horror.

"Help me," Tirzah called out to the sheep. "My sister is coming at me with a spindle."

Tirzah's silly song and their little drama spread a smile across Milcah's face, taking her away from her pain. Just then, the ground rumbled. The girls looked around, thinking a rockslide had started. What they saw was far off, at the edge of the camp. A dark cloud billowed up from the ground, filling the air with brown blooms that burst slowly in tendrils, floating toward the heavens like stray locks of hair.

At the base of the cloud, fire flickered, then burst into a furious orange ball that shot up with fiery arms, searing the sky. Greasy soot spewed from the fireball in long, black tongues, twisting through the roiling cloud. From under the skirts of the cloud, fissures raced across the desert, knife-sharp crevices that thundered open. Milcah and Tirzah saw people, small as mice, swallowed into the earth.

They stood, gape-mouthed, as sheep climbed each other's backs, panicked.

When Tirzah began running toward the chaos, Milcah threw herself on her sister.

"No. Wait. Just wait!" she screamed.

Hearing Milcah's screams and smelling death, the flocks broke into full flight away from doom, and the girls ran after them.

FLAMES SPEWING FROM abysmal fissures consumed Korach and his closest companions. The smell of their scorched flesh seared the air. Their bones, burnt to ash, swirled upward, the sooty tongues that Milcah and Tirzah watched from afar.

Those who stood with them began to run, but the cracking earth dropped them into its molten mouth.

Gaddi felt the ground part beneath his feet.

"What have I done?"

He fell forward, hoping to grasp a rock, a root, something. In the dust and commotion he saw those around him falling into deep crevasses. The earth was eating them alive, burying Korach and his followers under a rage of rubble that crushed bones and filled mouths, smothering them, returning them to dust. The earth that once nourished them now consort to a punishing God.

Gaddi heard the cries and moans of those around him. One voice, in particular, echoed awfully in his head until he realized the cries were his own. His fingers dug into the earth, clutching, as he tried to climb out of a collapsing world. A boulder tore into him, knocking him deeper into the abyss, burying him half-alive as he realized he had thoughtlessly compounded one error of judgment with another. He, who others had thought so wise, would die for a stupid mistake. Tears flooded his eyes as cinders from the fires rained down upon him, burning the flesh that was still exposed until the earth swallowed what remained of him.

WHEN HUR DID not find his father in his tent, he ran wildly into the chaos of panicked people, bellowing animals, and tangled tent ropes, asking if anyone had seen Gaddi. They paid no attention. Most were stunned or frantically speculating about what might happen next. Some feared the sky would collapse, shattering its blue dome against the ground, destroying the heavens.

He saw a friend of his father's clutching a boy in his arms, both of them crying as the man stumbled away from the chaos.

Hur grasped the man's shoulder and asked, "Have you seen my father?"

The man turned to Hur, the boy's arms clinging around his neck, his small head rigid with fear, their faces streaked with soot.

"Your father?" All he could say was, "Gone."

"Gone? What do you mean 'gone'?"

The man jerked his head in the direction from which he had come.

The great fire had consumed itself and now smoldered, blazing up here and there as it ate the remains of bodies caught in the cataclysm.

Hur pressed on. As he approached the epicenter, at the blistered edge of camp, the few people left alive yelled, "Help us!" or "Come no closer!"

He stopped and saw, ahead, a crevasse piled with boulders, shreds of tents, and human limbs. He feared his father had been caught in Korach's web of deceit and lay somewhere in the smoking, rubble-filled devastation. His face a stricken mask, Hur turned back toward the tents of Manasseh.

NOA HAD STRUGGLED through the night, bearing down as the women's chants rose to urge her on, resting on their arms in between, sweat streaming from her body, her hair damp, curling down her shoulders in tangled ropes. Nechama had turned the child within and now saw a circle of dark hair.

"Only a little more. One push. Two. Three at most and your child will be in your arms," she urged.

"I cannot. I am so tired."

Malah's arms ached from supporting her sister. She wondered if she had the strength for such a trial. Images welled up: The unseen man who planted the seed, his smell, and the feel of him inside her. Seglit and how the balance between them would change. The child within her, Boaz's child, rightfully. Malah imagined handing a perfect boy to his father, and she forgot her tired arms.

Their mother began humming an old tune that the sisters loved, a wordless tune that had lulled them to sleep when they were little. Now she added words, singing of the child to come and the joy he would bring. It was not a perfect song, but so heartfelt that, in the next contraction, the baby's head crowned. Noa grunted as her baby breached her opening and new life burst forth.

Nechama caught the wet, wrinkled baby, held it upside down, and tapped its back until its lungs filled with air for the first time, and it cried. Nechama called for linen and fleece, wrapped the infant, and handed it to Noa's mother while she asked Noa to bear down one more time to expel the placenta.

Hur's sister called loudly, "Liri." knowing her younger sister would be awake and listening. "Call mother to come."

Almost immediately, Tamar rushed in, followed by Liri.

"Prepare food for the 'laborers,'" Tamar ordered her younger daughter, then addressed the women. "We will have a feast . . ." She pulled open the wrappings to see the sex. "Yes, a feast for our son."

On her way to fix food, Liri passed Hur coming the other way.

"Brother, I am an aunt," she said proudly.

Hur rushed to the tent door and called, "May I enter?"

"A moment. A moment," his mother called out.

Hur stood impatiently outside, wiping his hands on his robe, wiping away the smoke and the horror of what he had seen, the scarred earth that swallowed those who stood with Korach, all buried alive. Filled with dread that his father was among them, he imagined his cries. A wave of nausea swept over him. He needed to see new life.

Finally, his mother called, "Enter, father, and hold your son."

Noa, wrapped in a warm robe, her face washed, her hair plaited, held a tiny, dark-haired boy. Swaddled tightly, only his head was visible, with lashes so long Nechama had to wash them to reveal his carob-brown eyes.

Hur walked toward his son and wife, seeing nothing but them. Then, he remembered and stopped to kiss his mother. Her face, shining with joy and triumph, told him that she knew nothing of what had occurred beyond this tent. He continued to Noa. Heart pounding with far too much, he kneeled before her. Wondering at his clouded eyes, Noa offered their son to him. Hur held his son and wept.

WHEN IT WAS confirmed that Gaddi had died in the Korach rebellion, the house of Manasseh mourned. Hur had lost a father and gained a son on the same day. In honor of his father's memory and his mother's loss, the feast for his son was postponed for seven days of mourning.

Ignoring the question in his heart, why his father sided with Korach, Hur railed, "What did my father do to bring God's wrath down on him? He was upright. This God. Cannot even see into the heart of one man. Who can rely on such a One?"

"Hush. You foolish son of mine. Do you want to bring down God's anger on this family a second time? The gods do with us as they will."

In her heart, Tamar held God accountable.

As she did with everything in life, Tamar upheld propriety. She presented Nechama with a jar of olive oil and a red-trimmed robe as payment for guiding her grandson from womb to world. She arranged the feast for the baby who would be Gaddi's namesake. She mourned publicly as befitted her position and kept her grief to herself.

Noa had come to admire the way Tamar ordered her household and modulated her temper to fit any circumstance. If Hur inherited his father's position and she were thrust into Tamar's role, she wondered if she could temper herself, knowing her father's volatility coursed through her.

As Noa worried Tamar's mantle would fall on her, Malah saw Tamar's crown on her own head. Malah convinced herself that Noa would not care to become Tamar. She told herself that Hur would get his due when his time came, but now Boaz deserved the bright light of leadership, second only to tribal leader Gamaliel.

And Gamaliel was dying. Over the years, worms from the waters of Egypt had weakened him, killing him from the inside. When the men of Manasseh met to choose Gamaliel's successor, Gamaliel's son was rejected as weak, with all the stature of a downy-lipped girl.

Hur's name was raised, matched with "upright" and "brave." Then cut down with "inexperienced" and "young." Long before the men met, Malah had worked her young wives' network. She suggested to one, who suggested to her husband, "Why not choose Hur, but place Boaz as regent until Hur ripens?"

At the meeting, the man offered his wife's proposal. The problem of leadership was thorny, the men were tired, and here was a simple, acceptable solution. They praised the proposal, though Boaz saw Malah's hand in it.

Boaz said, "I would be honored to serve as tutor to the next leader of Manasseh, instructing him by example. If you judge my example as worthy."

Malah had determined that Boaz be the one. And so he was.

Noa knew what Malah had done, seizing for Boaz what should have come to Hur. But, with a baby at her breast, she had no energy to act against Malah's machinations or anything else. Exhausted, Noa relinquished.

"Let Tamar provide guidance. I will hold my tongue."

Tamar, seeing the men of Manasseh had chosen experience over youth, sought Boaz.

"I know you will provide excellent education for Hur's leadership," Tamar said, deliberately attaching the word "leader" to her son rather than to Boaz. "You will find him an ideal student, with all the qualities presently in place."

Boaz heard Tamar's subtext clearly.

"I hope I will prove a worthy model."

They understood each other perfectly, and warily.

CHAPTER 21
YOELA ASCENDING

TAMAR BRUSHED AWAY Malah's bid to supplant her as she might a sand flea. Tamar was mother to Manasseh's chosen leader and that is how it would remain.

"You poisoned my well," Malah accused Noa.

"Your well?"

"You spoke against me to Tamar. Why should I not have Tamar's place if Boaz has Gaddi's?"

"Tamar does not consult women beneath her, least of all me," Noa remarked, cooing to Gaddi as if his were the only needs that concerned her.

"Liar."

Noa's placidity, meant to rankle her sister, did. Malah stamped off, vowing that her son, not Gaddi, would one day lead Manasseh.

Although it was at her sister's expense, Noa thought, "I am learning."

Hur was satisfied with the tribal elders' decision. When the time came, he would reach for leadership and it would be his. Now he wanted freedom, not the yoke of leadership. He wanted to hone himself and the young men of Manasseh in order to triumph when it came time to regain their ancestral lands.

And he sang his son's praises to all who would hear. To Haddad, who told of his own new child.

"A girl—Keturah," Haddad said. "And the next will be a boy, a hero of Midian."

"A girl, a match for Gaddi. We will bind our peoples together."

"You say. I say she is too beautiful for your son."

"Stand in line, my friend. The offers of beautiful daughters have already begun."

They boasted back and forth, delighting in each other's company, sitting under the tasseled shade of a palm, eating dates, and drinking sweet water. But Hur felt the Scarface lingering at the edges, a dark chaperone.

YOELA HAD COME alone to the feast for Noa's and Hur's son. Noa wore a gracious smile, acknowledging congratulations from women who meant it and from women who wanted to raise their ranking with Tamar. Yoela noticed Noa's tired eyes and knew she was overwhelmed. Noa said nothing, but tried to add a smile to her eyes. Yoela pressed into Noa's hand a bead from one of her own earrings into which she had figured a sign against the Evil Eye and threaded it onto a slim, child-sized thong. She stayed only a few moments longer.

When Gaddi was a few weeks old, secure enough in life, Noa snuggled him into a sling and made her way to Yoela, who sat weaving at a loom outside her in-law's tent, her hair tucked beneath a tightly bound headcloth.

Yoela's hair was her glory. With her hair bound up, the golden glow and her inner glow were gone. Although a covered head was the sign of a married woman, the convention was as loosely applied as the covering. Yoela's binding was more that of a prisoner. At her son's feast day, Noa had been too tired to notice. Now she stared, then cast her eyes elsewhere.

Yoela saw Noa's face and said, too softly for others to hear, "The man I am bound to does not want other men to see my hair. He says it tempts them." She shrugged. "You can see Barzel's property is safe."

"Has he bent, a bit?"

"Him? No. I wish he would not just bend, but break."

Noa had never heard Yoela speak so violently.

"I'm just complaining. I have no one to complain to, so it must be you. Sit by me. I promise I will stop. We have your pink-cheeked son to talk about."

"I have brought you a salve. Malah says it will help."

"Oh, I have learned to endure that part. Come. Sit." Yoela patted a stack of goat-hair panels beside her.

Noa eased herself onto the stack of sun-heated panels and felt its warmth spread through her. She lifted the knot of the sling over her head and laid Gaddi next to her. He flung out an arm, which she swaddled, and he settled back to sleep.

Yoela reached over to push the cloth away from his face, then turned to Noa. "May I?"

"Please."

She examined his face, his puckered suckling mouth, the rolled edges of his ears, opalescent as a seashell. Brushing aside a heartbeat of jealousy, Yoela relaxed, and they talked as they always had, until Yoela jumped up and pulled Noa's hand.

"Come, let me take you to the place I found."

Noa stood, gathered Gaddi, and offered him to Yoela, who cradled the baby as she headed toward hills aproned by tumbled rocks. Twisting through a break between the hills, she came to a sunny niche. On one side, a flat rock formed a lintel above a shallow, shady grotto.

"Here is my place. Wait," Yoela said, as she handed Gaddi back to Noa. She got down on hands and knees and, like a dog digging a hole, scooped sand from the desert floor toward the back of the grotto, then patted it in place to form a backrest for her friend.

Noa told her the tale of Gaddi's death and baby Gaddi's birth. Yoela relayed the gossip of the clan of Zerach: the aunt whose big toe twitched when she lied to her husband; the cousin who thought he was bedding his wife's twin sister and told her how much prettier she was, not recognizing it was, in fact, his own wife. Noa shared the gossip of Manasseh. They let their tales spin them away and laughed until their sides ached, then shushed each other when Gaddi stirred from the noise.

Yoela unwrapped her head, shook out her hair, and lay back, luxuriating in the small freedom. Noa fingered a sunny lock, had a thought, unwrapped Gaddi, and laid the naked baby on the bed of Yoela's soft curls. Startled, Gaddi blinked and grasped his mother's offered finger. The fresh air stimulated him and he arced a golden stream of urine. Noa tried to catch Gaddi and his stream before it wetted Yoela, who struggled up, causing the arc to catch Noa full in the face.

"Some mother. Serves you right." Yoela laughed.

"You can say a strange male lay in your hair," Noa teased as she rewrapped her son.

"Barzel would kill me."

Her face tightened at the thought that he might do it for a lot less.

They were silent. Noa fussed with Gaddi, then said, "If you manage to have a son, it will change things. You'll see. It will elevate and protect you."

At the smell of his mother, Gaddi turned his head toward Noa, his open mouth searching for food. She put her baby to her breast and said, "Tell me a story."

Yoela took a deep breath and began. "Long ago, Ba'al, the great god of thunder was creating thick, black clouds to hurl a storm upon the world."

"Like the One God at Sinai," Noa interjected.

"Silence! I am telling a story."

Gaddi, sucking himself to sleep, began sucking more vigorously at the sharp sound of Yoela's voice.

"At the end of his cloud-creating, Ba'al squeezed out one more small cloud. He herded the clouds and made them run across the sky, bawling and tumbling over one another like black sheep. The small cloud, the last one, could not keep up. She drifted to the southlands where the sun threatened to eat her."

The grotto was cool, but Noa's legs stuck out, warmed by the sun. The contrast and Yoela's voice lulled her.

"Her father Ba'al lived in the great mountains to the north. The small cloud was alone. Burnt by the sun above, the cloud sought refuge among a cluster of peaks. Here she settled.

"Hiding among cracks and crevices, the cloud gathered strength. Every morning she covered the small canyons with a veil of mist that allowed creatures to venture out and do their work until the sun drove her and them back until nightfall. One beetle drew her attention. Long-legged, like others of its kind, this black dancer-on-the-sand had grace and purpose. That is how the cloud saw it.

"One morning, the beetle—call her Oza—saw a large shard of bark. She raised it above her head and struggled the heavy shard toward her kin, to build them a home.

"The others saw her strength and were jealous. They knocked the bark from her, injuring one of her legs. Then they tore at the bark, each one trying to gain advantage until they shredded it into a hundred useless pieces.

"When the sun reached the height of the heavens, draping its fiery robes over the earth, the beetles fled to their crevices. All but Oza, who lay broken as the bark. The sun played with the edges of her shell, burning it until it curled, crisping the delicate gossamer wings that lay beneath. Oza lay dying. The cloud summoned all her strength and hovered over Oza, covering her until shadows of dusk cooled the canyon. And Oza found the strength to crawl to safety.

"The cloud had exposed herself in order to save a beetle. Now she was as fragile as . . . as . . . a baby's breath. 'Oh Father Ba'al,' she cried, 'save me. Give me back my strength, I beg you.' But Ba'al was far away and did not hear. The cloud child withered until only a strand of mist curled near the base of a cave, a cave like this one."

Yoela's voice rested.

"This cannot be the end. It is sad. Far too sad. Go on, Yoela," Noa demanded.

Yoela quickly recast the ending on a rising note, but her heart was not in it. Noa sensed her sorrow. They lay looking up at the wedge of cloudless sky beyond the lintel, until Yoela said, "It is time to return."

She bound up her hair, and they left.

With Gaddi tied to her side, Noa continued home, troubled by Yoela's melancholy. She turned her mind to the forests and running waters her father had promised, now far in the future. Noa wondered whether she should ask Boaz for a place before the Judges of Hundreds, whether inheritance was still worth fighting for.

Then, for a brief moment, she was washed free of her wonderings. With the memory of Yoela's voice in her ears and the sweet smell of Gaddi at her side, she hoped God did not notice her momentary completeness.

WEIGHTED BY THEIR terrible penance for the spies' report, the people pegged their tents for permanence and laid out small plots for barley, wheat, lentils, and melons along the broad wadis that scored Kadesh Barnea. The men lashed blades to wood plows and drove their donkeys across the desert, carving troughs for irrigation.

The women bent their heads to spinning and sewing, grinding grain and baking bread, and raising the generation who would enter the promised land.

As barley and wheat grew, so grew Malah's belly, which she paraded with pride, especially when she met with her group of wives, whose young children crawled over them and curled in their laps. She was the center of attention, each young mother vying to offer advice to Malah, wife of Manasseh's headman.

One evening, as Malah sat with Boaz at the tent door, a bondsman arrived with news of a stolen ram and the name of the thief. As the servant drew close, Malah breathed in a familiar scent. Her hidden place swelled, remembering her gown thrown back as her legs were parted. While Boaz gave the bondsman instructions, Malah looked straight at the man, and he at her. Boaz saw.

The next day, Boaz sent a squad of servants to seize him and sell him to a passing caravan. Malah never saw the man again. She bore Boaz a fine, healthy child. Nechama, who guided the baby out, handed the tiny, red-cheeked child to her exhausted mother and saw Malah's face darken with disappointment when she saw it was a girl.

Malah quickly fixed her face, claiming, "One day my daughter will be the first among the women of Manasseh."

Remembering the pomegranate seeds Seglit spat out to emphasize Boaz's impotence, she said, "We will call her . . . Rimon."

The women clapped their hands and laughed. And that is what she was called.

SEASON CROWDED SEASON. It was a time of increase for the daughters of Zelophechad. Noa's second pregnancy drove out all thoughts of promised land.

Hoglah, too, was pregnant. She, who expected nothing, was elated by her luck: first a husband, soon a child. Even sharing Bar-On's tent no longer felt burdensome. Her sisters offered a thousand ways to avoid the old man's cranky demands. She dutifully thanked them but was, in truth, grateful for his presence. His wheezing on the other side of the tent wall told her she was not alone. Except for spring sheep shearing, Asaf spent more time traveling the desert with small caravans than within the camp of Manasseh.

He discovered that his knowledge of Egyptian ways and goods provided easy entrée to the peoples of the east. And he could make his words dance. He hawked wool and hides, beads and tools for seeds, figs, oil, whatever product looked like it might turn a profit. He had an eye for the gullible and for those who fancied they had the wits to win a gamble.

When his need for a woman came upon him, he drew weak women like moths to the flames of his flattery, providing juicy moments of danger to women with dry lives. And he had a tale or trick for every item he sold. A phallus-shaped tool, whose base was carved with coupling gods of Egypt, brought children to childless women, he claimed, adding that only he knew how to make it work. Barren women fumbled off a bracelet, an earring, bits of worn wealth, desperate to trade for fertility. His smooth tool provided Asaf an opening. He left his seed in the tents of the foolish and, sometimes, his implement worked, bringing babies to the barren.

He sold Hoglah's salve of sheep grease and ground herbs to cure sores, strengthen limbs, and lessen the pain of arthritic joints. His sales songs were so convincing even he half-believed them. Hoglah did not know why the salve she made sold so well. She was simply happy to contribute to the household increase, thinking her salve as special as her sisters' cheeses.

Asaf gulled men with a deluge of words that flooded the minds of his listeners while his hands took advantage. This is how he had outwitted a man in a dice game, carrying off the hand mill that helped win Hoglah. The man heard that Asaf had used substitute dice, created for the purpose.

On a later trip, Asaf sauntered into the same camp, not recognizing the hand mill's former owner until the man was nearly upon him with a club. Asaf ran and hid until the next morning when he joined caravan companions headed south. Indignant at suffering such treatment, Asaf told himself that he traded fairly when it suited him. When truth was convenient, then truth was on his lips.

Asaf aspired to trade in the most costly goods: frankincense and the Balm of Gilead that grew among springs along the Salt Sea. The Balm of Gilead healed wounds and hid the stink of sacrifice with its holy odor, but the powerful faction that controlled its trade blocked Asaf. In raw goods he could do no better than the thick, sticky asphalt that pitched up from the depths of the Salt Sea.

"Pitch from the place of its birth," he cajoled Egyptian embalmers, who used asphalt for mummification. "Preserve your dead with the best."

At home, he complained to Hoglah, "Who but a hard-working trader would trade in pitch?"

She fussed sympathetically as she picked off pitch stuck to his robe. While Asaf was away, the hand mill that lured women to her tent kept her days from being lonely. Women brought wheat and barley, and Hoglah delighted in demonstrating how to stream the kernels into the hole at the top of the mill and grind out silky flour.

Her sisters chided her for being so generous with her time, but her grindstone snared Hoglah a friend, a young woman as shy as she, who had tagged along with an older sister. The young woman had a crooked back, yet her family had managed to marry her off because her spirit was as sunny as her back was crooked. She and Hoglah often met to work side by side.

Hoglah's evenings and nights were lonely, and she pined for Asaf. His return brought color to her cheeks, her breath came fast, she fluttered around him, plumping pillows for his back, feeding him date cakes, setting bowls of cool water to wash his hands and feet. In the evening, Asaf regaled Hoglah with tales of his journey.

"The peoples of the east, they all sing praises of your salve. 'There is none like it,' they say. A widow with a terrible canker—rubbed it in and . . . Ho! . . . she was cured."

Asaf did not say who had done the rubbing.

Hoglah, puffed with pride, imagined people telling their neighbors, "Yes, it was made by the middle daughter, the one they call Hoglah."

But Asaf was on to the next incident. " . . . then I showed the man how much the beads weighed. I had three strands of different weights. I put one on a scale and showed him how much that weighed, then two together and a different weight, then the first again, with a third and yet another weight, telling him numbers faster than the gods can throw lightning across the sky. 'Wait, wait,' he pleaded to catch up . . . 'Another weight you want,' I teased, and threw yet another number at him."

As Asaf told the story, he juggled imaginary beads from hand to hand, dancing from one leg to another, then portraying the fuddled buyer until Hoglah laughed out loud.

When Bar-On grumbled from the other side of the tent wall, Asaf continued his animated tale softly, but added a pantomime of pinched-face Bar-On. Hoglah's silent laughter reddened her face and made her sides ache with merriment. At moments like this, Asaf truly did love her. She was his best, most grateful audience.

Hoglah's sisters saw what sort of man Hoglah had married and hoped they saw nothing worse of him.

"What if Asaf does not return from one of his trips?" Noa supposed.

Noa and Malah were kneading dough in their bread troughs. Ora, Noa's new baby girl, lay swaddled beside her. As they dug fists into the dough, they kept an eye on Gaddi and Rimon, who pushed toy donkeys that Hur's younger brother had carved.

"Hoglah would be free to remarry and free from Bar-On . . . *if* we could find someone to take her," said Malah. "What if she remarried, and Asaf returned? Hoglah with two husbands."

They laughed at the thought.

"And what if Asaf does not return and Hoglah does not remarry?" said Malah, suddenly serious. "She and her child would have nothing. They might become enslaved to Bar-On. Or worse, he could sell them."

"That will not happen. Land—not love—is what drew Asaf to her. He will wait for the land. There. I've said it."

"And what of our claim to land you were so hot to pursue? Boaz is no youth. What if I am widowed, as seems likely while we wait to enter this much-promised land? What will Rimon get? If you are going to do something, do it."

"Yes. I will. But first let me feed my daughter," Noa said, putting baby to breast, feeling her life seep away in small increments.

MILCAH MARRIED THE man chosen for her and buried what was left of her dreams of Oholiav. The family found a man from Manasseh. Dor bore none of the age or authority of Boaz, none of the youth or courage of Hur. He expected little in life but hard work. He was colorless as a sun-bleached noon, neither blessed nor bad, an average man.

Before Milcah's marriage, Hoglah determined to dispense the wisdom of a married woman to a maiden, and found Milcah and Tirzah with the flocks in a sunny hollow.

"Milcah," she began, her voice deepened with gravitas. "There is something you should know."

Hoglah looked down at her own child-swollen belly to signify her womanly knowledge. Then she looked at Tirzah.

"Run to that kid wandering at the edge of the flock," Hoglah ordered. "It is in danger."

"What are you talking about?" Tirzah shot back. "I'm with these flocks every day. No danger."

Milcah sighed quietly, and said to Tirzah, "Go, please your sister."

She knew what was coming and had heard it already from Rina, a far better source.

"To have relations with your husband is a wonderful thing. He wants it. And you will want it, in time. It is like . . ." She struggled for a description. "It is like the moment before you sneeze. You feel something coming. You cannot stop it. And when it comes, it takes you over and feels good."

Tirzah, who had hidden to hear Hoglah, called out, "Do you wipe your nose when it's over?"

"You . . . evil child." Hoglah scooped up gravel and flung it in Tirzah's direction. "What do you know about anything?"

Tirzah, who knew more than she should, danced out of the way. Milcah laid quieting hands on her sister's shoulders.

"Tirzah is like a sneeze herself. She can't help it." Taken by Hoglah's deflated face, Milcah continued, "Now I know what to expect. You explained it so well."

Hoglah brightened. "Yes. I knew you would appreciate it." She scowled at Tirzah.

But Tirzah had her. For the next few weeks, she burst out, "Ah-CHEW!" when she passed Hoglah, then crinkled with glee as she ran from her sister's rage.

Milcah married Dor when snow dusted the peaks surrounding Kadesh Barnea. The third of three sons, he had little to offer besides hard work. Too poor to provide a tent, Dor and Milcah moved into Zelophechad's chamber. Ada now shared the other side of the tent only with Tirzah.

"Soon I will be alone. Then I will be ready to join my husband."

WHEN HER SECOND child was newly walking, Noa became pregnant a third time but lost the child soon after she could feel its first movements. Hoping to soothe Noa, Hur spoke softly and kept their two little ones near. Tamar told Noa that most had lost one or more, and sent for Nechama to bring potions that would cleanse Noa's womb and her heart.

As the weeks passed, Noa recovered, but she roiled with inchoate needs.

"I am a daughter. I am a wife. I am a mother. I do my jobs. I do not complain," she told herself. "But something is missing."

She could not think of a soul to tell. Her mother would voice empty aphorisms. Tamar and Malah would dismiss her yearnings, each in their own way. Hur would try to fix the problem without understanding it. She could not burden Yoela, whose burdens were far worse.

She was not even sure what was missing.

"Am I selfish for wanting more?" she wondered. "And will we ever reach this promised land?"

Aloud, she complained, "Why do you children always need something?"

She needed to fill more than a slot in tribal society, but she did not comprehend her need to be Noa.

THE DAY NOA was certain she was pregnant again, Yoela appeared at her door, swinging her skirts, pulling at the knot that bound up her hair.

Yoela hugged her and laughed. "Another one on the way?"

"Yoela, what wonderful thing has happened to give you life again?"

Yoela loosed her hair, then kissed Ora's head.

Her brother looked up at Yoela and said, "Did you know I can make wind from my bottom."

"Oh," Yoela said, "that is a good trick, Gaddi."

"You are you again. How?" Noa asked. "Barzel has softened?"

"Barzel? Not him. No, I have determined to become master of my situation," answered Yoela in a voice bright and brittle.

"I know you will. Sit next to me as I master this loom," said Noa, as she shoved her shuttle tight against the yarn.

They sat and talked as the two children played until Gaddi pulled at Yoela's skirt and demanded, "Tell us a story." She gathered both children onto her lap and began, "Once there was a baby hedgehog whose prickles tickled him . . ."

Too soon, Yoela finished the story, lifted Gaddi and Ora from her lap, and said, "Give me a hug, Noa, and I'll be on my way."

They stood. Yoela lingered a moment, then left, calling back carelessly, "I love you, Noa." While she walked, Yoela tucked her hair up and the sleeves of her robe slipped back. Noa saw purple bruises on her upper arms.

Two days later, Noa looked up to see Malah approaching. Malah rarely came to her these days, so she tilted her head as if to ask "What brings you here?"

"No one wanted to tell you. So it must be me. Yoela. They found her body . . ."

Noa's chest tightened, strangling her breath. Malah saw the anguish twisting her sister's face. She did not know what to say, so stood before Noa, the space between them awkward and tense. Finally, Malah closed the gap and grasped Noa to her, breaking the seal of her pain.

Noa collapsed against her sister, sobbing raggedly, her words muffled by Malah's shoulder. "It is my fault. I did not stop her from going back to Barzel."

"It was not Barzel," Malah whispered.

"She was with me only the other day. I saw what Barzel does to her."

"It was not Barzel. It was Amalek, the evil ones."

"Amalek? What do you mean?"

Malah looked down at her feet, used the great toe from one foot to brush off an invisible fleck of dirt from the other. She did not want to explain.

"What do you mean, Amalek?"

Malah bent her head and mumbled, "Parts of her, strewn on the desert."

"How do they know it is Yoela?"

"They found her . . ."

Malah could not bring herself to say "head" nor describe what Amalek had done to Yoela's eyes, so said, "Her hair. No one has hair like hers."

Noa covered her eyes, trying to destroy the picture, then sank to the ground. Full of fear, her children ran to her, pressing themselves as closely as possible, Gaddi burrowing under his mother's arm, Ora clinging to her skirt and frantically sucking her thumb. Malah removed her headcloth and eased it beneath Noa's face so she would not choke on the desert dust, then sat and stroked Noa's hair until the sun cast purple shadows over the tents of Manasseh.

NOA MOVED THROUGH her duties, stunned, tears leaking down her cheeks at odd moments. Gaddi offered his toy donkey, Ora held her hand. Nights were worse. Hur held her when she woke, terrified by her dreams.

Her mother attended her. Tamar, too, but after a few days commented loudly to Hur as she left their tent, "She was not so gripped by the loss of your unborn child."

"How can you be so unfeeling?" he returned. But he felt as she did.

Hur waxed and waned in his attempts to break through the shell Noa constructed. He wondered if he had died, would Noa grieve so much.

Haddad had taken a second wife and, while visiting the Midianite's tent, he listened to his friend boast. "They fight for my attention, each bringing better than the other."

As the men sat together, Haddad's first wife brought them a platter of vegetables stuffed with roasted grains. The second, no more than a girl, shyly offered them barley beer and date cakes.

"Tell me your secret?"

"Secret? You need no advice from me. Is your woman lacking something you like?" Haddad asked, coloring his question with sly humor. "Maybe a second wife would open her eyes."

CHAPTER 22
LEARNING TO LIVE

THE TRIBES LEARNED to plant and to harvest, husbanding every drop of water, every seed, every tumid head of wheat and barley. They wasted nothing. The margin of error was as thin as the arm of a starving child. After the wheat and barley were cleaned, they poured it into tall jars. The sight filled their hearts, and they were as jealous of their hard-won grain as a pharaoh of his gold.

When the days became short and the dark season was upon them, Noa bore her third child, a boy. A week later, Milcah bore her first, a girl they named Sarai. Hoglah's first child was nearly a year and another on the way. Counting Malah's daughter Rimon, Ada thanked Asherah for her garden of six grandchildren and congratulated herself for making such fruitful matches.

Noa's mood matched the season. She did her duties perfunctorily, feeding her newborn, sleeping by her husband's side, carrying out the unending jobs of wife and mother. Her face showed nothing, not even the grief that still clung like cobwebs.

Milcah, who bloomed with the birth of Sarai, suggested, "Why not return to the judges and pursue our claim for land?"

"But we have so long to wait."

"Why not fill the wait with something you care about?"

Noa looked at Milcah with new eyes.

"It would gain justice for us," Milcah urged.

That evening she said to Hur, "I am finally ready to face the Judges of Hundreds. Boaz said he would secure my place. But that was before our three children. Would you support me, as you are the rightful head of Manasseh?"

"Why did you wait until now? Now, when we all must wait?"

"I was not ready," was all Noa could say.

"Yes, I will support you before Boaz. But that is all."

Boaz was not optimistic.

"The Judges of Hundreds will not be easy. A plea that sets a precedent is difficult. Especially when this land of our fathers is merely a promise."

"But the Judges of Fifties gave me the right to pursue . . ."

"I will speak with the chief judge, Naftali ben Nun. But I have little hope. Even if he agrees, they do not meet often. It may take months."

He spoke with Naftali ben Nun, who grudgingly agreed only because Boaz's name carried weight. He told Boaz the Judges of Hundreds would meet the day after the new moon, three days hence.

"Send her then," Ben Nun said.

When Hur told Noa, she wailed, "Three days? I cannot prepare in three days."

"Just present what won the Judges of Fifties. And perhaps, 'thank you, husband.'"

"Forgive me. Yes, thank you. And, please, if you would play lead judge and hear my practice plea."

"A practice plea before a practice judge. A fair match. But I will not accompany you to the *bet din*. Remember, this is your petition. Not mine."

THREE DAYS LATER, Noa waited her turn. Because her claim was squeezed into the list late, Noa was one of the last to stand before the Judges of Hundreds in the cold of the waning day.

Finally, she was called before the three judges, who sat under a tent awning. The judges at right and left were muffled in their cloaks. Naftali ben Nun sat in the middle, straight as a stake, folds of cloak hanging from angular shoulders. Her head tilted in submission, Noa raised her eyes and saw the face of a griffon vulture, big beaked and bony.

"Proceed," he ordered.

Wrapped against the chill wind, she feared her words would be blown away and told herself to speak clearly. "But," she reminded herself, "not too loudly." Naftali ben Nun did not look like he would tolerate impertinence.

Noa told of how she and her sisters wanted to perpetuate their father's name and had no brothers to do so. Inheritance would extend his name through them and, she remembered to add, through their sons.

"Your father, he who was Zelophechad?"

"Yes, honorable judge."

"Zelophechad, the Sabbath-breaker."

Noa gasped. None but the Guardians of Truth had ever said a bad word about her father, in her hearing.

"He was a good man, an honest man. If he breached any new law, he did so in ignorance."

"Ignorance is no defense," the judge thundered.

Noa shrank back, not sure what to say next. The judges on either side looked into the middle distance. Noa took a deep breath to calm herself and pointed her argument toward a common ancestor.

"If we had been sons, we would have helped build the house of Israel—Jacob, our father. But we are daughters. Five dutiful daughters," she said in a voice meant to be meek. "It is our desire to receive permission to help build our people, as any son would."

"Who put such ideas in your head? Your father, the Sabbath-breaker? It is not a woman's place to build. It is a woman's place to serve her husband."

Ben Nun's voice was as unyielding as his face.

Noa was about agree, but realized that no matter how agreeable she tried to be, ben Nun was her adversary. Heated by anger, her reasons came roaring out.

"If women were more than a thing bought, a step above a slave, my beloved Yoela would be alive today. She served her husband and he served her: with the back of his hand, with a rod, with whatever came to hand until she was purple with bruises. Oh, how Barzel ben Zerach tore down his house by driving Yoela to her death. Where is the justice in that?"

"Enough. You foolish girl." Ben Nun's voice was as cold as the day. "The house of Zerach is honorable beyond your knowing. And arguments about a land so far in the future are not worth my time. Promised land? 'I would like this, oh judge.' 'I am due that.' No more of promised land before the Judges of Hundreds. Not while I live."

Noa realized she had lost. Her eyes bore into him. She had nothing more to lose.

"Justice," she blazed, "cannot be found here."

Rigid with fury, she turned on her heel and strode home. As she left, she growled under her breath, "And may God count your days short, oh exalted judge."

Three weeks later, Naftali ben Nun fell over after a heavy meal, dead.

Those who heard Noa as she left the *bet din* told others what she had said. A rumor grew that her curse caused the judge's death. Some remembered she had predicted her father's death.

"There. She *is* a witch," they said.

And the rumor circulated again, quietly among the tents.

WOMEN WHO HEARD the rumor avoided Noa, fearing the odor of witchery would taint them. Anger and frustration so curdled Noa that even her sisters gave her wide berth, all but Milcah, who feared Noa's isolation compounded her misery. Despite Milcah's attempts to engage her, Noa remained apart.

When Noa learned that Barzel planned to marry again, she arose from her darkness, imagining a path toward justice paved by vengeance. She knew that one of Malah's group would attend the wedding. Wedding guests brought food for newly married couples to eat during their days of seclusion, and Noa planned a special present for Barzel.

Noa and Malah usually molded their cheeses in segments of hollow reeds. Tall as a fist and perfectly circular, their cheeses were a delight to the eye as well as the mouth. This time, Noa molded her cheese in the way of most women, simply tying it up in the cloth used to drain the whey. She mixed in chopped leaves of the saltbush to cover the toxic taste of henbane.

The morning of Barzel's second wedding, the winds began flirting with the skirts of the tents. Teasing gave way to tearing as the wind picked up. Gritty veils of yellow dust swirled like wraiths.

Noa left her children in Milcah's care and pushed through the *hamsin* winds to catch Malah's friend on her way to the wedding. She depended that Barzel would be so filled with himself that he would enter the marriage booth, take his new wife, then consume Noa's revenge, leaving none for the young woman who replaced Yoela.

Her present tucked within her robe, Noa waited until Malah's friend and her family emerged from their tent, heads bent against wind, parents holding toddlers, grandparents clutching the hands of older children, fearful the winds would carry the young ones off.

"A moment, please," Noa asked as she walked quickly alongside. "Please, take this present for the couple when they are in their marriage booth."

"But," said Malah's friend, recognizing Noa's face through the swirling grit, "I thought you were a friend of . . . eh . . . Barzel's wife who died. Forgive me, I cannot remember her name."

"Yes, I was," Noa replied. "Surely Barzel is marrying to ease his loneliness. Please, take my present for them. No need to say who it is from. It would only bring sadness to his eyes, remembering she who died."

She thrust the wrapped cheese toward the woman, not seeing that she clutched a child within her robes.

"Please, give it to my sister." She tipped her head toward the young woman next to her. "Her arms are free. We must hurry. The wind . . ."

They had reached the large wedding canopy whose palm fronds the wind was flinging off like chaff from a winnowing basket. Ben Zerach's women were gathering foods and wedding accessories and hurriedly moving them into a nearby tent.

Malah's friend and her family entered the tent, as Noa looked on. Once they were within, Noa left. Inside the crowded tent, the sister saw a mat full of foods for the guests and laid the cheese among them.

Noa lay awake that night, tossed between the terrible thing she had done and the anticipation of hearing of Barzel's death.

The next day the camp of Manasseh learned that a plague had struck the wedding. One moment guests were enjoying breads and cheeses, melons and date wine as winds lashed the tent walls. The next, they were falling against each other, gagging and gasping. Earlier, Barzel had rudely left the guests in order to take his bride right away. Neither bride nor groom was among the people affected.

When Malah told Noa that a plague had struck the guests at Barzel's wedding, Noa's face became chalky as death.

"And, Barzel," Noa asked, "was he among them?"

"No."

"How many dead?" Noa asked, her voice as drained as her face.

"What is the matter with you? You look terrible."

Noa waved Malah on. "Please, tell me."

"Many are sick, but none are dead . . . yet. Perhaps God struck them ill for disobeying this new law that says we cannot eat milk and meat together. Barzel's clan, they gorge like animals. Even my friend says so. And they dance like those who worship Moloch. Likely the plague is God's work. That is what they are all saying."

"Yes, I'm sure that is it," said Noa, her voice faint with fear.

Malah squinted at Noa, searching to detect what drove her sister's strangeness.

Later, Noa searched as well. She could not believe what she had done. And she had acted not in fury, but with deliberation. Worse, still, Barzel lived. She dreaded her terrible deed would become her and imagined a descent so steep that she would end like their addled cousin who sat and rocked all day, tied to a tent pole so she would not wander into the desert.

Although none had died, Noa feared she could not hide what she had done from the God that saw all. Noa vowed she would never hurt another soul. Deep in the night, when she thought Hur was asleep, Noa rose, huddled within her robe, and sat in a corner, facing away from their bed and their children.

She whispered, "Please cleanse me and let me live again. Pray separate my husband from all evil I have caused."

Night after night, she pleaded with God. Hur heard Noa's pleas and wondered if the rumors of her witchery were true. He loved Noa. She was a dutiful wife and a fair mother, but he feared she had gone from miserable to half-mad. He remembered what Haddad said. Hur wanted what his friend had.

He went to his mother's tent and, before he could voice his dilemma, Tamar said, "You must take another wife."

"And put Noa aside? For the sake of rumors?"

"No. Simply take another wife. Whatever Noa did or did not do, rumors leave an ugly stain. Cleanse away the stain by taking a second wife. It cost me something to bring these rumors to rest. I have had to make promises to keep some from making trouble and others for challenging your judgment in not putting Noa aside. Your justice-chasing wife is causing you an injustice."

Tamar took her son's hands in hers and said, more softly, "Noa has wits and courage. When you are sole leader and these rumors are long gone, she will be a fitting mate, just as I am. But even I knew to bend to my husband."

"I need . . ." Hur began, then hesitated before admitting, "I need the warmth of a wife."

"Take another wife, a softer woman who will bend to your needs."

Hur made up his mind to follow his mother's advice.

THE MEN SAT together within Boaz's tent, eating what the women had prepared. The women ate outside, around the cooking pits, gossiping and reining in noisy children. Noa, beginning to wean their youngest, spooned thin wheat gruel into his mouth. Sarai, who Milcah called "my gift," lay on her mother's lap, giggling, as Tirzah tickled her toes.

After dinner, Hur and Noa returned to their own tent where Noa nursed the youngest while the two older children lolled on their bedding.

"I am taking a second wife," Hur announced.

"What?"

"Yes. Her name is Ahuva."

"Like that? Am I the last to know?"

Noa was so struck she did not know what else to say. With their youngest in her lap, Hur had chosen a time when Noa could not even raise her voice.

"No. I came to this decision by a difficult path. You have given me excellent children. You are a good wife. But this chasing after justice. And . . ."

He could not bring himself to speak about his jealousy of Yoela, dead or alive, rumors of sorcery, and Noa's strange, guilty prayers in the night.

" . . . and I need someone to care for me. There. It wounds my pride to say it, but this is how it is."

Beyond the still-open tent door, Noa saw tents pitched in a tight and stifling geometry. She wished for a view of the open desert covered by a quilt of stars. She wished she were what Hur wanted. She wanted to cry, not because Hur was wrong. He was not.

She bent her head to the baby at her breast and, as evenly as possible, asked, "How will we manage this?"

If Noa had answered with a heart full of love, asking him to reconsider, Hur gladly would have dropped his intention. But her response convinced him that his path was true. Noa said nothing more.

So they enlarged the tent and hung a wall to provide Hur with private quarters. He married and brought Ahuva into their home. Only a few years younger than Noa, she seemed a child. Malah remarked on her resemblance to Noa, who saw Tamar's hand in the match. When Ahuva asked Noa how to plait her hair in the style of a married woman, Noa showed her and used the demonstration to look at their images side by side in her mirror. What Malah said was true.

Noa's reputation and her coolness cowed the new wife. At first, Ahuva could not do enough for Noa. As she begged to learn her duties, she began to copy Noa's gestures and the rhythm of Noa's speech. She pleaded to know the secrets of Noa's cheeses, causing Noa to remember her terrible deed.

"If she is the worst penance I must pay," Noa told herself, "I cannot complain."

Ahuva was observant and soon understood why she was chosen. On the nights Ahuva lay with Hur, Noa lay in the dark listening as her husband groaned with deep satisfaction as Ahuva inflamed him with honeyed words and sounds, and with couplings that Noa could not imagine.

"She is stealing me, as fast as she can," Noa said to Malah. "Words, weaving, how I walk. What should I do?"

"She can steal and steal, but she will still be a poor copy. Will she ever be as outspoken? As contrary?"

"Malah!"

"Oh, you opened that door for me." She laughed. "I say things only a sister can say. And, more . . ." Malah softened her voice. "She will never be as courageous, wise-hearted, or so devoted to something outside herself."

Noa caught her breath. Before her stood a Malah rarely revealed.

"That is all you will get from me."

Before Noa could respond, Malah had turned and left.

Strangely, Ahuva's presence melted the tension between Noa and Hur. Over time they had built enough reserves so, once the bonds of love and sex were loosened, they became comfortable with each other.

Noa counseled Hur on how to build leadership in Boaz's shadow, and Hur came to depend on her judgment.

Boaz now sat with the Judges of Tens, thus raising Hur's position. In the hottest part of the day, when labor paused, Hur sat in the shade of his doorway and listened to petitioners: gossip that cost a marital match, a knife for a ewe that proved barren, a set of weights and measures that favored the seller.

Noa sat out of sight, weaving and listening. Occasionally a case would stump him, and Hur would send the parties away, saying, "Return tomorrow." Then he conferred with Noa. Rarely did a ruling elude their reach, and a new bond grew between them.

THE WILDERNESS PROVIDED little sustenance, no matter how hard the Israelites worked to nourish themselves. Some women were so undernourished their wombs withered and they were cast aside. Stories were told of those who became prostitutes, getting wages in lieu of a fruitful womb. Propagation of every sort was an act full of awe and fear of failure. Yet, the tribes increased, but slowly.

The daughters of Zelophechad were counted as favored by God: five daughters, four with children. Soon after Hur took a second wife, Boaz determined that Tirzah must come to the canopy. Adam was an easy choice.

At dawn, the day before the wedding, Tirzah came to Noa in a panic. She entered the tent, glanced at Ahuva, and pulled Noa outside.

"What will I do, Noa, when they come to examine the cloth? They will see nothing. Adam and I, we . . ."

Noa looked Tirzah up and down, hardly believing Tirzah had already crossed that flesh-and-blood divide. Quickly readjusting, she replied, "I understand."

Noa stood thinking, as Tirzah impatiently banged her hands against her sides, looking nothing like a graceful bride-to-be.

At last, Noa said, "Let us go to the flocks and solve the problem."

Leaving her children with Ahuva, Noa made a quick detour to see Nechama, then they zigzagged around tent pegs, donkeys, and women carrying jugs to the well. The breaking light filtered through the palms, fingering them with the promise of warmth. As they left the line of palms, Noa saw women waiting their turn at the well, glad for a chance to share the news of their lives.

Rarely did Noa's duties allow her beyond the confines of camp. This day, Tirzah's need quickened Noa's step. Tirzah, forgetting her predicament, skipped alongside, excited by the promise of adventure with Noa, colored by the memory of dancing with Noa at the Sea of Reeds. Ahead, they saw a brush pen where sheep and goats milled, waiting to graze the folds of the far hills.

Nearly there, Noa's eye caught movement at the periphery. She turned to see a gazelle standing on hind legs, reaching into the branches of an acacia tree to nibble leaves.

Arriving at the pen, they found the bondsman who slept by the family's flocks to protect them from poachers, animal and human. He was surprised to see Noa, but it was not his place to inquire.

Noa urged him, "There, just up the track, at that far tree, a gazelle awaits your spear. She will make a good meal. Quick, before she moves on."

The guard rushed off for a chance at easy meat. Noa smiled at Tirzah. "A timely gazelle," she said, then pointed at a fat ewe. They pulled her down and lashed her front legs together as the rest of the flock edged away nervously.

"I am heavier," Noa said, "so I will hold her down. Use this knife to nick her in the fold of her leg, where the blood lies. Feel for the throbbing thread." She handed a small clay vial to Tirzah. "Here, take my kohl jar to catch as much blood as it will hold."

Tirzah did as she was told, filling the vial, then stanching the ewe's cut until the blood clotted. Noa pulled a twist of cloth from her sleeve and unfolded it to reveal grape seeds she had begged from Nechama. She laid them on a flat rock and carefully crushed them, then sprinkled the fragments into the kohl jar so the blood would stay fresh and flowing until it was needed.

Then she stuffed the cloth into the top of the jar and handed it to Tirzah, saying, "Take care with this. Your honor depends upon it."

Tirzah nodded, as solemn as Noa had ever seen her.

As they returned to the tents, Noa said, "When you go into your marriage booth, take the jar with you and pour the blood out on the cloth."

"How can I repay you for saving me?"

"Return the jar to me . . . full of kohl."

The next day, after the nuptials, the bride and groom were escorted to the wedding booth. Inside, Tirzah pulled the kohl bottle from her robe, split the sheep's blood on the cloth and grinned. Adam's eyes widened at his wife's clever ruse. He fell on her with a whoop and they rolled together, laughing, and stained with sheep's blood.

TO ENSURE TIRZAH'S success, Malah organized a party for her, serving triangular cakes shaped like Asherah's pudendum. When Tirzah discovered she was pregnant, she laughed so hard that Adam warned her against harming his child, which made Tirzah laugh even harder.

So the daughters of Zelophechad increased their tents. As did the whole of the twelve tribes, until the camps at Kadesh Barnea could hold no more. Some, living at the outer edges, moved on to other oases, causing skirmishes with Midianites, who now saw the Israelites as competitors.

In the tent of Haddad, his first wife stooped to hand him a cup of tea and complained, "That Israelite you call your friend, he and his people are bringing trouble to our lands."

"Ach. You sound like the Scarface. Few are more upright than Hur."

She pinched his earlobe, saying, "Some day you will hear me."

Haddad flung his arm out to slap at her. "Leave me be."

As she retreated, she muttered, "Your children will hear even if you do not."

CHAPTER 23
WRAITHS

TIRZAH SOON REALIZED pregnancy was no laughing matter and not to her liking. Consumed by nausea, she lay on her bed in her in-law's tent, writhing and whining.

"I'd rather fight Anak and his giant sons."

"This is nothing. It will pass and you will live," countered Noa.

"Perhaps pregnancy does not suit you, as it does me," Hoglah said.

"Do you want to attract God's displeasure?" Noa hissed, annoyed with both of them.

Hoglah gathered herself and her two children and left in a huff.

Milcah sighed and offered, "If you are feeling that bad, I will watch the flocks today."

"You cannot manage with a baby at the breast," Noa said.

"The rest of you have more to cope with. A suckling child is always right there. Not running. And I am only giving Tirzah a day, two at most."

So Milcah relieved the night watchman, who growled about her late arrival. She pointed the sheep and goats toward the hills, Sarai nestled in a sling knotted across her shoulder. Noa walked out a little way with her, one child in her arms and two at her skirts.

"I wish I could go with you. I long for only the voice of the wind. But grain must be ground, bread made. How many loaves for you and Dor?"

"Enough to carry us through another day or two. I pray that Tirzah becomes quickly accustomed to her new body. For her sake and ours."

They parted, and Milcah drove the flocks forward, a small waterskin slapping against one hip, Sarai asleep in her sling on the other hip.

The folds of the hills were already dotted with black goats and white sheep. Manasseh's shepherds had pushed their flocks out earlier than she, so Milcah had to drive hers farther into the desert, toward a trio of hills whose folds were lined with green.

She found a low stone in the lee of the near hill, arranged Sarai on her lap, then pulled out her drop-spindle and began spinning wool, letting her mind roam where it would. The animals followed their mouths up the slope, their necks bent, their teeth busy ripping at the meager forage.

Sarai's pink bud of a mouth began to suck energetically, a dream of milk, then a cry that signaled Milcah's rush of milk. She laid down her spindle, fit her child to her breast, and felt complete. A soft breeze ruffled Sarai's dark, silky curls. Milcah smoothed her daughter's hair and sang a wordless song.

Sarai slipped back into a milk-stupored sleep, her mouth twitching, almost a smile. With Sarai swaddled on her lap, Milcah picked up her spindle and noticed that a few of the sheep had strayed far up the hill. She would have to climb to retrieve them. A distant stir caught her eye. Near the horizon, she saw a small column of dust. She glanced at the shepherd's staff leaning against the rock, then chided herself for her nervousness, saying, "Just the daughter of a wind demon."

She bent her head to her thread, but could not concentrate. She broke the thread and, while twisting the broken ends together, she looked up again.

The swirl of dust, now closer, revealed two men on camels. They rode at a lope, like raiders. Milcah looked behind her, to see how far the closest shepherds were. She dropped her spindle and swept Sarai to her chest, remembering the stories of Moloch and his fire-filled, baby-eating belly.

She stepped behind the rock, lifted her skirts, tied Sarai tightly against her belly, and let her skirts drop. A pregnant woman had no child to seize. Sarai stirred, but briefly.

"Thank you," Milcah said for Sarai's silence, walking quickly toward Kadesh, whose lines of palms were specks in the distance. A broad, dun-colored plain stretched between Milcah and the oasis. It offered no cover. She hoped she would reach people before the camel riders noticed her.

"Oh, please give us safety," she begged silently as stones wedged in her sandals, cutting her feet. She feared to stop and shake them loose.

She felt the ground thudding. She thought she heard their camels snort, but far off. Milcah rushed on, trying to keep terror at bay.

Then she heard them shout. Her heart was pounding. Her lungs hurt. She stumbled forward, hoping Sarai would not wake and cry.

They shouted, words she could not understand, but close enough to hear. Milcah turned, holding her belly with one arm, shielding her face from the sun with the other.

The riders were closer than the length of a camp circle. Chimeras, their faces wrapped, all but their eyes. Milcah, blinded by the sun and the sweat pouring into her eyes, called out, "Please, I am with child. An unborn child. I have nothing."

The camel riders consumed ground, then they stopped. Milcah could see the heat pulsing from the flanks of their camels, trembling the air. One pulled his headcloth free of his face and shouted to her, the same words as before. But she could not understand. She realized, terrified, that as she could not understand them, they could not understand her.

The other said something to his companion, and the two of them laughed. Salvia dripped from the lip of the first man's camel, a long thread flecked silver in the sunlight. Milcah locked her eyes on the pendulous thread so she would not see the men. The two laughed again, then wheeled their camels.

Milcah let out her breath slowly, jaggedly, watching as they started back across the plain.

"Thank you, my precious gift, for your silence," she whispered to her daughter. "Thank you, my God, for sparing our lives."

Her legs shook so badly she waited a few moments before she felt steady enough to turn toward Kadesh. Her eyes clouded by sweat and tears, she thought she saw one of the riders turn. By the time she was sure, he had beaten his camel to a gallop and was bearing down on her, one fist full of reins, the other wrapped around the haft of his spear as he leaned forward toward the blade cutting through the air.

Milcah watched him come for her, as if it was happening in a dream. The edges of her vision blurred until all she saw was the point of a spear and a camel the color of desert. She smelled salt then something terribly sweet.

"DON'T BABY ME."

"You were asking for it," Noa responded.

She turned to leave Tirzah curled miserably on her bed, a shard of dry bread and a waterskin—all that Tirzah could consume—beside her.

She stopped by her mother's tent. Outside the entrance, her mother stirred a pot of soup. Dor, just returned from repairing a section of irrigation ditch, poured water into a bowl to wash his hands and face.

"Milcah? Sarai? They are with you?" he asked.

Noa explained what had happened. Dor thought they were foolish to allow Milcah, with a child in her arms, to take Tirzah's place, but he held his tongue. He guessed that Milcah had volunteered.

When evening began to cast purple shadows and Milcah had not arrived, Dor became disturbed. His eyes darkened with anger.

"How could they have let my wife and my daughter go out by themselves," he growled to himself on his way to find the night watchman, who was playing the bones with his fellows.

Mild-mannered Dor, seized by fear, roared, "Up! We seek my wife and daughter."

Together they left the safety of tents to find Milcah and Sarai.

From afar they saw a flock, skittishly circling near the base of three hills. The rising moon colored the milling animals a milky blue. Dor squinted, to see better in the dark, and the flock became a smooth, white whirlpool swirling around a dark center. The watchman feared they found what they were looking for.

They reached the milling flock and pushed a path through the animals. The sheep and goats were not willing to stray from their shepherdess, but not willing to approach death. A space separated the animals and the body at the center.

Milcah lay on her back, her limbs splayed at odd angles. Her robe was scalloped with red-brown stains. Sarai had slipped to one side and, there, the robe was dark and wet with blood.

The men stood above Milcah and Sarai, while they absorbed what had happened.

Finally, the watchman urged quietly, "We must take them back."

Dor nodded, unable to talk.

Larger than Dor, the watchman assumed he would carry Milcah and stooped, his arms poised to lift her body. Dor stopped him.

"My wife. My child. I will carry them."

The watchman tipped his head in acknowledgement.

"Let me at least help you lift them." He gently extracted Sarai. "Look away, sir."

A gaping hole ripped her small, still chest. The watchman nestled the body in the crook of his left arm as he tore off his headcloth, then wrapped Sarai's body in it as Dor struggled to lift the body of his wife. The hair at the back of Milcah's head was matted and sticky with blood.

Once he held his wife in his arms, Dor started walking toward Kadesh. The watchman, walking beside him, held Sarai in one arm and drove the flock home.

NOA AND MALAH stood near the edge of camp, shivering in their robes, sheltering near a saltbush. Malah stamped her feet to stay warm. Noa tore off a gray leaf from the plant, chewed the salt from it, threw it down, then tore off another and another, chewed leaves scattered around her skirts. Their eyes strained from staring into the dark, searching the horizon.

When Noa spied something moving toward them, she let out a whoop.

"Shhhh," scolded Malah.

Noa's shout returned an angry response from the nearest tent.

"May Amalek take you," someone cursed.

Noa shuddered at the mention of Amalek. As they waited, the two men moved slowly toward camp. From the way Dor arched backward with his burden, the watchman knew Dor's arms burned with effort, but he knew that no amount of coaxing would allow Dor to be relieved of his burden.

When the shapes on the horizon became distinct, Malah gasped. Noa, wild with dread, ran to meet them.

They laid the bodies of Milcah and Sarai on rugs in Ada's tent. Knowing Milcah's mentor would want to help prepare her body, Noa asked Malah to find Rina. Malah was relieved to escape the sight of the torn child.

A bowl of water at her side, Noa cleaned the blood from Sarai. When the water turned red from rinsing, Hoglah emptied it far from the tent and refilled it with clean water, bowl after bowl.

She wiped the tears streaking Noa's face. They worked without speaking.

When she was finished washing Sarai, Noa asked Hoglah to fetch their mother's needles. She wanted to make her niece as whole as possible. Hoglah returned with the packet, untied the cloth, and held out the needles. Noa threaded the copper needle with a length of sheep gut, then gently began to stitch together the ugly hole that split Sarai from belly to backbone.

Rina ran in, breathless, with Malah behind her. She heard a man sobbing on the other side of the tent wall, and male voices of consolation. As Ada held Milcah's head in her lap, Malah worked to remove her blood-matted robe. Rina bent to help. When Milcah lay bare before them, Rina noted the gash on her stomach where the sword had penetrated. But it had not penetrated deeply and the blood was already clotted. Rina bent to Milcah's chest, listening. Then she laid two fingers on the large vein in Milcah's neck.

"Bring a mirror," she whispered.

Malah ran for hers. Rina grabbed the mirror and held it to Milcah's lips. A small, barely visible cloud of moisture formed. Rina looked around at the others, rubbed the mirror clean on her sleeve and, again, held it to Milcah's lips.

"She lives."

THEY BURIED SARAI the next day. Dor wrapped his daughter in fabric stitched with sun colors that Milcah had made for Sarai. Milcah was barely aware, drifting in and out of consciousness as her mother and sisters took turns watching over her. Rina brought food, as did Tamar, Nechama, and Milcah's close friends. But she ate little besides gruel and bread, the same foods Tirzah could manage, Noa noticed.

Confused and barely lucid, Milcah sometimes turned to reach for Sarai as she felt her milk let down. Nechama and Rina knew young mothers whose milk was scant, who would be grateful for the extra nourishment. But neither would ask.

When Milcah became aware of herself and her surroundings, her head throbbed with the horror of what happened. The images flashed in her mind, and she breathed in ragged gasps.

"Sarai," she sobbed. "She saved me. I killed her."

"No, no, no. You did not kill her. You tried to protect her," her mother countered, having heard how they found her.

"If I had not gone out. If I had hidden among the rocks. If I had . . ."

Milcah choked on revulsion and guilt.

"At least what they did was swift," said Malah. "What if you had not hidden her? What if they had taken her? Who knows what greater horrors might have happened."

At that, Milcah's overwrought brain reeled out images even more frightening.

"Stop, please stop."

Nechama glared at Malah for her foolish chatter as she pulled a small pot from her kit and rubbed a smear of dark paste against Milcah's upper gum. Nechama used the opiate sparingly, in difficult births, because paste from the poppy cost her dearly in trade. She knew it would ease Milcah's pain.

THE MOON WANED, then waxed again before Milcah's wound healed. Though her body was whole, her soul was frayed. The light of her life, a child with silky curls and a smile that warmed her world, was no more for no reason other than the pleasure of two men who played with death and thought nothing of it.

Milcah's robe hung on her as if the person within had withered. Her family tried to engage her. They spoke brightly to her, as if she could not hear. She could not.

"God will redeem you and will avenge Sarai's death. God will be good to you, I am certain," her mother said with as much certainty as she could muster.

Noa revisited her accounting: The Guardians of Truth who killed her father. Hur's father, buried by Korach's evil, God's wrath, or simply chance. Yoela, torn between Barzel and Amalek. Her own awful attempt at vengeance. And Sarai, an innocent infant killed for no reason whatever. In Egypt, at least they could anticipate Pharaoh's evils. Here, evil had no order at all.

Noa wondered if God's order was larger than she could see. Perhaps it spanned generations and existed for their children's benefit, or their children's children. How far forward would such an accounting be paid? Should she trust that it would be paid? But who could trust such a cruel and distant accounting? It made her head throb. Few, besides Moses, could see the incremental transformation of a people.

Tirzah was not one to examine, but a kernel of guilt caused her to conceal herself among Adam's family, so to avoid Milcah. Guilt over Sarai's death grew in her like a disease, transforming itself to a deep, calcified wrath, pointing itself outward.

"The Midianites . . . they are no better than the Amalekites. They would kill us all, if they could."

"No one will kill my child," Adam swore.

"Hur and this Haddad," Tirzah continued, hardly hearing Adam. "Befriending the enemy. And Asaf. He spends more time with strangers than with his own people."

"Enough," said Adam.

For Tirzah, it was not quite enough.

"We can't depend on God to avenge us. To be weak is to see the face of death. I will take life."

"Tirzah. Sit," Adam demanded. "Give the child in your belly a rest from your wrath."

MILCAH AND DOR passed through their days like shadows. Dor heard the sympathies and the outrage of others at their loss and simply nodded. The edges of Milcah's sleeves became stained and crusted. When the hem of her robe frayed, she did not bother to repair it.

"Just do," her mother urged. "Work until you are weary and too tired to remember."

Milcah dutifully followed her mother's advice, but she worked with her eyes cast inward, to the horrors of her heart. She slept more hours than a child, curled in a corner of the tent.

Noa sought out Rina and implored, "Please, return my sister to us. You, who are like her second mother."

Rina met with Nechama and together they devised a plan. One day, while visiting Milcah, Rina said that Nechama needed the help of someone caring and quick.

"Nechama immediately thought of you."

"That was another me."

"No," Rina urged. "That is your true self."

Milcah shrugged. Rina noticed how worn both Milcah and her clothes looked.

"Perhaps you can act the part of the old Milcah. Nechama remembers her well, and needs her."

"Surely there are others to choose."

"How many with your skills, with your carefulness . . ."

Milcah did not respond.

"Perhaps to help Nechama just for one moon's cycle? Not long. Her brother's daughter may be able to help if it does not suit you. But what can a girl know? And Nechama asked specifically for you."

Milcah said she would answer her later, but Rina pressed her, knowing that if she left, Milcah would do nothing.

Grudgingly, Milcah agreed. She feared anything that might take her away from the memory of her beloved Sarai, even from the memory of her murder. But her heart hinted it felt good to be needed. The next day, Rina brought Nechama, who spoke of her needs and how Milcah could help.

When a birth was at hand, Nechama sent for Milcah, and she learned how to clean babies that Nechama eased from women's wombs. At first, Milcah saw Sarai in each girlchild born, her loss so fierce she could barely breathe, her arms trembling from the memory and the need to hold her daughter. Too responsible to allow harm, Milcah willed herself to heed the needs of each newborn handed to her. Nechama could sense the struggle, but said nothing, knowing that Milcah's real work was to tame the pain within.

The moon cycled through its phases once, twice, three times and still Milcah came when she was summoned. She fetched water, wiped the sweat-drenched foreheads of laboring women, and learned the songs that kept their spirits and their straining bodies focused.

Nechama taught her where to press to help a new mother bear down. For practice, she used a sheep's bladder with a gourd sewn inside, showing Milcah how to insert her arm into the bladder's tight opening and rotate the gourd-child. Using a goat's intestine for the umbilical cord, Nechama urged Milcah to practice tying off the cord with a strand of dried gut from her birthing kit.

One evening, after many months and many births, Nechama sat on her low stool before a mother of three, whose fourth was striving to emerge. The woman's feet were planted on the floor, and she squatted atop Nechama's birthing stool. The woman knew what she had to do. Her arms akimbo, the woman pressed them against her hips for leverage. Grunting and moaning, she pushed.

Sitting at Nechama's feet, Milcah's view took in a heaving belly and the swollen vulva below. Between contractions, the laboring mother collapsed onto the stool and into the arms of her sister and cousin. As the laboring woman strained again, Milcah watched the slit stretch to reveal a disc of dark, wet hair. Another contraction and the disc pulsed as the mother pushed.

Suddenly, Nechama slid off her stool and stood, her hand offering the stool to Milcah.

"This child is yours to catch."

Nechama grinned broadly as Milcah, her arms shaking with nervousness and excitement, slipped into place.

As the mother strained and the baby's head crowned, Milcah gently pushed her fingers against the edges of the mother's vaginal opening so it would not tear. Then, in a gush, the head emerged, the tiny shoulders shot forward, and the rest of the body followed. Milcah caught her first newborn, slick with vernix the consistency of soft, white cheese.

"Like a baby lamb," Milcah murmured, having helped her share of ewes.

"Beauty once again enters the world through your hands," Nechama whispered.

After the newborn was cleaned and swaddled, the new mother beckoned her sister to bring a basket from the back of the tent. She lifted out an oval egg the size of the newborn's head and offered it to Nechama as payment for her services. Stealing an ostrich egg from the nest of its mother was a feat, and a feast, as one egg might feed a dozen people.

Nechama accepted the payment and immediately extended it to Milcah, saying, "It belongs to she who caught your child. But," she added, as she handed Milcah the heavy egg, smooth and white as marble, "I will feast with you, in honor of this new child."

She turned back to the mother, who cradled her newborn in her arms. "Two great gifts, one from Asherah to you, the other from you to us. We are all blessed."

Not every birth was as easy and as blessed. Some ended with stillborn children, some with mothers so weakened by effort and blood loss that they died even as their babies were being born. Sometimes both mother and child died. Bearing life in the face of so many deadly possibilities was a miracle.

Nechama's skills were recognized as a hedge against death, and she taught Milcah all she knew. She showed Milcah how to make infusions that helped pregnant women hold their pregnancies. She explained which herbs and foods helped mother's milk. Over time, Milcah, too, became regarded as a life-giver.

WHEN TIRZAH'S TIME came, she insisted that Nechama, not Milcah, assist her. Tirzah was fierce for her unborn and feared retribution from Asherah or Milcah for Sarai's death.

"If you should be the one to help bring out my baby," she said to Milcah, "and if something bad happened, well . . ." She implied a world of dire possibilities.

Milcah eased her sister's mind with a small lie. "Then you will not mind if I assist Rina's cousin. I did not want to say 'yes' in case her time came at the same time as yours."

"Don't set aside an opportunity because of me."

Nechama had detected two in Tirzah's womb and, when her time arrived, Tirzah bore them one after the other during a sweat-drenched, miserable night. She howled in rage at her pain, stretching Nechama's patience and assaulting the ears of all.

Tirzah insisted on Gibor as the first twin's name, before she noticed his right foot was bent, a clubfoot child. When Adam heard how the second boy eased down a moment later, he named him Yared.

When Adam's family learned about the clubfooted infant, they asked which foot, knowing that a bent left foot was an ill omen.

"I told them, 'No, it is the other foot that is ill-formed,'" said Hoglah, hoping to cheer her sister.

"Leave me. I don't want to hear any of that," said Tirzah, sending Hoglah away in tears.

Before the twins' naming feast, Tirzah tried to switch their names.

"'Hero' is not a fitting name for a damaged child."

Adam saw how it would be between Tirzah and her clubfooted son.

His voice shaking at Tirzah's dismissive attitude, he raged, "You think you can do what you like, but you will confuse God and bring curses down on all of us. I will not allow it. Gibor is his name."

Tirzah had never heard Adam push back with such vehemence. She was stunned, realizing her place on the ladder might be challenged by these children. Yet, when Tirzah thought about Yared and how perfect every part of him looked, she promised herself, "He will be mine to make."

THE SLAYING OF Sarai opened a chasm between Milcah and Dor. At first, Dor's pain flashed in every direction. As time passed, the sword of blame steadied on Milcah. He considered putting her aside and marrying again. But he was too poor, and he needed a wife. Milcah felt Dor's disapproval and poured her energy into saving babies. With no way out, they stayed together, focusing on daily needs and terse notifications.

"I've made your supper. It is ready."

"Asaf has shorn our sheep. Here is the wool, ready for your spindle."

"For you . . . a fine plough point. The new father's payment for my services."

"Tomorrow I will plough our plot and it will be ready for seed."

Despite their distance, they worked to plant seed within Milcah's womb, each believing that new life would repair the damage. But no seeds were planted, giving Dor another reason to blame Milcah and draw further away, even as he wished for a way back.

Milcah blamed herself, remembering that she had not been filled with the light of God at Sinai, as had her sisters.

"Misfortune does not happen for no reason," she told herself.

When the bile of self-blame became too great, Milcah found comfort in her "children." They lived, thanks to her. And she lived for them. As they grew, they ran to her when they saw her coming, pulling Auntie Milcah to show her a palm-leaf doll, a twisted scrap of cloth woven just for her. Her value rose in the eyes of her community and, over time, Milcah learned to value herself.

Noa noticed the changes.

"Perhaps I, too, will find what I seek if I make Milcah my model," Noa murmured to herself as her fingers worked wool in her mother's tent.

"What did you say?"

"I will pursue our inheritance rights again," Noa began.

"Oh, my dear, why? Judges high and low accepted Ben Nun's ruling. You won't be heard until my generation passes away. Are you wishing I will soon sleep in the dust?"

"No. But this land is in my dreams, sleeping and waking. It gives me a path and tells me who I am."

"Who you are? You are you. You are a daughter of Zelophechad, a leader among the tribe of Manasseh. What more?"

"That is my family. That is not me."

"What is the difference? That *is* who you are. What more is there to life besides your family?"

"What makes me different from Malah? From Hoglah?"

"Malah is older. Hoglah is younger. Malah has bigger breasts."

Her mother slapped her thigh and laughed. Noa's children, napping in the corner, stirred.

"Malah, Hoglah . . . neither would ask this question. Only you, my difficult daughter."

"Perhaps you are right. Am I pursuing justice? Or simply pursuing myself?"

"Pursue patience," her mother advised. "Your time will come."

And it was as Ada said: crops must be watered, grain ground, yarn spun and woven, children raised. While waiting for her time to come, Noa helped Hur adjudicate for Manasseh. They learned judicial wisdom together as the years passed.

CHAPTER 24
FROM GENERATION TO GENERATION

AS THE YEARS passed, so did many of the generation that had brought their families out of Egypt. Sometimes Noa felt an urge to approach the Judges of Hundreds again, but always her hesitation was compounded by sick children, an argument with Ahuva, a jar of grain eaten by rats, a hole in the tent. Life intruded and time blurred. No one knew when they would leave Kadesh Barnea, or if they would ever leave.

The justice of inheritance seemed remote, but the daily plight of women found Noa close by. As she and Hur became learned in the law, the women of Manasseh discovered that Noa provided shrewd advice on problems a man might dismiss. One by one, they came, sitting with her as they spun wool, no more remarkable than any two women spinning wool and talking.

"I am newly married," said one young woman, "and my sister-in-law accuses me of stealing her bracelets and earrings."

"And you did not steal them?" asked Noa.

"No. They were given by my husband as my bride price."

"So he stole them? Or, perhaps your sister-in-law is lying?"

"I fear . . . yes. He did. Once I thought about it, I remember her wearing the earrings before I married."

"Then suggest to your husband there must be some mistake, but to preserve peace within the family it would be best to buy you new ones and give the others to his sister. In that order."

"What if he says 'you are women and I can do what I want'?"

"Tell him the law says 'Do not put a stumbling block before the blind.'"

"But I'm not blind."

"If he hid his acts from both of you, you were blind to his deceit. The law covers all sorts of blindness. And it is a law for all. If he refuses and you must approach a *bet din*, return to me, and I will help smooth the way."

"Thank you. You are as good an Advocate as they say. What can I do to repay you?"

"Pursue justice. That is enough."

As she left, Noa hoped the young woman's marriage, and her husband, would improve, but feared she would experience more of the same.

Then she smiled. She had never heard anyone use such an honorific in addressing her. It felt good.

"When the time is right, I will follow my own advice."

WHILE THE ISRAELITES wondered when they would leave for their promised land, the Midianites, who lived on lands to the east, came to resent them. Before the Israelites settled at Kadesh Barnea, the Midianites had often stopped there. They told their children about the cool nights they had spent under the palms they thought of as theirs.

Their children said, "The date palms that were once ours now shelter strangers from Egypt who speak a strange tongue and worship a god no one can see but them."

Their loss filled them with hate.

Now Haddad was a rising leader among the clans of the Midianites. He saw that the tribes from the land of the Great River were marked for favor and thought to wed his tribe to Hur's. His daughter Keturah's body had budded, filling him with dread that his honor would be soiled with lost virginity.

"Our daughter Keturah is of an age to marry," he said to his first wife. "She is of similar age to Hur's oldest son, Gaddi. A match with Gaddi would be well made and wise."

"Why marry our daughter to a son of slaves? Those who steal our lands?" she argued.

"We will strengthen ourselves by such a match."

"We will weaken ourselves with such a match."

"We weaken the other by embracing them, drawing them into us. And that is that," Haddad finished.

But Keturah's mother had other plans. She did not want to marry her daughter to strangers who worshipped a strange god. She spoke in her daughter's ear of Midian glories and losses, especially the theft of Kadesh Barnea.

Malah, too, taught her daughter. Rimon heard of Beer Sheva, the well that Abraham had bought long ago. She heard of the cave and field he had purchased in the hill country, the honeyed land they had been promised, the house they would have.

Seglit whispered a different story in Rimon's ear. "Look at life as it is. Don't be a fool full of dreams."

Rimon heard her mothers' words, but her thoughts ran elsewhere. She nodded dutifully at their admonishments and nurtured her own visions. In the heat of the day, when most rested, she met with Tikvah, Hoglah's oldest daughter, and a few others, celebrating their bloom just by being. They assessed the most handsome young men, imagined bride-price gifts they hoped to win, and assured themselves they would not be like their mothers.

Over the years, the once-spirited chatter of Malah's group had devolved to discussions about nostrums and carping about husbands' bad habits during the odd moments when they managed to meet.

Malah remembered well the evening when Boaz, honing his knife on a sharpening stone, bent his head so that his hair, now more gray than black, parted to expose the back of his neck. Scored with lines like a dry, cracked riverbed, it was the neck of an old man.

She looked at her own hands and saw knuckles bony and swollen with grinding grain and kneading dough day after day. Age and the sun were stealing her beauty and that of Seglit. Each looked at the other, smug in seeing a line etched deeper in the other's face, a ropy blue vein stringing down a forearm.

They turned the mirror on themselves only to apply more henna and kohl to cover graying hair and dulled eyes. When a smear of henna streaked the edge of Seglit's temple, Malah smiled at her sweetly, delighted that Seglit's vanity was on askew.

Rimon was their shared, contested glory. Now of marriageable age, Rimon had hints of Malah about her, but the provenance of her tilted nose was unknown as was her hair, an explosion of coiled ringlets that framed her face like a dark, glowing corona. One evening, while trying to pull a comb through Rimon's hair, Seglit ceased her effort to run a hand around the girl's finely boned wrist.

"These and your ankles are more mine than your mother's. You are more like me in shape. After all, your mother's frame is much more . . . sturdy."

Spontaneously, Seglit pulled off one of her daintiest bracelets and offered it to Rimon.

"Here, my heart, this will show off your wrist—and will attract eyes."

She arched her eyebrows knowingly as she slipped the bracelet onto the girl's wrist. Rimon smiled, tolerantly, and arched her eyebrows right back, wondering if she had time to run off and meet Tikvah.

Rimon's other aim was to avoid her mothers' dramas. Once, Noa stepped in unnoticed while Malah and Seglit slung insults, contesting each other's mothering tactics. They were in the thick of it, hurling verbal volleys.

"You wait for my daughter like a spider in a hole, ready to jump her with your skinny spider-hair arms," Malah threw at Seglit.

"You," returned Seglit. "You infect her with the smell the dung beetle spews when it eats the shit of the scorpion."

Noa burst into laughter, breaking their viperous entanglement. The two women yanked themselves erect and glared at Noa.

"You two. You should hear yourselves. Even Yoela, telling stories, could not have thought of such things. You should hold a contest. You are the experts. Who better?"

And that was what they did.

On Rosh Chodesh, the night the moon returned from darkness, they celebrated. Matching women's cycles with the moon's cycles, Rosh Chodesh was meant to be holy, but Malah's and Seglit's celebrations were hardly that. Women came to be entertained by word-sparring, storytelling, and song.

At the entrance to the women's side of the tent Malah had laid a pile of sweet, brown carob pods, curved like cupped hands and rattling with seeds. The women shook the pods while ululating their approval of the most outrageous verbal concoctions.

Seglit's women cheered her on while Malah's group crowded in with "Let her speak." Sometimes Malah and Seglit charged into such ridiculous territory they collapsed against each other in laughter. At this point in their lives laughter was a release at least as potent as sex or sarcasm.

The women ate dates and cakes washed down with barley beer. Some beat tambourines. Others got up to tell their best tales: bawdy and beyond belief. No one was disappointed.

Embarrassed by these entertainments, Rimon fled to her grandmother's tent where she was sure to find Milcah. She was drawn to Milcah, the antidote for her mothers' emotional extravagance, and imagined midwifery for herself.

Like Rimon, Boaz left the tent on the evenings his wives put on their entertainments, saying to himself, "They are women. This is what they do."

Some among the priestly class heard of the raucous Rosh Chodesh parties and set out to end them. In the month of Sivan, as the women inside were clapping to the rhymed tale of Seglit's cousin, men from the tribe of Levi broke into Boaz's tent. They came with sticks and started beating the women and driving them into the night, roaring at them:

"Sacrilege. How dare you desecrate a holy day?"

"Whores! Go home to your husbands."

The women scattered into the dark like mice.

The blunt end of a stick caught Malah's cheek, and it swelled, red and purple.

Boaz returned to find Malah and Seglit in a corner of the tent, Seglit pouring water into a bowl so that Malah could refresh the cloth compress she held to her cheek.

"What happened here?"

When they told him, his first response was, "Is Rimon safe? With Milcah?" Then, "It is my fault. I should have forbidden such foolishness."

"What are you saying," demanded Seglit. "We were bothering no one. Does our faith forbid laughter?"

"They are like the mob that killed my father," Malah spat, cupping her hand over her cheek to mute the pain. "I thought we were finished with those . . . those . . ." She could not find the words, and her jaw had begun throbbing.

"I'm afraid we will never be done with them," he said. "You cut back the branches, yet they rise from the roots."

"Well, then, we must cut the roots."

"But the roots are part of who we are as well."

AMONG THE MOIST rushes edging Egypt's River dwells a great slayer. Over the years, the prick of the anopheles mosquito, seeking a blood meal, infected and killed more Israelites than all of Pharaoh's slave masters. Some survived the blistering fevers and chills and struggled back to health, only to be struck by bouts throughout their lives. Tamar, the wife of Gaddi, he who died with Korach, suffered bouts of malaria, but suffered stoically.

"The slave masters did not kill my husband and this will not kill me."

Although malaria and age weakened Tamar, a stroke that paralyzed her right side struck the critical blow. More so than the zealots' attack, Tamar's stroke brought the wild nights of Rosh Chodesh to an end. Seeing the matriarchy of Manasseh on the horizon, Malah decided to cloak herself with the stately bearing of a headwoman.

As Tamar declined, Noa and her sisters-in-law tended to her needs until she melted into the arms of her ancestors. As Tamar had done for Gaddi, Hur mourned his mother's death with calibrated emotion in public and true grief within his tent. Tamar's passing also caused Hur to see the world anew. In his eyes, the older generation was no more.

"I should take my rightful place as tribal head, rather than wait," Hur said to Noa. "Boaz is old and fading. His is only the face of leadership. Everyone knows it is me who leads and judges."

"And how will you pry the title from him?"

"The older generation are few, and soon we will set forth for our lands. We know we must fight for them. That's how it will be. Boaz is too old for battle."

"As you see fit," said Noa. But she worried that if Hur wrested tribal leadership from Boaz, he would expect her to take his mother's place. Malah would fight her for a position she did not want.

Malah, too, was shaken by Tamar's death.

"Boaz will be next. And what will happen to me and my daughter?"

She feared she would lose claim to his land and the thick-walled, two-story home, plastered and painted, that should be hers.

Malah sought out her sister and demanded, "Noa, why have you allowed this to linger?"

"What has lingered?" Noa looked up from her loom.

"The claim for our land. You won over the Judges of Tens and the Judges of Fifties. Why did you stop?"

"Ben Nun refused to hear our plea."

"But he is dead. Many years."

With her shuttle in one hand, Noa flung out her other arm to encompass the loom, the tent, everything.

"All of this, every day of work . . . and children. The days slip away. What did you think? That I have been dreaming away my days, fanned by servants, drinking cool, scented water?"

Malah stiffened at Noa's sharp reply. Bridling her tongue, she continued evenly, "Now that our children are nearly grown, we must pursue this again. How can I insure a good match for Rimon? If Boaz dies before we reach our lands, Rimon will have nothing."

"It seems we will all die here. And these lands will be a match for our dry bones."

Noa said nothing about the pain of accusation and rumors of witchery that plagued her the last time she stood before the Judges of Hundreds.

"I thought I had a sister with a fierce heart. A heart bent toward justice. What I find is a sister with a heart like a soggy stew."

As Malah stamped off, Noa asked herself, "What happened to the fearless Noa? The Noa I once was?"

Unexpectedly, Hur strode into the tent to rummage through a small basket of flints.

"Hur, do you think that petition for my father's land . . ."

"Can it wait?" Hur scrabbled through his belongings until he found the chisel he sought. "Gaddi and I are striking flints and—can you believe it—he is showing me a better method."

Hur rushed from the tent, full of fatherly pride. Noa pushed Malah's challenge under the detritus of daily life.

HOGLAH DID NOT ask Asaf for much. The one thing she urged was that the family celebrate the fall harvest together, and Asaf had always honored Hoglah's desire.

This year Asaf did not return for the festival, and she received no word of him. Although her sisters had included Hoglah and her five children in all the festive meals, Hoglah cried herself to sleep each night. She confessed to Noa that she feared something terrible had happened to Asaf. Noa feared something terrible had happened to Hoglah.

Noa's fears were confirmed when a trader from the tribe of Reuben told Boaz that Asaf had married a Moabite woman. Boaz was circumspect and kept the information to himself until he learned more.

The Reubenite trader felt no such obligation and word got back to Hoglah, who threw herself on her bed. Her weeping brought a sharp response from Bar-On, who had also heard the report.

"You daughters of Zelophechad, you think you are high born. You are nothing but the spawn of a man stoned for stealing wood on the Sabbath. And your husband Asaf's long lineage as a son of Manasseh—a story backed by silver. A talking ass would be closer in blood. There, now you know the truth. And you will pay as he did if you want to remain in this shelter."

"But I have nothing to pay with," Hoglah wailed.

She fled with her children to her mother's tent. The hung wall shifted yet again, expanding Ada's space to allow Hoglah and her children to crowd in, and contracting Milcah's and Dor's share of the tent. Milcah persuaded her husband that it was a temporary shift, but the noise of five children and Hoglah's weeping took a toll on everyone's temper.

When Hoglah asked Boaz what she should do, he said, "Wait. This will resolve itself. It is likely just an evil-tongued rumor."

Yet, to ensure that Hoglah did not lose all of her possessions as well as a husband, Boaz sent one of his men to Bar-On's tent to retrieve Hoglah's belongings, especially the hand mill.

Fall cycled into winter with no word of Asaf. As winter ebbed, another trader returned telling Boaz a tale of Asaf's marriage to a rich Midianite widow "as old as your sister-in-law." Boaz could not ignore the fact that two separate witnesses had told him the same story.

He called Hoglah to his tent and said, "I'm afraid the rumors are true. Your husband has left you, still married. If Asaf does not return, your portion and that of your children will fall to Bar-On."

"Bar-On said Asaf paid him for his name. He is no relation to Bar-On at all."

Assessing the dire implications for Hoglah and her children, Boaz said to Hur, "Bar-On could fight for rights of inheritance, saying Asaf sold him what was his. And he could do with Hoglah, her children, and her belongings what he will. Even if Bar-On does not succeed in his claim, Hoglah will remain 'chained' to the marriage, and Asaf may return to claim these lands."

When Hur told Noa, she exploded.

"This is not an empty debate. Either way Hoglah will be plundered."

Anger coursed through her, down to hands that felt Asaf's neck between her fingers, his easygoing eyes staring back, for once not so full of lucky-me. She was frustrated with Hoglah, a bewildered accomplice to her own predation, at the mercy of whatever would come next. Knowing they were all willingly taken in by Asaf, Noa was determined to protect this most vulnerable of her sisters.

"If Bar-On presses to inherit and wins, he will get the lands that should go to Hoglah," she said to Hur. "Worse, he could sell her and her children into bondage. Hur . . ."

"Yes?" he said, knowing what would come next.

"Secure a place for me before the Judges of Hundreds."

"I HAVE A taste for game," Adam announced.

"So, feed your desire," Tirzah answered.

Hunting pleased Adam both in the act and in the eating. And it gave him time with his sons, Gibor and Yared. In the hazy light of dusk, the three of them crouched behind a low screen of bean-caper bushes. Ignoring flies and cramped muscles, they awaited the arrival of gazelles at acacia trees that stood an arrow's shot away.

Though Gibor and Yared had emerged from their mother one after another, they were unlikely twins, especially after their surge into puberty. Yared, who had descended second, was first in height, strength, and daring. Like his mother, honey-colored hair framed his head in soft waves. Though he had the slim build of an adolescent, his sure stance and swelling muscles attracted glances and flirtatious giggles of girls who had begun eyeing their prospects. Yared emanated energy as though the very air was charged by his presence. Yared also had Tirzah's temper.

Gibor poured his energy into simply moving forward, leaning on his crutch, dragging his clubfooted leg. Adam had carved the crutch from acacia wood and shaved it smooth as a priest's linen robe. He had made many over the years and, although Gibor could now make his own crutches, Adam insisted on continuing this act of love. Unlike Tirzah, Adam saw beyond Gibor's infirmity. Gibor welcomed the care his father invested.

Gibor moved slowly, but observed what others moved too fast to see. It was he who had discovered gazelles browsing the leaves of these acacias.

A few months before, as the brothers stood at the edge of camp, a sand viper slithered before them, linking S-curves so quickly it appeared the snake was dancing across the desert. Yared instinctively jumped back. Gibor could not, but pointed at the viper, who was headed toward a pile of rocks.

"Watch how clever he is. Only a few points of his body ever touch the sand. He gets where he wants without burning his belly."

To cover his embarrassment at jumping, Yared picked up a stick and started after the snake.

"You be the eyes. I'll be the arm."

"Leave him be," urged Gibor. "Find me a tamarisk, and I'll show you your next bow, strong *and* flexible."

While other young men had learned to plough and hunt, Gibor was carving a niche for himself as a crafter of bows, arrows, spears, plough blades, and other tools of work and war. Adam, seeing his son's future, brought him hollow reeds for arrow shafts that Gibor fitted with flint points. Yared brought feathers that Gibor trimmed and bound to the shaft, which he nocked and balanced for precise flight. Adam displayed his son's weapons with pride to potential customers.

As they waited quietly for the sun to sink and the birds to settle, Adam whispered, "I told your mother to have a pot of lentils for us when we return. I am hungry already, and we may have to wait."

"If *I* had 'told' her, she would have bitten back. Like she always does." Yared's voice was low, but full of venom.

He and his mother had argued earlier, as they often did. She was determined that Yared be exactly as she wished him to be, the son into which she poured all her aspirations. Yared had other ideas. Sometimes he did not have another idea, but simply did not want to be bound by his mother's demands. Their increasing conflicts pained all of them.

Gibor had hoped for a quiet evening with his father and brother, leaving the turmoil of his mother behind. He noticed a pair of bean-caper seeds: one swelling and full, one withered.

"Her temper is like my foot—a defect. But not everything."

"Why should you defend her? She pays no attention to you. Have you never noticed?"

"Stop," Adam hissed. "She is your mother. That's the end of it."

Ahead, a gazelle edged into sight, its tan coat barely visible in the shadows. Followed by a yearling, it stepped cautiously, looking up into the trees as if anticipating a leopard.

CHAPTER 25
JUDGES OF HUNDREDS

ONCE AGAIN, NOA stood before the Judges of Hundreds, hoping she appeared calm. When she last stood before judges she was little more than a girl.

"How did I have the courage?"

"Oh, judges are distracted by ripe youth," Malah answered airily.

"If that is true, what will win them now?"

"The arrow of justice arcs true," Milcah assured her.

Noa was not so sure, but Milcah's words gave her strength.

The Judges of Hundreds sat before a small tent set up exclusively for their use within the precinct of the tribe of Benjamin. Shaded by palms, the tent was supplied with mats and pillows, a table with three cups, a tall jar of water, and a boy to serve them. When court was in session, they sat on stools before the mouth of their tent. When they tired or needed to discuss the merits of a case, they withdrew within.

In the heat of the day, people came to be entertained, their interest juicy as just-cut melon. If a case hung on legal technicalities, their interest shriveled, leaving only a small rind of listeners. If a case flared with hot-blooded contestants, crowds gathered.

Noa stood before the judges, her skin filmed by nervous sweat under her robe. Streaming down through wind-whipped palms, the sun flashed on and off, blinding her. Cautiously, she stepped forward a few paces to gain the shadows, hoping the judges did not think her too bold.

Noa had consulted with Hur on the thrust of her petition, but he did not accompany her. Win or lose, the judges' decision would be hers.

Her sisters—save Tirzah—stood just behind her, at the front of the crowd. Malah noted more women than usual, older women and mothers with babes on hips, bouncing them to keep them quiet. Rimon stood next to her mother, her chin tipped upward, concentrating on being elsewhere. Malah reached for her daughter's wrist and squeezed it.

Hoglah's children pressed close to their mother, their faces clean and hair untangled, their sand-scrubbed clothes as presentable as possible. Although she faced the judges, Noa felt Milcah's warm, secure presence just behind her.

She wondered who these judges were and to whom they owed allegiance. The judge on her left looked younger than she. His beard was trimmed in the style of warriors who tested themselves in skirmishes against desert bands. The planes of his square face looked chiseled, and she imagined him eating rocks to break his nightly fast. A smile rose at the picture of pebbled crumbs dropping into his lap. She quickly subdued it lest he think she was smiling at him. She doubted emotion would soften this judge.

Noa quickly scanned the judge on her right, who looked neither hard nor soft, smart nor stupid. If she saw him walking among others, she doubted she would recognize him, except for the milky stains that striped the left edge of his robe. She hoped this judge, like her father, was careless only about appearance.

She focused her attention on the center judge, who directed the proceedings. His face was scored by his years and by gravitas. His thinning hair and beard, streaked with gray, hung straight, strengthening a sense of vertical clarity. He sat upright on his stool, half-a-head higher than his fellows, his long fingers cupped over each knee.

Noa was struck by his eyes. One looked directly at her. The other searched for something at the periphery. It wandered, unanchored from its mate. Noa wondered if he was able to see in both directions, or did the straight eye take precedence? Suddenly she felt a tug on her robe and the heat of a body behind her. Milcah had stepped forward to jolt Noa's wandering attention.

"I am so very sorry, honored judges. The sun . . . the sun blinded my eyes, and . . . You will not see inattention again."

The lead judge was familiar with reactions to his eyes. He ignored her inattention and simply repeated, "What brings you before this *bet din*? Speak up."

Noa breathed deeply and drew herself up. Anticipating this question, she launched the answer she had practiced. "As you know, the former head judge of the *bet din* you now lead—the Judges of Hundreds—refused to hear cases based on a promised land so far in our future. But, with all my heart, I believe that future is nearly upon us."

Noa stopped to catch her breath and to see if the lead judge's good eye was on her, or if it, too, wandered. He waved her on.

"We have accorded you a hearing because, yes, our time here draws to an end."

"My sisters and I, we have no brothers. We fear our father's house and his name—Zelophechad ben Hefer—will wither because daughters cannot inherit. Yet, we have all been careful to marry within the tribe of Manasseh to preserve claims promised to each tribe for when we reach our land."

The lead judge nodded with an implicit " . . . and?"

The warrior judge leaned forward, his forearm on his thigh, as if to hear more closely.

"But," Noa breathed deeply again, "even careful plans can go astray."

She looked around, her arms shrugging "What can you do?" She saw that she drew in the crowd, who leaned toward her, confirming her simple truth.

"Careful as we were, the fate of the children behind me lies in question."

Noa turned and swept her hand toward Hoglah's children, standing meekly with their heads bowed, as they were coached.

"Through no fault of their own, they may have nothing." In a low voice, to avoid frightening her nieces and nephews, she added, "Their fate—bondage."

Noa told of the examination into Asaf's background and explained that they had just learned it was based on a payoff and a lie. She told further of Asaf's flight and of his new wife and life among Midianites to the east.

The square-faced judge squinted and drilled his question. "So you say that you—all of you—were taken in by such a one?"

Noa did not know how to reply. She felt stupid, admitting "yes."

"Please explain," the lead judge prompted her.

"Yes, we believed this man Bar-On. We had no reason not to. But bribery and lies go against the law. I hope trust does not. If that were the case, I would trust no one, not even my own blood," she finished with some heat.

Some of the crowd supported her passion. Some laughed.

"Silence!" roared the lead judge, then turned back to Noa. "If you wish to bring a suit against this man Bar-On, that is another matter. Continue with your case."

Noa dipped her head toward the judge in thanks for pulling them back to the point.

"The lack of law for brotherless daughters does not end with my sisters and me. Not only my sister Hoglah's five children, but the daughter of my older sister is also at stake."

Malah nudged Rimon a step forward, turning her as she went so that the crowd and the judges could admire her beauty: a bloom of dark ringlets cascading over her shoulders, framing a face with rose-dark cheeks and almond eyes. Rimon's face clouded at being put on display, but the crowd murmured its approval. Malah lowered her own eyes modestly and allowed herself a slight smile of triumph.

"Rimon is the only child of my sister Malah," said Noa. "The wife of our uncle Boaz, leader of Manasseh. Her situation is as ours."

"Make sure she marries into your tribe," advised the judge.

"Certainly, but even if she does marry within our tribe and her husband dies, the property reverts to his brothers, not to her. So she still will be left with nothing of her father's inheritance."

"And," Noa continued, "to marry within clan or tribe . . . If the parents are poor, they may not have that choice." She thought of how Yoela's parents sold her to the family of Barzel. "Without a law, my father's house, all that he and we have built, may vanish like the morning dew."

"We can understand your concern. But who among us can guarantee the path of our life? Only God knows."

With his one good eye, the head judge considered Noa and the crowd behind her. Like the dun-colored robes they wore, the people were frayed by wear. Like the flocks they depended on, they jostled among themselves, trying to catch the shade of the palms above and avoid being singled out for scrutiny. They worked hard and long for a life of little security.

"Oh, judges, all the more reason for a ruling," Noa said. "What you say is true—there is no way to be certain of life." She shaped her hands as a funnel. "Without law, justice can slip away, even through a small hole."

"Are you saying our law is not good? That there are holes in our law?" the warrior judge challenged.

"No. But perhaps the law . . ."

"Who are we to challenge God's laws?" he broke in.

"Perhaps . . ." Noa started again, leaving a moment of silence to allow the crowd's rumble to fade so all could hear her next words. "Perhaps God leaves gaps in the law to test us, so that we can learn from them. Perhaps it is for us to help God make the law whole."

"Are you saying we partner with God, like common traders? That sounds like blasphemy."

"I fear my words are at fault. I am speaking my thoughts poorly."

Noa had thought her interpretation was sound and would please and impress the judges. Now she desperately ticked through phrases in her head to come up with something more palatable.

Finally, she said, "I beg you to consider our case and allow us to inherit the land promised to Manasseh and to our father Zelophechad, that his name may not fade from the earth. We implore you to allow the law to include the daughters of Zelophechad and all brotherless daughters. Perhaps God wants us to learn from His laws, to complete them and, in doing so, make ourselves the people He hopes we will become."

Finished, Noa bowed slightly before the judges and stepped backward slowly. She had done her best and had nothing more to add.

"Well spoken, daughter of Zelophechad," said the lead judge.

The mild judge nodded, yet raised his eyebrows as if agreeing and querying at the same time. The warrior judge—Noa could not gauge his stony face.

"Your petition is thoughtful," continued the lead judge, "and requires thought on our part. We will take time to consider. Return tomorrow to learn our ruling."

With that, the three judges rose and entered their tent, the lead judge beckoning the boy who served them.

"*I* WAS WON by your words," said Milcah.

The sisters, all but Tirzah, sat in their mother's tent. Noa knew that Milcah spoke from her head as well as her heart. She valued her younger sister's opinion, as did most who knew Milcah.

When Nechama's hands had become too old to bring forth babies, she gave her birthing goods to Milcah, acknowledging for the community what all had known for a while. Milcah had gained fame when she reached into the birth canal of a favored daughter of the tribe of Efraim and untangled the cord that had wrapped itself like a snake around the infant's neck. She rescued more than one tiny life by cutting open its dying mother's womb and lifting the infant out alive.

She believed God guided her fingers, and she derived deep pleasure from having brought so many across the perilous threshold of birth into the world of sun and rain, warmth and cold, joy and woe—life.

When Nechama bequeathed her birthing stool, she said to Milcah, "We are rarely given what we want. But look what you have done with the life you *were* given."

Milcah had felt a sharp but brief stab of pain, thinking of Sarai. Her love and loss of her daughter had supplanted feelings for Oholiav. And if Dor was not Oholiav, he was enough.

Two of Hoglah's children sprawled at their mother's side. She urged Tikvah to rise and brew them all some tea. The girl protested, unwilling to unwind her gangly, pubescent body from the edge of her mother's lap.

"Look, it's only there."

Hoglah pointed at the glowing embers just to the side of the open tent doorway. Tikvah got up.

Malah, reminded of her own daughter's part in the day's events, said, "I am sure Rimon's appearance added favorably to our cause. And, certainly, the judges know she is the daughter of Boaz, leader of Manasseh."

Noa smiled. Malah's imperious declarations rarely rankled her. They were so much a part of her sister's nature. They told Noa the world was in order. She looked toward her mother, whose old bones rested uncomfortably against a cushion in the corner, and wondered if her mother saw her, saw all of them, each by the odd bumps and grooves in their nature.

Increasingly, her mother's spirit turned toward the world of her ancestors. If she died at this moment, only Tirzah would be missing, Noa thought, just as Tirzah burst through the doorway, nearly knocking the pitcher from Tikvah's hands.

"Good evening and good news."

Their mother lifted her eyes, briefly, shining at the sound of her youngest daughter.

"So, what is your news, oh fearless one?"

Tirzah ignored Malah's sarcasm, aimed at Tirzah's role in Adam's warrior group, one of many that had formed among the tribes.

"Adam fights alongside a judge. They test themselves." She threw out her forearm like a shield. "The judge complained about having to sit for the *bet din.* Something about a long ya-ya-ya on daughters' inheritance. Didn't say the outcome. He did say the one who spoke presented fair. It must have been about us."

They gasped. Hoglah clapped her hands, disturbing the child curled on her lap. Noa permitted herself a small smile of hope.

NOA STOOD BEFORE the judges, her hands folded together, her body contained and quiet. The crowd, curved behind her, was larger than the day before. Many had returned to hear the outcome.

She hoped for a good outcome, but did not hope too much. She had determined to absorb whatever decision was given without her face telling her story.

The judges exited their tent and arranged themselves on their stools, adjusting their robes and their composure. Despite the hot breath of the *hamsin* winds, their faces revealed nothing. The tall judge fixed his good eye on Noa before saying, "Noa, daughter of Zelophechad, you stood before us yesterday and presented your petition for inheritance, for you and your sisters, your father having no sons."

Noa dipped her head in agreement.

"Your words were convincing. They have merit . . ."

Noa allowed herself only a quick intake of breath.

" . . . but a ruling for your inheritance would set such precedence . . ."

Suddenly hot and faint, Noa struggled to remain upright. At that moment, all she wanted was a "yes" or a "no."

Tears rolled down Hoglah's cheeks. Milcah saw that Noa trembled. She whispered to Malah, and the two of them moved to Noa and grasped her arms to hold her up.

Without warning, the third judge, whose robes now showed only faint signs of stain, stood up.

"There is yet another matter," he said, his voice ominous. "A matter that I alone know of."

The other two judges looked up at him, surprised.

"This woman," he pointed to Noa, "harmed my family. With evil intent."

The sisters stood, transfixed.

"She tried to poison my family. At the wedding of my wife's cousin, he who was Barzel ben Zerach."

Malah felt Noa stiffen. Without dropping Noa's arm she called back, "But that wedding was years ago."

"My wife recognized her only yesterday." His stabbed his finger toward Noa. "She remembers *this* woman thrusting a cheese as a gift. My wife thought it strange and the taste of the cheese stranger still." His voice deepened with anger as he called out, "Strange because it was full of poison!"

A low rattle, like locusts, rose from the crowd as it twitched with rumor and speculation.

"Everyone fell ill," he called out, then turned his face, no longer mild and forgettable, directly toward Noa. "Do you deny giving this 'gift'?" He spat out the word as if the word itself were poison.

"I did . . . I did offer . . ." Noa stuttered, clutching her sisters' supporting arms.

The square-faced judge stood, but the lead judge waved him down, saying quietly, "Let us hear this out."

"And did you mix poison into your gift?"

"Poison? Only an herb, for taste," she lied, fearful of this sudden eruption of the past. In her mind, her lie gained ground. "An herb Barzel had a taste for, I heard."

"And who did not hate Barzel?" Malah demanded, unwittingly adding fuel to the fire lit by the judge. A few women's voices in the crowd ululated in agreement with Malah's assessment. "He beat his third wife so badly she lost the child within her belly. Who did not sigh with relief when this unfortunate woman's brother spilled Barzel's evil blood in the dust?"

Upon hearing her sister speak up in such voice, Noa burst in, "He killed his wives slowly. He killed one as close to me as my own soul. And . . . and . . . I heard no one of the guests died," she finished lamely.

"So. You did try to poison Barzel ben Zerach and, instead, succeeded in poisoning all of his guests," said Noa's accuser. "Intent-to-kill is at the root of your deed. And intent means something."

At that point, the lead judge rose, saying, "Yes, intent is a serious matter and, as such, we must consider this accusation. As law states, two witnesses must step forward." He turned to his fellow. "If tomorrow you will bring your wife and one other who witnessed this deed, we can proceed."

"EVEN BEYOND DEATH this cursed woman will not leave me alone," Hur thundered when he heard what Noa had done to avenge Yoela. "And what would you have me do? Do you think I can save you? No one knows better than you that the law stands."

After Hur's initial eruption, the family decided to plan a strategy. Hur had insisted that, as his wife was at the heart of the matter, they should meet in his dwelling. Boaz, too tired to cling to even this remnant of leadership, did not argue. He felt unwell and said to his wives, "Tell me what was decided. Hur will find the right path."

"I will stay with you," Seglit said.

The men and women gathered on their respective sides of Hur's tent. They had only an evening to find a way to defend Noa and their honor. Each side was hot and crowded with people, opinions, and the pungent smells of wool and anxiety. Flickering oil lamps tossed shadows back and forth, adding to the sense of confusion and urgency.

On Hur's side, the men crowded around a platter holding cups of tea and piles of seeds. Opinions and seed hulls flew. Boys packed the spaces just behind the men, eager to take part. As the men argued strategies, so did the boys behind them. In lowered voices, they supported or argued against fathers' and uncles' views, keeping an ear to the flow of talk at the center.

Yared agreed with his father's opinion that they should challenge the accusation. Gibor was more circumspect. Gaddi, Noa's oldest, who wished the problem swept away as soon as possible, supported his father's inclination toward a negotiated settlement. Ahuva's son, who usually challenged Gaddi reflexively, backed him this night.

The women's side was a cacophony of contention. Tirzah's fury to fight against the accusers buffeted Milcah, who had her arm around Ora, Noa's daughter. Ora quivered with outrage over the accusation and the possibility of humiliation if her mother were guilty. Noa sat next to her mother, both crumpled in a corner.

Hoglah, who feared that somehow she was at fault, organized her children to heat water and serve tea. Tikvah stepped carefully with the bubbling jar, but Ahuva's ten-year-old suddenly stuck out a leg, causing Tikvah to stumble. Hot water splashed onto the younger girl, mapping wet channels over her dusty leg. She howled and pulled her leg close as Ahuva reached for her.

The girl stopped sobbing long enough to spit out, "Clumsy," at Tikvah.

All were aware of Hoglah's diminished status, which devolved to her children. Tikvah bit back an ugly reply and stifled the urge to grate the girl's leg with her ragged toenails. She was learning quickly that those at the bottom must learn to pick their way carefully.

Malah made an excuse to relieve herself and slipped outside. Thankful the night was dark, she allowed her eyes to adjust, then pulled her headcloth forward to shield her face before setting out, a rod-straight wraith walking quickly toward the tents of the tribe of Efraim.

The night was dark but not silent. She heard murmurs from within the tents she passed. Men still sat before embers here and there, looking up briefly as Malah strode by. One called after her, "Hey," seeing if he might waylay a woman on her way to an assignation. But Malah's shadow had already become a shadow.

Sporadic bleats rose from the brush pens at the edges of camp. Out alone, skirting barely seen obstacles, Malah was anxious. Her destination, wrapped in the dark folds of night, seemed farther than she imagined. She feared she had missed the borders of Efraim until, finally, she made out the tribe's fluttering standard, an adder snaking its way across the folds of Efraim's flag.

Relieved, Malah allowed herself a moment to breathe in the night air, softly sweetened by white broom blooming in the wadis. It reminded her of the smell of the man who planted his seed in her. She felt an unexpected stab of desire. Then hurried on.

To avoid being seen in the tight intersection ahead, she veered toward the sheepfolds. On the far side, a trio of watchmen bent over something. One of them threw his hand downward and cried, "Two!" She bent her head away and nearly tripped over a tent peg, dodging another one as she navigated back among the tents, hoping her divergence had not put her on the wrong path.

Earlier, after the judge's accusation, Malah had learned the way to his tent, signaled by a loom with a striped pattern. Now darkness tricked her eyes and she found herself in a bewilderment of tents, anxious and near tears with frustration.

"Why is it that I must clean up the messes made by my thoughtless sisters?"

Gripped by self-righteous anger, Malah drew herself up and, at the horizon, caught sight of the rising crescent moon. The right horn pierced the night sky, a crooked finger in the heavens. Malah relaxed her shoulders and allowed herself a deep breath as anxiety and anger dissipated at this sign of Asherah. Suddenly, she saw the tall loom with the 3-2-3 pattern of dark and light stripes. She sent a silent message of thanks to the heavens.

Next to the loom, she noticed the gazelle horn used for beating in the weft. "Careless. Laying there for anyone to take," she thought. This hint of the weaver's failing gave her confidence in her mission.

Malah eased herself down next to the loom. Her hand found the horn and thumbed its ridges like a talisman. The side of the tent was rolled up only a few handbreadths, so all she saw was the backside of a woman sitting on a fleece.

"Please tell your mistress I have vital information about her daughter," Malah whispered urgently.

The woman startled and hissed back, "Who is that?"

"The sister of the midwife who will attend the daughter of the judge."

"I am the mistress of this family," the voice answered, lowered to match Malah's. "You are speaking of my daughter. What do you want?"

"Let us speak here, by your loom."

"I do not meet with strangers in the night."

"I am of Manasseh, a lone woman among the tents of Efraim. *You* are the safe one. My news is urgent."

"I will come with one of my women."

"This is for your ears only. For your daughter's sake. Only a few steps separate us even now."

The whispered exchange ended, and Malah heard a faint sigh of cloth shifting. Malah stood and stepped away from the loom, grasping a tent pole for support, ready to disappear into the night. She waited.

Finally, she saw a form approaching, and a woman breathed into the night, "Who is there?" When the woman did not hear an immediate answer, she turned. "Eh, a trick."

Malah quickly stepped forward. "I am here."

The woman challenged, "What concerns you with my daughter?"

With the ends of their headcloths wrapped to conceal all but their eyes, Malah and the cousin of Barzel began a dark, muffled exchange. Malah began by praising the woman for the wisdom to choose Milcah as midwife.

"But," Malah said, "I have a story to tell, one that happened long ago, one that is darkened by the death of a young and innocent woman."

Malah related Yoela's story, without giving her name. She saw the woman's eyes narrow, guessing the identity of the husband who abused his wives.

"She was like a sister to my sister and to me."

Malah had practiced this untruth, reminding herself that the goal was forwarding her daughter's claim to land. Whatever she had to say, she would.

"How does this concern my daughter," the woman insisted.

"The woman you accuse . . . her sister is the midwife who will attend your daughter. You have chosen the midwife well. Her hands are blessed," Malah said. "But if your accusation stands, she will not attend the birth of your first grandchild."

"And who will stop her? You?"

"Do not doubt that I can. Consider: your accusation or the safety of your daughter and the child that is the future of your house."

The woman did not speak. Ever attuned to drama, Malah swept her robes around her and left. Unsure of the outcome, Malah asked the night air, "Who would not act in her greatest self-interest?"

Having expended all of her heat, Malah shivered as she retraced her route. Despite the rising crescent moon, the way back seemed darker and devoid of people. She had to pick her steps with care so as not to step into the hot remains of cookfires covered by ash.

Shadows thickened as she passed. She feared they were evil spirits, as every man was now in his tent. From the direction of the sheepfolds, she heard the low "oooo-whoop" of a hyena, then a sleep-muffled curse, and the thud of a rock.

Finally she arrived home, breathless, chilled by fear. She slipped onto her bedding and reached for a fleece to cover herself with. When her hand found the warm wool, she wrapped herself tightly and waited for her body to stop shaking. As she fell asleep, Malah congratulated herself on her courage in the service of her daughter.

"Just as Noa said, I am completing God's intended work."

MALAH WAS AWAKENED by a sharp cry that dissolved into a low, animal moan. Seglit. With an awful premonition, Malah sprang up and tore through to the other side of the still-dark tent where she found Seglit sitting, holding Boaz's hand.

"He is gone," Seglit said.

Malah found Boaz's other hand. It lacked the warmth of life. No one among them was unfamiliar with death's gaunt face. Malah thought she had prepared herself, but at this moment she felt lost.

His two wives sat, enveloped by grief and disbelief.

Suddenly shaken by a vision of Rimon as a baby in her father's arms, Malah remembered that Noa's fate would be cast today. She prayed that her work last night would remove the barrier to Noa's progress, but feared that Boaz's death might muddy a delicate deliberation. Malah would let nothing impede her daughter's future.

"We must keep this between us, only until nightfall," she whispered to Seglit, fearing Rimon and the dead might hear.

"What do you mean?"

"His death. No one must know during this day."

"Why? His body must be cleaned and prepared. We cannot wait."

"We must, only until sunset. Our daughter's fate depends on it."

Malah explained, and Seglit agreed. Seglit would guard against intrusion while Malah promised to make sure Rimon was busy with Milcah. She was thankful she would not have to remain in the tent as the flesh that was once her husband stiffened.

In a rare expression of sympathy, she said, "I am sorry to leave you alone. I will return as soon as the *bet din* makes its judgment."

They remained in the dark, each wrapped in her robes and her thoughts, until daybreak. When sunrise found their tent and Rimon awoke, Malah hurried her off to Milcah's. Malah then went to find Noa to escort her to the *bet din*.

"I hope you will hold your thoughts until you see what will happen," she urged Noa as they walked. "I believe this accusation was just a boil in a pot. It will likely come to nothing."

Pressing through the crowd like the breath of God through the Sea of Reeds, Malah parted a path for Noa. They stood to one side of the arc of people, with Milcah and Rimon. Hoglah waited at home, too anxious to hear her children's fate in public.

The judges came forward and took their seats. The judge who had confronted Noa had been replaced by a short, hairy man. Malah saw the recused judge standing at the other edge of the arc.

The crowd had come to hear the results of yesterday's accusation. Some who recognized her looked toward Noa, whose face was colorless and set like stone. At last, the judge with the walleye stood, the better to be heard.

"In the matter of Noa, daughter of Zelophechad, accused of intent to poison, which event occurred in years past . . ."

He took a breath before continuing and the crowd leaned in.

"The witness withdrew her accusation. Mistaken identity. This matter is finished. As for the petition regarding inheritance of daughters who lack brothers . . .

"It will be forwarded to the Judges of Thousands, the highest *bet din* of the people of Israel."

The crowd bubbled with comments and opinions. The judge stirred them down by announcing the next case, as the sisters slipped to the edge of the crowd on their way home. Women reached out to Noa, touching her arm as she passed, and she acknowledged their quiet congratulations with a set smile.

The recused judge left, his face sour. First his wife accused, then she recanted. She made him look a fool before his fellow judges, and he vowed she would pay. He did not know that she had already paid, twice over. Initially, when his wife remembered Noa's face at the *bet din*, she was filled with the rage of retribution. She offered one of her best gold bands to a kinswoman willing to bear false witness.

"This, for you, as my second witness to a crime committed against our family. And your vow of silence regarding this exchange."

After Malah's threat to withhold Milcah, the judge's wife told her kinswoman no second witness would be needed. But the woman refused to return the payment.

That night, the daughters of Zelophechad and their families, busy with the rituals of death, did not celebrate Noa's victory. They readied Boaz for burial and praised his name. Noa was relieved to be in Boaz's shadow, but the accusation reminded her that no legal machinations could remove the stain of what she had done.

With Boaz's death, Hur's desire for unrivaled leadership was, in one stroke, resolved. As the sole leader of the tribe of Manasseh, the responsibility both weighed upon him and elated him even as he mourned.

Later that night, Hur said to Noa, "If I am the leader of Manasseh, I must model the straight path."

"And Gaddi? Will it still be right for Manasseh to match Gaddi with the daughter of the Midianite?"

With the highest *bet din* about to consider a woman's right to inherit, Noa did not want to soil her case with the possibility of a Midianite inheritor.

"Now that Manasseh has grown in numbers and in strength," Hur conceded, "perhaps we do not need alliances . . ."

" . . . with strangers," Noa finished.

She was happy that Hur's heart had hardened against matching their son with the daughter of Haddad. Hur wondered how he would break his oath.

CHAPTER 26
BLESSINGS AND CURSES

THE TRIBES HAD lived at Kadesh Barnea since the spies' bad report. Over the years, they became accustomed to the dry hills that framed their tents, the palms, and the sweet-water wells. It was said that Miriam's very presence caused living waters to flow.

Over the years, the generation that had fled Egypt was reduced by death. Miriam and her brothers were among the last of that generation. When she died, the wells that had been dug deeper and deeper into the sands dried up.

The people cried out to Moses, "There is no water to drink."

Grieving over his sister's death, Moses could not hear. God heard the peoples' cries and directed Moses to call water forth. Moses had little will to intercede, yet he silenced his mind and raised his staff over the rock that God had designated.

At that moment, a man shouted, "Why did you make us leave Egypt to bring us to this wretched place?"

In frustration, Moses cried out, "Listen, you rebels, shall we get water for you out of this rock?"

As Aaron stood silent, Moses struck the rock and broke his rod. Water flowed but God's forgiveness did not. Moses was forbidden from the promised land.

"THE JUDGES OF Thousands . . . theirs is the final decision on our land," Noa said. "But will they have time to hear me before we set out?"

Miriam's death marked the end of their time at Kadesh and everyone was too busy packing to note Noa's urgency.

The way forward led through the lands of the Edomites. Moses requested safe passage, promising that the tribes would turn neither left nor right and pay for any water their herds drank. The

Edomites refused, and the Israelites, journeying eastward, skirted their lands.

The young men, their blood hot for war, charged that they did not need to be escorted to the edges like trembling women. Old women complained that the move would kill them and, for some, the complaint proved true. Others feared disruption. As ever, the people grumbled. Except the children, who thought the journey a grand adventure.

When they reached Mount Hor, Aaron took off his priestly garments, put them on his son Eleazar, and was gathered to his ancestors. With the deaths of both sister and brother, Moses now felt utterly alone and knew his time approached. Increasingly, he depended on Joshua.

The Canaanites, hearing that Israel's tribes journeyed near, remembered stories of a weak slave people and sent a band to assault them. With Joshua at their head, the tribes overcame the Canaanites and the news spread. When Balak, king of Moab, learned of the victory, he consulted with Midian allies who recommended a prophet named Balaam.

"Here," commanded Balak, "come curse these people for me."

The elders of Midian and Moab paid Balaam handsomely to curse Israel's twelve tribes, now camped at Shittim at the northern edge of the Salt Sea. So Balaam made his way up the Mountains of Moab. From the ridge, he looked out on the silver surface of the Salt Sea, the tumbling Jordan River that spilled into the sea from the north, watering the great oasis of Shittim, with its canopy of stately winterthorn acacia trees and broad green meadows. Green meadows, black tents, white sands, silver sea . . . all laid out in beauty. God blinded Balaam with beauty. Instead of curses, he uttered blessings:

> How fair are your tents, O Jacob,
> Your dwellings, O Israel!
> Like palm-groves that stretch out,
> Like gardens beside a river.

Balaam's reports, carefully told to those who sent him, strengthened Haddad's plans for a marital alliance between his daughter and Hur's son.

His wife countered, "You would sell our daughter to our enemies?"

When his daughter Keturah heard of Balaam's blessing, praising the orderliness of the Israelites' camps, she cursed the priest to her friends. She was among the young Midianites who saw the tribes from Egypt as strangers who stole their land. Her mother had taught her well. Keturah met with Cozbi, another ripe young woman, to plan humiliations for the interlopers.

Malah's reaction to Balaam's blessing was different from Haddad's or Keturah's.

"From up there all may look orderly. Tell that old priest to come down here and see how things truly are," Malah growled to no one in particular.

She was tired of desert dust when a green land was what they were promised. She was tired of being a tent-dweller when she aspired to a mudbrick home. She was tired of moving from place to place. She was, simply, tired.

YARED AND HIS companion approached the well, intending to fill their waterskins. They were surprised to see three young women, laughing as they tried to roll back the rock that covered the well. He noticed the clan mark of a wolf on the ankle of one, the tattoo trailing a wolf's mane under her skirts.

"Not one of us," Yared thought, intrigued.

"Please, handsome lads, can you help us?" the young woman with the tattoo urged.

"Who are you?" Yared called. "We have not seen you among the tents of our tribes."

"We are from the tents of Midian, not far from here," she said. "Strange we have not seen you here before."

As they approached, the young men saw that the Midianite women were comely.

"Had we known what we would find, we would have come sooner," Yared's friend said, as they helped the young women roll back the rock.

"And you, who are your people?" Keturah asked, her smile a mask for her guile.

"We are from the tribe of Manasseh. My mother's brother—Hur, son of Gaddi—leads the tribe," Yared boasted.

Keturah could not believe her luck. She shot a look at her two friends. One raised her eyebrows and played her tongue across her lips.

"Will you lads help us draw water?" Keturah asked, bending to her jug so that her robe gaped open, revealing enough for Yared to respond:

"You call us lads. We are as much men as you are women."

"Then, prove yourselves," Keturah dared, handing him the jug, implying something else.

Aroused by this bold invitation, Yared took up her challenge.

"WHO WILL GO out and take back what is ours?"

The square-faced judge counted nine others willing to find those who had stolen the prized flock of fat-tailed sheep.

They were among the bands that formed at Kadesh Barnea to sharpen themselves in the art of war. When they first formed, Tirzah demanded she be included.

The judge countered, "Women are full of fear."

"Ho! Fear?" Tirzah's feral laugh caught them up.

Adam, amused, raised his eyebrows at the idea of a fearful Tirzah.

"You will be a weight when we need speed," the men argued.

"I vouch for her speed," Adam said.

"If you should be killed, what of your sons, especially the one . . ." implying Gibor's infirmity.

"I will not be killed. And I have sisters who can care for him," said Tirzah.

The men relented and, with spears and knives, they went out on forays from Kadesh Barnea. From her temperament to the color of her hair, Tirzah was a match for the name they had given her: Tanit, Little Jackal.

Tanit tied up her hair, wore a short tunic, and carried a long knife. On her first foray, she hung back briefly to assess the battle. Finally, plunging in, she helped slay one, then another. The men of her band were inspired by her fierce joy in battle.

After the twelve tribes settled at Shittim, Midianites and Moabites beset them, some to repulse them from their borders, some to steal what they could. By this time, Israelite warrior bands were battle hardened.

Now Tirzah bore a leather shield on her left arm, made from the hide of a gazelle Yared had killed. After the brothers brought back the carcass, Gibor began curing the hide, parching then rolling it with salt-laden soil until ready to scrape and grease.

"This is women's work," Tirzah scolded. "Don't put yourself in a worse light. I'll get one of Hoglah's daughters to cure it."

"Leave him be," Yared said. "Everything my brother can do he does well. And why Hoglah's daughters? Why not you?"

"Take your disrespect away from my face."

The encounter with Yared ended badly, but the shield came out well. As did the spear Gibor had fashioned for her. If Yared was embarrassed by his mother, Gibor strove to gain grace in her eyes.

At first, Tirzah had refused to carry a spear, saying a knife was sufficient, until Adam said, "If you run at your enemy and he holds a knife the length of a hand and you hold a spear the length of an arm, who has the advantage?"

As they went out to regain the stolen sheep, the spear felt good, the heft in her hand, the balance as she ran. Adam carried a bronze, Kenite-crafted sword, for which he had paid dearly.

In the pre-dawn glow, the small band said little as they trotted south along the swath of desert framing the Salt Sea. Speed kept them warm in the late winter chill and last week's rain softened the hardpan under their feet. As the rising sun crested the Mountains of Moab, its rays glinted bright and cold on the warriors below.

The sun was higher when they heard the sheep bleating, then saw them in the distance, milling under a lone umbrella acacia tree. The pursuers stopped out of sight to decide their strategy. Adam suggested circling to the southeast, attacking as the sun blinded the thieves' eyes.

They moved slowly, from bush to bush, until they saw their prey lazing near the base of the tree. They made little noise until they were nearly upon the logy men. As they ran, the slap-slap of their sandals gave them away. The thieves looked and leaped up as the Israelites stiffened their spear arms and attacked.

The thieves were fewer than they. The Israelites, calculating quickly, each spotted a man as they ran. Adam and Tanit, working together, pursued a tall, thin man.

"I'll run ahead," Adam panted, as they pounded forward, "and take him from the front. You . . . back."

Tanit grunted her agreement.

In the confusion of bawling sheep and fleeing men, pursuit was chaotic. Their man dodged among the sheep, grabbing fistfuls of wooly backs for leverage as he pushed himself forward through the frantic animals. Tanit stayed at his back while Adam cut around to the front.

He caught the thief making a break for the open sands, and pegged the man's foot with his sword. The man grabbed at Adam, and they clattered to the ground together. Tanit, close behind, dropped her spear and drew her knife. She leaped atop the downed thief, then aiming just below the ribs, she drove the knife in. When it was over, three thieves lay dead. The one Tanit stabbed crawled off to die, and two had fled.

"We can run them down," said one of the Israelites.

"Let them run. They will return to their people, and we will get a name for ourselves," said the judge. "In their telling, we will become greater in number, larger in body . . . and," he slapped his thigh, laughing, "fierce as the god Ba'al."

"And Amnon?" said one, quietly, as Amnon succumbed to a belly wound, his head cradled in the man's lap.

"We will carry Amnon home. Here . . ."

The judge grabbed one of the dead thieves' robes, and they lifted Amnon onto it. Four to carry him, the rest to drive the flock.

Once they were on their way, Tanit looked over at Adam and noticed a ragged wound in his thigh, still trickling blood. During the initial rush, he had been gored by the horn of a sheep, but was so full of battle he had not noticed. She pointed, and he looked down, surprised, as she pulled off the band holding her hair and bound it around the wound.

Adam looked at Tanit, her eyes alight, her hair tumbled around her face, streaked with dirt and the dark henna of crusted blood. The sight of her made him forget his wound.

When they returned, the owner of the flock thanked them each with a sheep and two for the widow of Amnon. He roasted one other in celebration and, after they feasted, they divided the meat that was left.

When Adam and Tirzah returned home, Gibor insisted on fetching Milcah to fix his father's wound. Milcah came with her unguents and needles and threads, but Adam said that the ragged edges needed only binding, not the needle. So Milcah cleaned his cut, trimmed the edges, smeared it with honey to guard against infection, and bound it so the edges would suture.

Then they sat outside at the smoldering cookfire, chewing charred, succulent chunks of roasted sheep, the grease smearing their mouths and hands. After she had eaten, Milcah cleaned her hands, wrapped the meat she saved for Dor, and returned home.

Across the Salt Sea, the setting sun limned a luminous rim atop the western mountains. The sky darkened and a full moon began its ascent above the mountains. Tirzah kissed her hand and raised it to the Queen of Heaven:

" . . . for giving us victory today."

As they watched, another darker orb slowly consumed the moon until the silvery light was completely covered and the double orb glowed the color of dried blood.

"A Blood Moon—a sign," Adam called. "But not our sign. I'm glad we did not see this last night."

Others had emerged to watch, with awe and dread, as their lunar timepiece temporarily disappeared behind the shadow of the orb on which they lived.

"Whose fate is the moon foretelling?" Adam wondered.

"I hope *our* next sign will be for our promised land," Tirzah said.

"And whose land would that be?" Yared muttered.

"What did you say?" Tirzah demanded.

"I said, 'Whose land do you plan to take?' "

"Our land." Tirzah's face was as full of anger as was her son's of defiance.

Yared remembered Keturah, lying on his robe, drawing him into her, fueling his passion to challenge his mother.

"How will you know which is our land when all you see are the dwellings of others?"

"It was ours before it was theirs."

"And whose before that?"

"God will show us our land," Tirzah countered.

"And if their God showed them the same land?"

"Our God is stronger."

"Stop," demanded Adam, disturbed by the railing between wife and son. "Whose land is it? He who takes it. That is always the way."

HUR SAT ON a rock at the edge of a spring-fed pool, waiting for Haddad. The rock was half-hidden among reeds and, as he sat there, he ran his thumbnail down a tall stalk, wondering how this meeting would go.

Hur had sent one of his men to request a meeting here, known as a neutral place. Now he chided himself as a fool for exposing himself, alone. He had brought his bow and a quiver of arrows, having said that perhaps they would hunt, as they used to. They had not seen each other for some time and hunting was a plausible, easy reason to meet. He brought his knife, too, as a hedge. He could not imagine that Haddad would betray him, yet he sat with his back covered by a screen of reeds.

Hur was certain Haddad had heard of Israel's move to Shittim, and was equally certain Haddad had heard of Balaam's blessings. As Hur rehearsed the words he would use, his mind wandered.

When Moses came down from the mountain, the laws he brought were meant to mold them as a distinct people sworn to remain distinct.

"But," Hur wondered, "Moses married a Midianite, so how separate must we be?"

He heard a rustling, reached for his knife, then looked up to see Haddad.

"Friend, did you not hear me?"

Haddad strode around the edge of the pool, and Hur rose to meet him. They embraced, but Hur noticed that Haddad had said "friend" when they used to call each other "brother."

"How is it with you?" asked Haddad.

"We recently buried my brother-in-law, Boaz." Hur raised an eyebrow, hinting at the change in his position.

Haddad was silent a moment, as he took in Hur's meaning.

"Ha! Making you sole leader of Manasseh. And a worthy one."

"One who waited. And how goes your . . ."

" . . . always the Scarface snaps at my heels, looking for weakness. I keep sending him off to battle. If he refused, he would lose face. One of these battles will solve my problem."

"He could gain a name by challenging you."

"He could, but he's better at scheming than fighting."

Haddad smiled with such naked satisfaction at his Scarface solution that Hur clapped him on the shoulder, laughing. "You!"

Their comfortable camaraderie reestablished, they busied themselves with checking their bowstrings and sighting the line of their arrows as though that were their goal. Then they set them down and continued talking. Eventually, Haddad reached for the topic he had on his mind all along.

"Your son, Gaddi, how is he?"

"Excellent," Hur replied. Then, realizing where this would lead, he drew back his enthusiasm. "But you know children are never exactly as you wish them to be."

"I know only too well," Haddad agreed, thankful for Hur's circumspection. "My daughter, a beauty, but . . ." Haddad looked around as if his praise might have attracted an Evil Eye. "She is hardly ready for a husband, I fear."

"A wise parent knows when the time is right. Your daughter is fortunate to have so wise a parent."

Their conversation slipped into stiff platitudes as they backed away from the oath they had sworn to bring their peoples together. They traversed to the abstractions of leadership.

Haddad sighed. "It is not easy."

"Yes. Now a wall surrounds me. I can go so far and no farther. Did I build it, or was it there?"

"Some of each. And it tests friendships."

They were no longer the careless young men they once had been. Haddad looked at Hur, trying to sound lighthearted when he knew this was likely the last time they would meet.

"The day is soon ending," Hur said as he got up and gathered his hunting gear.

Haddad did the same, then backed away.

"Good friend," he said, as he raised his free hand in farewell. "I will see you again. In time . . ."

"Yes, in time," Hur returned the lie.

Each fixed the face of the other in his heart, then turned and went their ways.

CHAPTER 27
SEDUCTION

BALAAM HAD NOT given satisfaction to those who sent him to curse Israel, and he sought to redeem himself in their eyes and in their purses. He heard that Cozbi, daughter of a Midianite tribal chief, plotted to seduce Israelites and drew other young women to her purpose.

Balaam allied himself with Cozbi and hatched an audacious plot that went beyond seduction. Not only would the Midianite women dilute Israel's future leaders through the vehicle of their bodies, they also would humiliate the interlopers' elders and worse. Cozbi clapped her hands with spiteful delight. Balaam remained more restrained but anticipated a return to rich living.

The Midianite women chose their targets and inducted young Israelite men into the mysteries of Ba'al-Peor, and Ba'al's profane sacraments. They brought their lessons to the tents of the twelve tribes on a spring day when the warming sun steamed away the end of winter. Cozbi flaunted across the Israelites' holy sector with her lover, Zimri, heir to the Israelite house of Simeon. Zimri, his loins aflame, saw nothing but the red red bower to which she drew him.

Pinchas, son of high priest Eleazar, found the two near the Ark of the Covenant, copulating with cries and groans, filling the holy sector with the sounds of sex. Bursting with zeal, Pinchas grabbed a spear and plunged it with such potency it pierced both Zimri and the bower of Cozbi's body.

The deed immediately rippled back through the tribes. Tirzah heard it at her mother's not long before she rounded the corner of her own tent to find Yared atop a naked young woman, her son thrusting like a ram. She froze, watching the sex-flushed rump of the woman beneath her son pulsate up and down. She smelled them, a pungent odor, sweet as honey, sour as sweat.

Yared turned his head, glared at his mother, and turned back, rapt in the rush of sex. Keturah also turned her head and fastened her eyes on Tirzah. Her face was shining, not with desire but with triumph.

Tirzah turned and ran into the tent to find her knife, just as zealous as Pinchas. She raised the knife above her head, and keened, "My son, my only one," before thrusting it.

ADAM AND GIBOR returned to find Tirzah slumped on the ground. Near where she lay, a stain spread across the dirt, blooming like an enormous night flower.

"Tirzah!" Adam cried.

Gibor, noticing the rise and fall of his mother's breath, eased himself down on his good leg and laid his hand on her shoulder.

"Mother?"

Tirzah, hearing familiar voices, mumbled a rambling string of words that made little sense. Moving as quickly as his leg allowed, Gibor entered the tent and readied a warm and secure place for his mother to lie. Then Adam carefully lifted her and carried her in. Gibor heated water while his father wiped the dirt from his wife's face. Tirzah's eyes wandered, her right arm twitched, her body a fugue of confusion.

Neither knew what terrible thing had occurred nor how to help, so Gibor sought Milcah, who asked Noa to accompany her. As Milcah applied warm compresses and coaxed Tirzah to sip yarrow tea, Adam and Noa tried to draw out a coherent story. The most they learned was "My son . . . gone."

Gibor went out to look for Yared, tracing a path through Manasseh, among the tents of Efraim, and into the grounds of the tribe of Benjamin. During his journey, he learned what strange events had happened that day. Gibor brought home what he had learned and found an excuse to call Noa outside, beyond his father's hearing.

He knew his aunt's eyes were clear, and he trusted her judgment, but he was shy to speak of what he had heard. He fidgeted, looking this way and that, but not at Noa.

"Gibor, tell me. What have you learned?"

"I fear for my brother. What happened was no accident."

"What did happen?"

"Midianite women took our young men."

"What do you mean 'took them?' Women simply do not come in and take men away."

"It was a plot."

"Does this have to do with Pinchas and what happened at the Ark of the Covenant?"

"Yes."

"And . . . ?"

"Today some of our young men went with Midianite women to their festival. Where they do things I can't speak of."

"So you are saying that these women lured the men away. Were others killed as Zimri was?"

"I did not hear of any. A sister of one said her brother swore her to secrecy. He told her how the Midianites honored their gods with drink and feasting, and . . . and . . ."

"Yes, I know what they do," said Noa, remembering the night of the Golden Calf. "And Yared? What happened to him?"

"He met with a Midian woman even before today. He would disappear, then return, full of . . . spirit."

"And the blood. It is blood that coats the ground where your mother lay."

"Yes."

"I found the knife." Noa drew the knife from among the folds of her robe.

He had seen the knife as soon as they had come upon his mother. Immediately, he used his crutch to shove it under the skirt of the tent, hoping his father would not notice. Now he looked at it closely. A smear of blood covered the tip of the blade. The haft was clean.

"Nothing deadly happened here," said Noa.

Gibor agreed, although neither found anything more positive to say.

Milcah stayed by Tirzah's side until morning. When Tirzah awoke, she rose to light a cookfire, wordlessly busying herself with getting water and grain to make gruel. When Milcah gently attempted to find out what had happened, Tirzah ignored her.

THE GYRE OF vengeance began the next day. Each tribe picked men to march on the Midianites. They arose in darkness and went forward as a storm. They were many, but knowing the Midianites might be more, they planned to take them from their beds.

The Midian tents stood near the base of the Mountains of Moab. As they drew near and the tents became distinct in the half-light of dawn, the Israelites saw a line of totems spread widely across the front of the encampment. As they approached, the totems took shape. Adam saw what remained of a young Israelite, pierced through from anus to mouth, his body sagging on a stiff pole. Bile rose in Adam's throat, now fearing what had become of his son.

Seduced, then delivered to Balaam, most of the young men who had come to the Midian camp were killed on the spot. A few, Yared among them, were chosen for worse. They were scourged, then impaled, their flayed bodies a fierce warning to those who would dislodge the Midianites or seek revenge. The young men died slowly. By the time the tribes of Israel arrived, some had still not reached their end, each in individual agony.

The Israelites stopped at the sight of their dead and dying sons and brothers. A quiet breeze floated through as, momentarily, the whole of Israel breathed as one. Above, a raven winged over a scene so still it might have been etched in stone, held forever in that moment.

Then Joshua called for the shofars. Those who carried them pulled the curved rams' horns from their backs and blew deep, raw blasts. The men's bile transformed to fury. They plunged forward, howling, spears and swords ready for flesh.

Anticipating the assault, the Midianites leaped from their tents, ready to slay the avengers, their women and children hidden in tents to the rear. Israel, possessed by momentum, killed whomever they came upon. They fought forward through the camp, driven by rage and from fear of dying as a totem.

As Israelites penetrated the camp, Midianites secreted among folds at the foot of the mountains emerged at a run. They planned to squeeze the Israelites from back and front, like the grasp of a scorpion before its deadly sting. They ran toward the backs of the Israelites, waving banners so their comrades could see them.

Some are born for words, some for action. Joshua was born for both. He knew how the hearts of men beat. He saw their patterns, as they were and as they would be. Unlike Moses, a reluctant leader, Joshua was built for battle and would lead this day and days to come.

He watched the Midianites emerge from the mountain folds and waited until they had committed themselves to battle. Then he loosed the wave of men he had held back.

Midian self-congratulations were short, their strategy outflanked by one who had schooled himself in the ways of war. Rushing from the rear, Israel fell upon their enemies, breaking as a blood-dimmed tide.

Dust and the frenzied din of battle roiled the camp. Blood foamed from the points of spears followed by agonized cries and the desperate breath of the dying on both sides. Adam, filled with fierce clarity, had screened his mind from the reasons for Yared's fate and all the clouded emotions it aroused. His eyes alert to those who might attack from back or side, he thrust with doubled-armed force, his sword seeking necks and bellies and any other point of entry. Before he took his son home, he would cut down many of his son's tormentors.

In another part of the camp, Hur's vision was blurred with Haddad's face as he last saw him. He feared Haddad would appear before him, and he would have to choose to slaughter or spare him.

Among the Midian hoard, Scarface did not wonder. He knew this was his chance. In the chaos of battle, he need only find Haddad from the back. With the end of Haddad, he could finally make his move and seize tribal power.

Hur moved forward with his kin, killing their way through those who would kill them. But his concentration was not complete so he did not see the Midianite sword that struck his thigh, drawing blood even as one of his kin pulled off Hur's attacker. His cousin found an empty tent, pulled Hur inside, and bound his wound.

"I will stay with you," he said, as his eyes looked to return to the fight.

"No. This is nothing," Hur said. "A scratch. Look, the blood is clotting. Return to help our kin. I will, too."

His cousin bolted past the tent flap as Hur sat on a pile of bedding. He thought of how his father and the other spies saw themselves as grasshoppers in the eyes of giants. Nothing here sized for a giant. Strange fate, he thought, that his son was born the very day his father was swallowed up with Korach's followers. His son was out there now, he and his companions fighting as men alongside their fathers.

At this, Hur shook off his thoughts and willed himself a single vision. He slipped outside the tent, gained his battle eyes, and plunged in. His respite brought strength back to his arms while the arms of those around him had become heavy. He drove himself on, lunging and thrusting, watching for danger at the edges of his vision, refusing to notice as he began to tire. Then he caught sight of Gaddi and Gaddi of him, and he found an extra cache of strength.

As men battled, the sun rose, heating the earth. Vultures launched themselves from ledges, their broad wings lifted by the rising air. Silently they circled, looking down to observe their future food.

The sun had passed its apex before the battle wound down. Dead and dying littered the camp as Hur and Gaddi fought within sight of each other until the fighting was done.

"God has given us this day!" the Israelites shouted.

They knew if they had not taken the day, that all—from Kenites at the Red Sea to Amorites near Mount Hermon—would mark the Israelites as slave-prey. And the land promised them would remain only a promise.

Midian women and children had fled into the hills. The young women who had allied themselves with Balaam stayed to help their warriors. At the end of the battle, some fled, some hid, and some stood their ground, their wrath making them careless of death.

The Israelites took the women as spoils, along with flocks and goods. When they found Balaam, they did to him what had been done to their brothers and sons. They cheered when he cried in terror and pain.

"How fair are *your* tents?" one jibed, mocking Balaam's blessing and eliciting a burst of laughter. They left his body for birds and beasts to feast on.

Gaddi and his age-mates found Yared, eased his body off the post, and wrapped him in a Midian robe. They carried him so his father would not see the suffering that death had fixed on his young face.

Hur, exhausted, trudged behind them. He kept his distance. He did not want to talk, even to console Adam. There was too much death for talk.

Behind him, Israelites had torched the camp. Before him was the way home. His head bent, he little noticed what he passed until he saw Haddad lying on the ground, his friend's eyes staring at eternity, his leg broken and bent, his blood spent on the ground.

Hur stopped. Then sank to his knees and wept. He forgot himself in a wash of emotion, shuddering tears of loss and exhaustion. Finally, he forced himself to gain composure. He closed Haddad's eyes and put his body in order. He found a cloth and covered him. He did not know what else to do but leave him for his people. He had nothing to give him. Then he remembered the knife. From his waistband, he took the tooled knife Haddad had given him so many years before. He set it in Haddad's right hand and wrapped his friend's fingers around it.

When he caught up with Adam, Gaddi, and the others, no one noticed that tears had striped his dirt-crusted face. They were as weary and battered as he.

The men returned to their camps, and the women, set free from fear, moved into action. They lit fires and heated water to bathe wounds and wash away the filth of war. Older children prepared food while the young raced around, also freed from tense waiting. Relief filled the camps, except where a body was returned and wailing rose in waves.

They divided the Midianite flocks and other goods. The women they had herded back were bunched together, like sheep at a market. Among them were those who had seduced the sons of the Israelites.

Word came from Moses that the women who perverted God's laws and killed Israel's sons must die. Each tribal leader assigned an executioner, but they were robbed of their bloody job. Mothers whose sons had been impaled attacked the Midian women with stones, raining down their pain.

Tirzah saw Keturah, who tilted her chin and leered, having nothing left to lose. For a moment, Tirzah thought to kill Keturah. Then she spat, turned, and walked away.

Tirzah would have nothing to do with her dead son. She could not bear to be near his body. She could not bear to be near anyone, so secluded herself behind the drape dividing the tent.

Adam knew the Israelites' stay at Shittim would be short-lived. He refused to leave his son behind, so asked an adept from the tribe of Dan to prepare Yared's body. He tried to help the embalmer, but when he looked on his dead son, Adam wept. It was Gibor who helped the man extract Yared's organs and coat his body with soda ash to speed desiccation. They filled the body cavity with pungent herbs, then wrapped it in cloth. As they worked, Gibor noticed the clotted gash on Yared's back, his mother's doing.

They kept Yared's remains within their tent, wrapped, ready for travel. When the priests heard, they railed against keeping the dead so close to the living, but Adam would not be moved. The silence in the tent hung like the curtain between Adam and Tirzah. Gibor saw that his parents were deeply damaged.

Those who survived the battle rejoiced. The fighters sloughed off the brutality of the day and told tales of victory and daring, raising tributes to comrades who had led them forward. They gathered in clans, and the smell of roasting mutton from Midian sheep filled the evening air, its savor rising on the smoke of cookfires. Their praises, too, rose to the heavens.

"Hear, o kings of the mountains," sang a man of the tribe of Naftali.

> I sing a song to the Lord
> Who heaps up the mountains
> And swells the waters of the seas
> Who makes the earth quiver
> And raises the praises of His people high to His throne
> Who gives us this day . . .

The women ululated, thrumming timbrels while men answered on drums.

The songs sung that evening were passed down as tribute to the first of the victories they were sure would come. They went to their beds filled with a potency that masked what they had seen and done that day. Yet, through the weeks that followed, many twitched at night as horrors surfaced in their sleep.

The day after their victory over the Midianites, Joshua rallied his warriors to armor them with praise and steel them for soldiering, knowing more battles lay ahead. Filled with glory, they told tales of their promised land: the pacts Abraham and his son Isaac had made with Abimelech, king of that land, for the wells at Beer Sheva. They reminded themselves of the price Abraham paid for the field and cave of Machpelah, where Abraham and Sarah and their descendants were buried.

"Four hundred shekels of silver—a fortune. We will regain what we paid for."

The land may have been promised, but it would not come cheaply. It came with a clause: God in the heavens would provide the spirit; those below would provide the strength. The price would be more lives, on this side and that, until the cycle of blood was stilled by exhaustion.

CHAPTER 28
THE PENULTIMATE JUDGE

THE JUDGES OF Thousands, the highest *bet din* of the people, had summoned Noa to present her petition for inheritance. On a mild day, the broad court around the Tent of Meeting would have been thronged, as her case had gained fame and most knew its history.

This day, rain-dark skies kept crowds away. Noa feared that the lack of a crowd would strengthen a decision against her, as her passion and tenacity on the path toward justice had gained public favor.

The sweep of ground before the Tent of Meeting was nearly empty. Only Milcah, Hoglah, and a few others whose families depended on the decision stood braced against the rising wind. She squinted to see the faces of the three judges, but they were blurred by gloom.

Knowing this *bet din* was the end of her journey, the highest court of Israel, Noa had practiced her presentation, again and again. As she offered her argument for inheritance, the sky began to release its burden. Fat drops fell, muffling her voice. Her words did not ring with as much passion, and few were there to hear.

She silently cursed the weather as she waited to hear what the judges would decide. The lead judge cleared his throat, his voice sonorous. "Your words are measured. But do they measure against natural law? If a woman can inherit, perhaps so can a slave."

"Sometimes not much difference," a bold woman challenged.

"Quiet!"

Noa's chest tightened.

"Yours is a matter with consequence for all our generations," the judge continued. "And our judgment will set a standard for all Israel . . ."

He stopped to let the import of his words settle, as though he spoke before a throng.

A slanting rain drove all but Noa and Milcah to shelter. The two stood alone on the rain-swept ground. Noa's hair was soaked under her sodden head covering and her robe was so wet she shrank from its touch. She was certain bad weather had put an end to her plea.

"Like the laws handed down by God," the judge said, "this judgment must come from the mouth of Moses. Your petition will sit with him."

Exhausted by rain, suspense, and judgment, Noa breathed jaggedly. She bent her head to show humility and to hide tears indistinguishable from the rain. She had been sure this would be the last step of her long journey.

"Sending it to Moses is how you can reject me without taking responsibility," she said as she turned to go, knowing the rain muffled her words.

Noa waved Milcah away. Anger was her chosen companion. No one crossed her path on the way back to her mother's tent. Noa's anger found voice as she walked, and she shrieked to the heavens and to the God who sent the rain and everything else. Anyone passing would have taken her for a madwoman.

As Noa approached the tents of Manasseh, the rain and her anger abated. She shivered under her wet robe. Entering her mother's tent, she stamped her feet to shake off sand and chill.

Milcah said, "I waited for you to tell them."

Noa did not answer. She found a blanket, stripped off her wet clothes, and wound the blanket around herself. She noticed her mother, now little more than a sack of bones. Ada swallowed the gruel Milcah made for her each day, but reluctantly, as though weaning herself from life.

Noa crouched to adjust the pillows behind her mother's back, while she gained a calm voice.

Malah opened her mouth to say something, then thought better of it. Her sisters waited.

Finally, Noa announced, "The judges are sending our petition to Moses."

"*Eikha*, that is the end of it," Malah lamented.

"No," insisted Milcah, "Moses is the highest and fairest judge."

Hoglah, fearing she would have to serve as an example again, insisted, "I cannot stand before Moses."

"I will go," said Noa. "But I know it's just to make me look a fool. Like today."

"Moses would not waste his time for such," said Malah.

Their voices banged around the tent with opinions, solace, and advice on the upcoming meeting with Moses. Ada was no longer able to follow their conversations, but she detected one voice was missing.

"Where's my little Tirzah, my laughing one?"

The sisters became quiet.

"Yes, where is she?" Noa grumbled.

Milcah laid her hand on Noa's shoulder, dissipating her sister's anger. "Remember when Tirzah tied a rope around her waist and flapped the end, crowing she had a man's member?"

Noa smiled, wistful for their long-ago youth.

"A willful child became a willful woman," said Malah.

They missed Tirzah the child. Whatever they thought about her now, each shivered at the horror of Yared's death.

Their mother's thin voice called out again, "My sweet daughter. Bring her to me so I may smile before I sleep with my ancestors."

Before they could respond, a man approached the tent and called in, "I was told I would find Noa, the daughter of Zelophechad, within."

Noa answered, "I am she."

She moved to the doorway to see who called for her. Immediately she saw he was of the priestly class.

"I have come from Moses, who will hear your petition for inheritance," he said, clearly annoyed by his damp task.

"Now?" Noa was so startled she blurted out the single word.

Malah stepped in. "Please excuse my sister's lack of hospitality. You have caught her by surprise. She will be ready in a moment. Please, wait a minute."

"No, not now. Tomorrow. Early. I was directed here by Hur, son of Gaddi. Tomorrow I will return to his tent to bring Noa, daughter of Zelophechad, to Moses," he snapped.

"She will be ready. We are so grateful that . . ."

But the Levite had already left.

WHEN NOA RETURNED home, Hur asked if the Levite had delivered his message.

"Tomorrow he will bring me to Moses."

"So," said Ahuva, "the last step in your journey."

Noa turned to Hur. "When I first sought a share of the promised land, I never thought it would go so far or take so long. If I had thought that one day I would be summoned to Moses . . ."

Hur saw something in her face akin to fear.

"Moses is no god," Hur said. "He is not even a king. Remain respectful, but he is a man, simply that. Your purpose is true and your petition has meaning far beyond Zelophechad's five daughters."

He smiled and held her hands in his. "You will go, fearless, to Moses. And you will know I am with you."

NOA AND HER escort passed among the tribes of Asher, Dan, and Naftali on their way to the Levite camp and the tent of Moses. Displeased by his mission, the young Levite strode ahead in cold silence. Noa sensed his disapproval.

Yesterday's rain had diminished to an early-morning drizzle. Noa's still-damp robe quickly became wet and heavy. She lifted her skirts to keep her hem from gathering a fringe of grit, fearing that a bedraggled appearance would go against her.

The Levite deliberately outpaced Noa so that every few strides she had to run, holding her skirts. Breathing shallowly to keep up, she inhaled a pungent reek rising from wet wool as shepherds drove bawling sheep from brush enclosures. Women cursed as they tried to light fires on damp coals as husbands squatted in twos and threes, talking while waiting for the morning's meal.

Children, rubbing sleep from their eyes, hopped around the mouths of tents, delighted by the newly wet world. A boy floated a piece of wood in a water-filled scrape. Two girls kneeled near their mother, pinching and twisting figures in a long loop of yarn, shifting the yarn shapes from one set of hands to the other.

As Noa and her escort rounded the province of the Ark, Noa worried that she did not know the protocols of meeting with the leader of all Israel. Would there be offering plates to contribute to, greetings to say in a certain order? At that moment, they arrived. The Levite simply waved her toward the open doorway and, suddenly, she stood within.

Standing near the doorway, Noa was blinded by the dimness within. She slipped off her sandals out of respect and surreptitiously rubbed one foot with the other, trying to scrape off the grit.

As her eyes adjusted to the low light, Moses came into focus. He sat, supported by pillows, on a rug-covered, raised platform. His silvered hair and beard framed an aged face tempered by stoic serenity.

A brief glance told her, "Old and tired, like my mother."

Horrified that he might be able to hear her thoughts, Noa focused on her hem. She felt him looking at her, but he did not speak. A tumid quiet filled the tent. Still breathless from the race around the camp, Noa let out her breath haltingly.

Finally, Moses said, "Sit. Please." His words came slowly, as if they were reluctant to leave his mouth. He waved his arm toward a nearby rug.

Keeping her head down, Noa sat and arranged her skirts, hesitant to look directly at Moses.

"I understand you seek a portion . . . for yourself and your sisters," he said slowly and deliberately, "in the land God has promised us."

Noa remembered hearing that speech did not come easily to Moses.

"Your case was submitted . . . by the Judges of Thousands. Now I want to hear . . . from you."

Noa considered, where to begin.

"Life does not always go as one wishes."

Immediately she stopped. Her opening sounded like a complaint. "Yes . . ."

Was he agreeing with her or only urging her on? Their halting dialogue made her shoulders ache. If he allowed her to stand, as she did before the *bet din*, she would be able to think. She took a deep breath and looked up.

"Please, sir," she murmured, "may I stand?"

"As you wish." He waved her up.

She stood, but kept her head lowered. Her palms were damp from tension, and she surreptitiously wiped them on the sides of her skirts, hoping Moses would not notice. There was little he did not notice, and he recognized the effect of his presence on petitioners' palms.

"My plea, sir, is not so much for me as for my sister who does not have a strong voice."

Mortified that Moses might think she was also alluding to his voice, Noa was struck silent. She willed her heart to stop thudding, then slowly raised her head and her eyes. Now she noticed that his aged face was suffused with an ageless glow. And she saw a trace of a smile at her discomfort, a conspiratorial smile that invited her in on the humor.

"Everyone begins here in discomfort," his smile seemed to say, "even I."

She looked down, allowing a smile to crease her face, before she composed herself and began again. "Our father died, and we are five daughters with no brothers."

"And your request?"

Noa paused.

"With no brothers, who will build our father's house in the land promised to Israel? If the daughters of Zelophechad cannot inherit, our father's name will have died with him. Worse, we are at risk. My sister Hoglah's husband ran off. What will be with her and her children? If brotherless daughters cannot inherit, we may become little better than slaves, which—I fear—will be the fate of Hoglah's children. As I said before the judges, perhaps God wants us to help complete His laws and, in doing so, advance justice. And fashion ourselves as the people He hopes we will become."

"If this is the core of your . . ."

" . . . and . . . and," Noa broke in, emboldened to say more, "are not the souls of women as worthy to God?"

She silenced herself, worried she had piled on too many words and thoughts, blathering before a holy man. Alarm chased triumph across her face as she realized how impertinent she sounded. Tensing, she expected the air around her to burst into flame and consume her.

Moses looked at her questioningly, then guessed her emotions. He smiled again, this time with compassion, so profound that its radiance filled the tent and Noa. She felt at one with the world, caressed by care that banishes fear. The tent pulsed like a heart and time flowed where it would, transcending earthbound regimes, enfolding the two humans in its current.

A VOICE ECHOED, and Noa struggled to remember where she was and why. Finally, she heard Moses say, "In truth, the answer to your appeal . . . it is a matter for the highest Judge of all."

His eyes held hers. A father's eyes. Suddenly, Noa wanted to pour out all her pain. The stoning of her father. Yoela. Sarai. Yared. Her guilt for the deaths she could have caused. She opened her mouth to begin, but her eyes, full of anguish, already told Moses what to expect and he stiffened slightly, anticipating her flood of grief.

Noa noticed and was suddenly certain their slow-tongued leader evoked this outpouring in many. She did not want to further burden him. She closed her mouth and said nothing. He nodded, thankful for her unspoken understanding.

"Be patient for your answer," Moses said, "as this matter will affect . . . not only the daughters of Zelophechad . . . but all Israel."

"I am grateful that you will put our plea before the One Judge," Noa replied as she stepped away slowly, careful not to turn her back on the man who spoke with God.

Outside, the drizzle had dissipated. Now more a mist, it bathed her face. She let her headcloth drop to her shoulders and felt light. The surly escort was nowhere apparent. Glad for his absence, she made her way home, thinking about all the steps she had taken to arrive at this point, knowing that whatever the outcome, there was no higher judge, and she would never have to present a plea again.

She considered Moses and the tremendous burden it must be to master one's own tongue and lead an entire people. She realized how small her concerns were in comparison.

Along her path home, she determined, "If Moses worked to master himself, so shall I try."

Noa's rash act to kill Barzel troubled her less when she was young, when she was filled with the righteousness of revenge. Now, with the outcry at the *bet din* and the accounting of her own mortality closer, she wanted to cleanse herself and her family of the stain of attempted poisoning. As she walked, she considered the path of a *nazir*, setting herself apart to seek redemption.

Noa walked past rain-slicked tents, past spider webs silvered with mist and shrubs jeweled by raindrops, their purple blossoms unfolding, a sign of spring. Soon it would be the feast of unleavened bread celebrating their escape to freedom. Afterward, summer would thicken the air with dust and heat. But now the air was cool and washed clean.

From Shittim, Noa looked toward the sere mountains that lined the western edge of the Salt Sea. They said the land on the far side of those same mountains was green with trees and grasses and blue with rushing streams, just as Noa had imagined.

"If I cleansed myself," she thought, "I would be at peace, no matter what the outcome of our inheritance.

"How little of my life I've spent alone."

Like most, Noa labored through her days from one chore to the next, tending the needs of family. She remained within the fold of family as protection against enemies, wild beasts, starvation, and a world that could rock into chaos without warning.

By the time Noa arrived home, the sun had broken through, burning off the mist and any doubts of her direction. She told Hur, Ahuva, and their children of her meeting with Moses, what he said and what he was like. Then she announced she had decided to become a *nazir*. They all looked at her, speechless.

Hur finally found words. "As your husband, I can deny you."

"Will you?"

"How badly do you need this?"

Her eyes answered.

"For only one cycle of the moon," he conceded.

"I am grateful."

"The *nazirim* live apart in those . . . little huts," said Gaddi, embarrassed by his mother's strange choice. "Why do you want to do that?"

"I will live apart to cleanse myself."

"From what?" Ora demanded.

"Will you come home to make us dinner," asked Noa's youngest.

"What does a *nazir* do?" asked Ahuva's son.

"I cannot cut my hair. I cannot drink strong drink. I cannot approach the dead."

"Mother," said Ora impatiently, "you don't do those things anyway. And he asked what you *will* do, not what you will *not* do."

Like her brother, Ora was annoyed that their mother would distinguish herself this way.

"I must put myself in order," Noa said. "There are some things only I know about my soul."

When Malah heard what Noa planned, she said, "Even if I possessed all the sins of our people, you will never find me living in the hut of a *nazir*."

CHAPTER 29
SEARCHING FOR A HEART OF WISDOM

JUST NORTH OF the camp, widely spaced brush huts and lean-tos served the *nazirim*. Erected in haste to match the insubstantiality of their lives, they stood flimsily between Israel's tents and the wild.

Nazirim came and went and Noa found a recently vacated hut to fill with the few things she brought: a small cooking pot, spoon, knife, grain, a jug of water, palm mat, sheepskin blanket, her spindle, and a small loom. She flung a length of tenting across the top of the hut and secured it to the corner posts.

Noa was pleased with the simplicity. The haphazard brush walls let in breezes and light, and the tenting above sheltered her from the worst of sun and rain. Absent were the noise and jostling bodies of five offspring squabbling over anything, trying out the people they were becoming. Absent were the routine negotiations with Ahuva over space and duties. During her first few days in the hut, Noa felt as though she had simply given herself a rest from the clamor of life.

"I am here to work, not to rest," she chided herself, feeling guilty for feeling so good. She needed focus, not respite, in order to cut out the rot she felt within.

At first, Hur and their children visited every day. Even Ahuva came, to tell Noa how well the household ran in her absence. After two quarters of the moon had passed, all came less frequently.

"They have their work and I have mine," Noa told herself as she sat at her loom, weaving pieces for her children's future, forgetting their next home might be within earthen walls.

Sequestered in silence, she wondered, "Who was Yoela to me that that I feel her presence still? Why are there such as Barzel?"

She thought of the brother of Barzel's third wife, he who killed Barzel. Disturbed that he had accomplished what she had not, she realized how far she was from her goal.

"Give me a heart of wisdom," she implored. "Give me a heart that is pure."

What she found were more questions.

"Ech . . . there is evil in me. But what should I have done? Does this God of ours plant evil in the world?"

MOSES KNEW HIS time drew near, and he had secluded himself, preparing his final words to the people Israel. He had received the answer concerning Zelophechad's daughters and their quest. He told himself there would be time enough to notify them after addressing the twelve tribes.

Facing the Jordan River and the land he would never see, Moses called the people from their tents to the foot of the Mountains of Moab. Moses stood on a low promontory with the people massed below. The people feared they would not hear, so great were their numbers. But Moses had purified his mouth for God's words to issue forth flawlessly and all those who listened, heard. He reminded them of the good that would come if they were faithful to God's laws and of the evil that would overtake them if they forsook the laws.

Some, like Milcah, sowed God's words in their hearts. Others heard what they wanted to hear. There were even those who stole into the tents of the listeners and, while the tents were empty, took what they would.

"It is not too difficult. It is not beyond reach," Moses said softly. "It is not in the heavens or beyond the sea. No, it is close, in your mouth and in your heart, to do."

The night before Moses's last discourse, a hyena sniffed around Noa's hut. Its gurgled growls and low chattering terrified her. She feared it would break into the flimsy structure and eat her. Afraid to move, lest it attack, she sweated under her blanket. Then, when the sweat dried, she shivered. Finally, the hyena moved off, and she fell into a shaky sleep, fearing the hyena was a sign.

Tired, Noa trudged toward the grounds below the promontory to hear Moses speak. He sang a song that told the history of their lives. Standing apart with other *nazirim*, she heard the blessings and the curses that would result, depending on the path each chose. But Noa's long nights alone had not revealed answers to her questions.

As she returned to her hut, Noa realized how much she missed the busyness of family, the chatter of children, now nearly grown. She did not want to miss a moment of their lives.

She thought of Yoela, the love that bound their souls together and the evil that had befallen Yoela. She thought of Hur, an essential thread in the fabric of her life, both trustworthy and trusted.

Of the words that Moses spoke, the ones she best remembered were, "I have put before you today life and death, blessing and curse. Choose life."

Noa had discovered no answers to the questions she had brought to the *nazir* hut. She feared there were no certain answers.

"Perhaps I can't know," she told herself. "But perhaps the way to atone is to 'Choose life.' This I can do."

Noa's time as a *nazir* had come to an end. Leaving her things to collect later, she hurried home to be with her family, to tell Hur the learning of her heart.

As she passed between stands of flowering broom throwing shadows near the close of day, she looked up and saw a great white bird circling above. Odd to see one in the evening, Noa thought. The sweet smell of broom blossoms filled the air, dizzying her with their scent.

Noa stopped, suddenly fatigued, then walked on, but more slowly. She looked up again when she noticed a shadow darkening above her. The white presence was circling down toward her. Disoriented, Noa felt she was falling. The presence reached her and wrapped its pearled wings around her, enveloping her. Gently, the wings tightened, squeezing breath from her body. She was not frightened. The embrace secured her as the world spun crazily. Her heart trembled, or was it the wings? A gauzy veil of blossoms covered her, then thinned to a mist. Noa thought, "I am in a cloud." The winged thing carried her upward, enfolding her ever tighter, absorbing her breath until, finally, Noa was released into its embrace.

THE EMISSARY ARRIVED at Hur's tent near dusk and announced to the woman who greeted him, "I have word from Moses for the daughters of Zelophechad. Please to follow me."

He had assumed Ahuva to be Noa. She, realizing his mistake, knew there was no time to find Noa among the *nazirim*, so begged the man to wait while she fetched Malah, who would know what to do.

As Malah strode toward the emissary, with Ahuva trailing behind, she called out, "I am the first daughter of Zelophechad."

"Moses himself would address you."

Winding through the tribal precincts, they arrived at Moses's tent and the emissary ushered Malah inside.

Moses raised his eyebrows in surprise when he saw Malah instead of the woman he expected. Malah saw his confusion and opened her mouth to speak, then closed it, unsure whether she should speak without permission.

"And you are?" Moses asked, inviting her answer.

"I am the first of Zelophechad's daughters. My sister Noa is ill," she explained, embarrassed to admit that Noa stayed among the *nazirim*.

Night approached and Moses knew his time was short. He wasted neither time nor words. "As God has said, your plea is just. Zelophechad's daughters will be given a hereditary holding among your father's kinsmen. In accordance with the Lord's command, this is the law of procedure for all Israelites: 'If a man dies without leaving a son, you shall transfer his property to his daughter.'"

Moses noted Malah's self-importance and added, "Of course, to *all* of his daughters."

"A God of justice . . ." Malah murmured, as she bowed.

" . . . and of mercy," Moses completed.

"Please give your sister my wishes for her complete recovery and for success in her land," Moses said, knowing he never would have what he wished for Noa.

Malah understood her interview was at an end and hurried home in the near dark. It was too late to seek out her sister among the *nazirim*. She would tell Noa at dawn's light.

CHAPTER 30
BEHOLD THE PROMISED LAND

AS THE GRIFFON vultures landed, they stood for a moment to steady their legs. Large and long-necked, they were as regal standing as they were in flight, their dark, glossy necks rising from white ruffs. Majesty faded as they vied for position, chesting each other while eyeing the body the night hunters had missed. In the slanting light of dawn, they hopped awkwardly and squabbled, casting hooked beaks heavy as hand axes.

Small Egyptian vultures looked for opportunity, their white plumage ruffled against the morning chill like the hair of children just awakened. As the larger raptors squabbled, one of the smaller birds stepped quickly toward the body, its beak, long and delicate as a bone awl, aiming for the eye.

As it moved, a challenger rushed the birds, its robe spread like giant wings. Then another caped body ran at them.

"Go. Grraggghhh!" screamed the smaller of the two, as she flew toward the birds.

"Thieves!"

The other dipped, scooped up a rock, and flung it as she ran, hitting the closest griffon vulture squarely on its side. The vulture croaked, rose awkwardly, and veered away.

Seeing Malah's success, Milcah scanned the ground for a rock, then flung it at another vulture. The two women screeched while pelting the remaining knot of scavengers until they drove them off, robbing them of their meal. The sisters turned to the body. Except for a certain tension around her mouth, Noa looked at ease, gently laid to sleep.

They stood, silent.

Malah reached down to brush back a strand of hair that fluttered across Noa's face. As close as a twin, yet so different.

"She looks asleep. Only asleep."

Was her soul still within?

Malah drew back.

Milcah saw her sister's fear and said, "Malah, if you would, bring my birthing bag."

Malah, too struck to wonder at Milcah's request, turned to do what her sister asked.

When she was alone, Milcah whispered, "Birth, death. The coming and going of life requires honor."

Her eyes filled with tears.

A gust dusted the desert floor, then died.

"You will never know that you won for us."

She looked for signs of violence, from animals, from humans, and found none. She felt Noa's arms, not surprised to find that stiffness had set in.

"A miracle nothing has touched you," Milcah said, her eyes on the vultures now circling high above, waiting.

"A miracle," she whispered, stroking Noa's hand. "You are a miracle."

Morning breezes rose and fell until finally, breathless from speed and shock, Hur, Gaddi, Hur's brother, and Hoglah's oldest son rushed to where Milcah knelt.

Malah carried Milcah's birthing bag, Hoglah at her side. Gibor trailed, moving as quickly as his crutch allowed.

"She died in the arms of God," Milcah said, hoping to ease Hur's grief. From her bag, she drew a long piece of linen, which would serve as a winding cloth.

Their faces blank with disbelief, Hur and Gaddi lifted Noa as Malah slipped the cloth beneath. Milcah wrapped the body, but before she covered Noa's face, Hur stayed her hand.

He laid his hand on her forehead, anointing her with love. His look said, "Please . . . open your eyes and live."

Never perfect, their lives had become so entwined that to lose her was to lose part of himself. He could not move, and they allowed him his time.

Milcah waited, then squeezed his shoulder—a sign to release her—and finished covering Noa.

Gaddi wept as he walked. After the battle with the Midianites, his mother's death was another introduction to the burdens of life.

That same day, Moses slowly ascended Mount Nebo. From the Mountains of Moab, he saw the whole of the promised land, all the way to the great western sea. He saw the land where they would go, but not he. And Moses died there.

FOR THIRTY DAYS, the Israelites mourned the loss of their leader. For thirty days, the house of Hur mourned Noa. Those who loved her needed no reminder of the fragility of life. Death was well known to all.

"Why Noa?" Milcah demanded. "The one of us who dreamed beyond her own life. Who pursued justice."

"And won. Now my children are safe," said Hoglah.

"If the ones in charge remember long enough," said Malah.

"But it was God who decreed."

"People follow decrees as it pleases them."

They fell silent for a moment.

"She was the star that pointed my way," said Milcah.

Their mother's eyes had already become dimmed and, upon hearing the word "star," asked, "Where's my little Tirzah, my little star?"

Because they had all gathered to mourn Noa, Tirzah was there to answer, "I am here."

Tirzah's pain at the loss of Yared had curdled to anger still so palpable that her sisters gave her room. Her mother addressed her alone.

"When I am called to sleep with my ancestors, bury me here," she insisted, though her voice was but a whisper. "Right here. With my husband, Zelophechad. I am too tired to travel farther."

When their mother died a few days later, her eyes and mind too clouded to realize that Noa had preceded her, they buried her and the bones of her husband together, placed with a view of the Jordan River and beyond. Her death marked a line between the past and the future.

TRIBE BY TRIBE, they waited impatiently for the call to begin the march into their promised land. Rolled rugs and baskets piled with household stuff stood near tents. Some had already folded their tents, readied for the backs of donkeys.

Milcah gathered a circle of the clan's younger children, helping them pass the time with a story. Gibor stood at the center of the circle, miming her story, using his crutch as a camel, a horn, a rainbow, making the children laugh with delight, taking up Milcah's story himself when she paused at the rhythmic sound of stone on stone off to one side.

Glancing sideways as Gibor continued her story, she saw Gaddi throwing pebbles at a rock.

Rimon and Tikvah stood near, their arms flung around each other. Rimon nodded toward Gaddi and whispered to Tikvah.

Gaddi noticed and called to them, "What are you saying about me?"

Relaxed, looking more boy than man, he appeared nothing like the young warrior who fought alongside his father or the son mourning his mother.

"We saw you talking with Talia today," Rimon challenged, naming a friend of theirs.

"We saw you talking with Talia yesterday as well," Tikvah added.

Gaddi blushed so deeply his ears burned.

He flung the next pebble at Rimon's feet and mumbled, " . . . business with her brother," and twisted away, trying to cover the spreading grin with a stern face.

"Ha, it's true. We've got you." Rimon laughed.

Milcah saw them bantering with each other. Gaddi squirmed comfortably under his cousins' teasing. She ached for Noa to see.

"Noa," she said, hope filling her heart, "we are almost there."

Michal Strutin is an award-winning author of eight books on natural and cultural history, including *Places of Grace: the Natural Landscapes of the American Midwest, Discovering Natural Israel*, and two volumes of *Smithsonian Guides to Natural America*. Her articles on travel and natural and cultural history have appeared in the *New York Times, Los Angeles Times, Tablet, Outside, Rolling Stone*, and other newspapers and magazines.

In addition to spending time with her family, she enjoys traveling, anything outdoors, and gardening.

Reading Guide

Judging Noa

by Michal Strutin

From the author

The full Reading Guide available at
http://binkbooks.bedazzledink.com/
for-readers-and-book-clubs/

While living in Denver, I had joined a group organizing a program for a Jewish women's camp retreat when women were striving to reclaim their place in history. The program organizer, who became a friend, focused the program on the little-known biblical story of Zelophechad's daughters. Based on a few verses, five sisters pursued their right to inherit land so they would not be reduced to bondswomen. Women inheriting land was unheard of for most of history, affecting the lives and choices of women for centuries. Even today, many women around the world cannot inherit. Yet, the Bible tells of a stunning conclusion 3500 years old. I had to tell their story.

Discussion Questions

1. Why do you think the Bible's editors included the story of Zelophechad's daughters?

2. What relevance does it have for life today?

3. What parallels—if any—do you see from then to now?

4. What is Noa's relationship to her friend Yoela.

5. How does Noa change over time?

6. What is Noa's relationship to her husband Hur, and how does it change over time.

7. Who do you think was the most compelling character in *Judging Noa*, and why? The second-most compelling character, and why?

8. How were their lives different from ours? How the same?

9. What interested you most in this tale?

10. What did you want to know more about?